THE GOLDEN AGE

THE LION'S DEN SERIES BOOK 3

EOIN DEMPSEY

Copyright © 2022 by Eoin Dempsey

All rights reserved.

No part of this book may be reproduced in any form or by any electronic or mechanical means, including information storage and retrieval systems, without written permission from the author, except for the use of brief quotations in a book review.

This book is for Carol and Ed McDuell.

1

Berlin, Thursday, March 14, 1935

Doctor Josef Walz stopped to adjust his tie and smooth his hair as he gazed through the gates of the Reich Chancellery Building on Wilhelmstrasse.

The famous building had housed the leaders of Germany from Bismarck in the nineteenth century to the present day. Now, standing in its shadow, Walz wondered what that old-school Prussian aristocrat would have made of the present occupant. Had it been only just over two years since Hitler became chancellor? It was almost hard to remember anything before the Nazis now.

In the courtyard of the former palace, soldiers marched back and forth as an officer barked orders at them. Behind, adorned in the ubiquitous red and white Nazi flags, the rococo monstrosity was crisscrossed in scaffolding. It was well known that Hitler abhorred the shabbiness of the structure and had handpicked the best builders and architects to upgrade it to his specifications. It was the Führer's home now, complete with its own ballroom and reception area. Rumor had it that the builders were burrowing down to create an air raid shelter. Strange for a country at peace.

Taking a deep breath, the doctor flashed the Nazi salute at the guard on duty and presented his papers and the invitation. "I have an appointment to see the Führer," he said, unable to quite believe the words that were coming out of his mouth.

The SS guard, a young man with insane blue eyes and arms like coiled steel, roared a greeting back at Walz, took a few seconds to read over his papers, and then handed them back and opened the gates.

Once he reached the building, the doctor was asked to present his papers twice more by the burly guards in black uniforms who were posted throughout its corridors. Following that, he was led up a marble staircase by another young SS man, whose slim frame and thick glasses seemed to make him more apt for civilian roles such as these. At the end of a long hallway, they were met by another guard who offered the Hitler salute before checking his invitation yet again.

Finally, Walz was shown to a leather armchair placed outside a large well-polished door—a small sign indicated that beyond were the Führer's chambers. As Walz sat down, a blond secretary stood up from a desk in the corner. She was tall and pretty, but lacking any makeup, and her hair was tied back in a dowdy bun—just the way Hitler insisted a German woman should look. She offered him coffee. The doctor accepted out of curiosity as to how good it would be more than anything else.

The secretary stomped away. Left alone, he stared at the oaken door. The muffled sound of men talking bled through, but it was impossible to make out any words, just an indistinct jumble of sounds.

The invitation to meet with the Führer had caused quite the stir in Walz's daughter's house when he announced it there over dinner the week before. Lisa and her husband Seamus were merely curious as to the reason, but Maureen's attitude,

Seamus's oldest daughter, worried him. She had laughed and told a stupid joke: *Who is the ideal Aryan? Why, someone as blond as Hitler, as tall as Goebbels, and as slim as Göring.*

A joke like that, said in the wrong company, would mean time in jail, or worse. It was a strange feeling to know one would be imprisoned or worse for expressing their thoughts out loud, but not an unusual one in Germany these days. His step-granddaughter really needed to curb her natural inclination toward disobedience, even when she thought she was among friends. Trusting no one was the safest policy these days. He would have to speak to her about it.

For his part, Walz had taken care not to mention to Lisa or his son-in-law that it was Otto Milch who had set up the invitation; he didn't feel it was wise to mention that name in his daughter's house.

Milch was the head of his own industrial conglomerate and one of the most powerful industrialists in the city. His companies had taken on the task of rearmament months ago, and he had tried more than once to get Seamus to sell to him. His son-in-law didn't know about his friendship with Milch. What was the benefit of telling him he spoke to his nemesis from time to time? Some things could never be shared. He was used to that. He'd been a single man for years before he found out he even had a daughter. Not every part of him was subject to change because of knowing he had a daughter now.

The old industrialist told Walz that the Nazi leadership was interested in his work, and had been for some time. He also coached him a little on what to expect when they met in the Kaiser's Club last night. Milch had visited the Reich Chancellery several times and knew Hitler and his inner circle well enough to give some insight into how Walz should behave beyond that door.

The secretary returned with a china cup and saucer and laid it down on the small table in front of him.

"Thank you," he said.

She returned to her desk without acknowledging what he said.

The coffee was better than he expected. A little bitter for his taste, but superior to most. The telephone on the secretary's desk rang, and he replaced his cup on the saucer in anticipation. The secretary thanked the person on the other end of the line and put down the phone.

"The Führer will see you now." She rose out of her seat.

The doctor stood and dusted nonexistent dirt from his pants and sleeves before turning to the young woman, who opened the door for him. As he stepped inside, the last words Milch had said to him were ringing in his ears: *If charisma, shrewdness, and energy are the mark of a leader, then it's no wonder this man is the most powerful man in the world.*

Hitler stood up from his desk in his familiar brown uniform, with glossy black boots up to his knees.

"My Führer," Walz said. He bowed his head and clicked his heels together. Milch had reminded him that giving the Hitler salute was expected of the citizens, but was rarely used among the higher echelons, except for the most sycophantic of flunkeys.

Hitler studied him for a long second with pale-blue eyes behind drooping eyelids. "Dr. Walz. Thank you for coming in today."

"Of course, my Führer. It's an honor to be invited." He tried to read the Führer's expression, to see what was going on in his mind, but he couldn't. It was impossible to judge the man's mood.

"Have you met Herr Göring?" Hitler asked, indicating a man who was lounging on a couch at the side of the large but sparsely decorated office. The air minister was massive, and the sweat on his brow was easily discernable. So was the reek of aftershave. He didn't raise himself off the sofa, merely offering a large damp hand for Walz to shake.

"A pleasure to meet you," Walz said.

"And you," Göring answered.

The door opened, and a very short man with receding, slicked-back hair stomped in and bowed to Hitler before staring closely at Walz.

"And this is Herr Goebbels, Reich Minister for Propaganda," announced the Führer. "Goebbels, this is Dr. Walz."

Walz bowed. "Good to meet you, sir," he said. He didn't know whether to compliment him. Doubtless, the man was good at what he did, but an executioner was efficient at cleaving off heads. Did that make him worthy of compliments too?

Goebbels nodded and shook his hand before taking a seat on the couch next to the Commander in Chief of the Luftwaffe. Ignoring Göring, he crossed one leg over the other and sat gazing at Hitler, waiting for his beloved Führer to speak.

Walz was reminded of Maureen's joke about the ideal Aryan: *Why, someone as blond as Hitler, as tall as Goebbels, and as slim as Göring.* None of these men came anywhere close to the physical ideals they espoused.

Hitler turned to his desk, shuffling some papers into a folder as the other three men watched him. Walz still didn't know what he was doing here, apart from the fact that the Nazi leadership was interested in his work and had been for some time. He knew what he hoped these men would say, but didn't dare to utter it out loud to anyone. An awkward silence descended upon the room; the only sound was of the Führer folding the papers.

A dagger of paranoia jabbed Walz. Had they found out about Lisa? Had they dragged him in here to make an example of someone with a bastard Jewish child? No. He dismissed his ridiculous thoughts, washed them away like blood from an operating table. But the residue remained.

After what seemed like an eternity, Hitler took a seat behind his desk. "Please join me," he said to Walz, gesturing to a simple wooden chair opposite him.

The doctor felt the eyes of the other men on him, as if they were judging his every move. He took the seat, saying, "Thank you, my Führer," just to break the silence.

Hitler clasped his hands together and leaned forward.

"Would you care for a coffee? I can have my girl bring you whatever you want."

"No, thank you, my Führer. I had some in the hallway as I was waiting."

"Was it to your liking?"

"Very much so."

The Führer sat back again. "Dr. Walz, I've been observing your work for quite some time with interest. In particular, that excellent article you published last year in one of the finest medical journals in the Fatherland."

"'Engineering a More Efficient Workforce'? I'm flattered that you have read my work." Walz felt like a student again, praised by the godlike professor.

"Herr Doktor, I'm fascinated by your ideas of cleansing the nation of those who offer a threat to its overall good health. It seems you're on the cutting edge of one of the most important scientific breakthroughs of our time. Your work could position Germany where it should be—at the top of the evolutionary ladder."

Walz felt the tension ease from his body. His fear about being accused of having a Jewish daughter faded from his mind. He said eagerly, "Yes. Science has proven the straight line between genetics and many of society's ills. It encompasses everything from alcoholism to feeble-mindedness."

Hitler nodded. His countenance changed to match the

grave nature of his words. "The useless eaters who are weighing down our society and keeping us from achieving our manifest destiny of greatness."

"Useless eaters, my Führer?"

"Those who suckle from the teat of the Fatherland without offering anything in return. Those who consume precious resources that could be used more fittingly to grow our power and influence. It seems your work promotes eliminating such miscreants from our nation."

"I believe it's possible. Through a rigorous set of guidelines and with help from the State, we could eliminate most of the unfortunates in our society. But it's too much to leave to the individual."

"I understand that much. If we left the running of our society to the man on the street, we'd end up back in the storm of the Weimar disaster, and democracy."

"That's why our nation needs men born with greatness inherent in them, such as our Führer, to lead us," Goebbels said from across the room.

Hitler inclined his head, taking a few seconds to bask in the glory bestowed upon him by his underling.

"The Führer's wise promotion of the Law for the Prevention of Genetically Diseased Offspring was a massive leap forward," Walz said, not to be left out.

Hitler seemed pleased. "Yes, it was one of the first priorities of my government. It's been almost two years since the law was enacted. Do you find we're seeing results? Do you think we need to do more?"

"I am seeing results, but the slow pace of sterilizations of those unfit to bear children has been frustrating at times."

Hitler raised an eyebrow and glanced at Göring.

"Perhaps we should issue a decree to speed up these sterilizations," said the air minister from his place on the couch.

"I was thinking the very same," the Führer said. "If you were issuing this decree, Dr. Walz, what would you want done?"

Walz felt a hot glow of pride at being consulted. "If we are to see the results all in this room desire, we need more investment. More investigations. More rulings on who isn't fit to bear progeny, and above all, more sterilizations. Hundreds of thousands of citizens are bearing children every year. Many of these offspring will grow up genetically flawed to a point where they may not be able to support themselves, let alone contribute to this great society we're trying to build."

Hitler blew out a breath. "Racial hygiene is paramount to the health of this nation as a whole. Without close monitoring, we'll sink to the level of Slavs, or even the Jews. Once that blood is born and flowing, nothing can be done. Do you agree with me, Doctor?"

"Of course, my Führer."

"I first read about the theories you've helped develop into reality when I was imprisoned by the same criminals who surrendered to the enemy at the end of the Great War. Göring was there with me—and took a bullet for the cause. I almost died myself that afternoon in Munich in '23 when we tried to steer this country back on to the right course. But divine providence was at work. I knew then, when the bullet hit six inches away from my heart, that God intended me to bring Germany back to greatness, and would protect me until I did. If I do nothing else, I will purify the German nation and return us to our Aryan roots. When making decisions to affect the entire course of a race of people, I think it's wise to look to history. Sparta must be regarded as the first state enlightened enough to embrace the ideas we're discussing today. Even in ancient Greece, they had the foresight to realize that the destruction of sick, weak, deformed children was more decent and, in truth, a thousand times more humane than the wretched insanity of our day, which preserves the most pathological subjects."

"I have read of the Spartan traditions," murmured Walz. "Every infant was evaluated, and if rejected, was done away with before it could consume further resources. And through these methods, the small nation of Sparta went on to become the preeminent military power in all of ancient Greece. People today are soft. Nature will always decide in the end. Liberal, and so-called 'humane attitudes,' will destroy us quicker than the Bolshevik hordes ever could. And the twin serpents of birth control and abortion deprive us of 100,000 healthy children a year in order to subsequently breed a race of degenerates burdened with illness." Hitler spat the last few words.

Walz clasped his hands together. "I'm glad you share my passion for a better nation and a better future, my Führer."

"It's my obsession." The veins in Hitler's neck were bulging. "Nothing could ever be more important than the racial purity and steadfastness of the German people. This revolution isn't just one of government or civic action—it's one of the very building blocks of our lives and existences. I need passionate, brilliant men to transform our society. The reason I called you here today is that I believe you are such a man. Are you?"

"I am." He felt so proud to be here, so lucky to be in this man's presence. Milch was correct in his assessment. The man's charisma was undeniable.

"Are you a member of the Party?" Hitler asked.

Walz's heart missed a beat. He decided it was safer to be honest. "Not as of yet, my Führer. I was always more concerned with medical matters than politics..."

Hitler waved his hand dismissively. "Well, I'm sure you can see now that the two are one and the same. You'll join the Party, and then our work can begin."

"Of course. What do you wish me to do, my Führer?"

"First, we need to spread word to the youth of our nation. Without them, our movement will crumble. We have plans to introduce the ideas of eugenics and racial purity into the curriculum for our schools. I would like you to help us design it."

"It would be an honor, my Führer."

"But that will be only the start of our journey toward a more pure and better future together. We must issue a decree to increase the pace of our work. We cannot allow our future to be dominated by those who could never contribute to our greatness. We have much work to do together. You will receive all the funding you need."

"Thank you, my Führer…"

"Also, we want to set up a system to streamline the work you do, to make it easier to accomplish our common goals," Göring said from the couch.

Walz wasn't sure if shifting his chair to address the air minister would be disrespectful to the Führer. He erred on the side of caution and turned only his head. "That's precisely what we need to achieve the monumental task facing us, Herr Göring. I've been carrying out sterilizations in my office, but not on the industrial level required to make sure the hundreds of thousands of unfortunates among us don't pass on their genes to the next generation."

"Can you imagine the reward if we succeed?" enthused Hitler. "A nation strong as steel."

"Where malady and feeble-mindedness is nothing more than a memory?" Walz asked. "It's something I've dreamed of for thirty years."

"Excellent." Hitler stood and shook Walz's hand again. "You have an important part to play in the future of the Reich."

"I won't let you down, my Führer."

"I know. You'll receive a letter at your clinic within a few days. I look forward to next time we meet."

"Thank you, my Führer. I look forward to it." He nodded to the other men, who stayed in their seats as he made his way to the door.

In the hallway, Hitler's secretary glanced up at him with a distracted look and indicated that he should take a seat in the leather armchair again. As he waited for an SS officer to escort him out of the building, Walz was barely able to keep a smile from his face. Were his days of crawling to Milch and the other fat cats at Kaiser's Club over? Would his work finally receive the national recognition it deserved? Would he be able to stamp his imprint on the future? Were his dreams of a better breed of human being to be realized?

Through the window behind the secretary's desk, the sun was setting over the city. It seemed like the end of his old life.

2

Saturday, May 25

Seamus Ritter stood outside the movie theater, jangling his car keys. The audience was still pouring out of the cinema onto Franzstrasse and he was waiting for his seventeen-year-old son Michael to join him after using the restroom. A vast Nazi flag flew above his head, draped over the theater's doors.

It was a few weeks since Seamus had gone to the movies with anyone. The American films he and Michael both loved were becoming rarer now. The Nazis had seen fit to censor most of them, but *The Call of the Wild* had made it past the censor's clippers, so they made an evening of it together. Michael groaned when the ubiquitous Nazi propaganda film came on first, but only loud enough that his father could hear. Even so, Seamus had shaken his head at the young man. A public cinema was no place to share opinions, even on the most trivial of matters, although he understood his son's amused frustration. The truth was that you couldn't even get to Mickey Mouse and his friends without enduring at least twenty tedious minutes of Hitler kissing babies or Göring parading around in his ill-fitting uniform to show the burgeoning military might of Germany's new Luftwaffe.

Here came Michael now. "What time is it?" the boy asked.

Seamus checked his watch. "Just past ten o'clock."

"Do we have time for a beer before we go home?"

His son was becoming a man before his eyes. "Don't you think you're a little young for that?"

"I'm almost eighteen."

"Next year."

"We don't have to go crazy."

Seamus sighed. "Ok. But just one or two. You have training tomorrow morning."

Michael's cheeks puffed out as he smiled. "I have training every morning."

"So, do you want to go to a bar or a café?"

"A bar."

"I know somewhere down the street."

Franzstrasse was illuminated by streetlights, and they had to zigzag through the crowds spilling out of restaurants and cafés.

"I'm going to count the flags until we get to the bar," Michael said. Back in the early days of the new regime, Michael had taken to playing this game—counting the Nazi flags hanging on each street as they went. Seamus didn't answer him, not wanting to encourage him. He hoped Michael wouldn't say anything out of turn—something derogatory about the government that could get them in trouble.

A squad of SA men stood smoking on the corner as they crossed to the next block. The unit was taking up most of the pavement, creating a bottleneck of pedestrians. Michael turned his body to edge past. He didn't get angry, didn't waste his time giving them icy looks, or throw a word their way that might lead to a fight. Clearly he knew better, and Seamus was relieved for that. Tilting against windmills in the country Germany had become was a deadly pursuit. Best to let the SA crowd the sidewalk and give them the widest possible berth.

"What did you think of the movie?" he asked.

Michael held his finger in the air, still counting flags. "Eighteen, nineteen. It was great. That was one enterprising dog. Can we get one like that?"

"No dogs. Things are too uncertain. We don't know where we'll be next year."

"Back in America?"

"I'm not saying that."

Michael didn't answer, just resumed his game of counting the Nazi flags. They walked in silence for the next couple of blocks until they reached the place Seamus knew. It was one of Clayton Thomas's regular haunts, and sure enough, the young journalist was sitting at the bar as they entered. He stood up with a broad smile on his face and a cigarette in his hand.

"Seamus, I didn't expect to see you here. Here, let's take this table... Barman, beers for my friends! Michael, how is the next great German athlete?"

"I'm great." He shook his father's best friend's hand.

"Wait, I said German. Is it German or American?"

"It's a gray area." Michael sighed as he took his seat. "Just trying hard to get my times down."

"Good for you. Hang on a moment..." Turning, the journalist waved at a statuesque blonde with permed hair who had just emerged from the bathroom and was gazing around her in confusion.

"Petra, we're over here!" He said to Seamus, "We only met last week, but she seems like a good sort."

"I didn't know where you'd gotten to," said Petra as Clayton pulled up a chair for her. She had deep blue eyes, and Seamus could detect just a hint of blusher on her cheeks and color on her lips. It was a risk to wear any makeup in public—one she apparently thought was worth taking.

Clayton took her hand as he sat down beside her. The conversation switched to German. Michael and his siblings had spoken it since childhood, and Seamus spent much of his youth in Berlin.

"Petra, I'd like to introduce you to two dear friends of mine, Seamus Ritter and his son Michael. I met them on the ship from America as they were moving over here back in '32."

She extended her free hand to both. "Pleased to meet you," she said with a friendly smile.

"This kid can run the 100 meters in eleven seconds," Clayton said.

"Not quite," Michael answered. "But I'm getting there."

"Do you run any other distances?" Petra asked.

"No, just the 100 meters. I'm a sprinter," he responded with some pride in front of the attractive woman. Female attention was certainly a fringe benefit of all the training he did, and he never shirked it. Seamus doubted Petra had much interest in a boy around ten years younger than she was, however.

"How did you choose that distance?"

"I started out running cross-country, but I was always better over the short distances. My trainers were the ones who pushed me to try the 100 and become a sprinter."

"The blue-ribbon event in the games," Clayton said. "I'm getting goose bumps just thinking about you in that stadium next year."

"Let's not get ahead of ourselves," Seamus said. "He hasn't qualified yet. I have faith in him, and he's working hard every day, but even getting to the Olympics would be a monumental achievement for someone his age."

Petra seemed quite eager to get ahead of herself. "Do you think you can win a medal? I've never met an Olympic sprinter before!"

"I'm not an Olympic sprinter yet, but I'm doing my best to be."

"And you're able to run for Germany?" she asked.

"You're just full of questions, aren't you?' Clayton said to his date. Before she had a chance to get angry, he spoke again. "I'll field this one, though. Michael is a citizen of both America and Germany, and so, gets the chance to choose who to represent."

"That's it. His three siblings are the same."

"Look at you," Petra said. "You must train all the time."

"About three hours a day."

"How long have you been running?"

"Two years. The local Hitler Youth troop organized it for me when they noticed I was faster than the rest during those endless drills."

Seamus winced with embarrassment. He knew that Clayton understood why his son was a member of the local Hitler Youth. Everyone in Michael's peer group was too, and not joining would have labeled him a pariah. Plus, he wouldn't have been able to access the coaches and training facilities he needed without joining. Clayton knew all that, but Seamus still wished Michael hadn't mentioned it.

"Michael just wants to be the best he can be," he said. "I support him in that, and am happy the coaching system is there to help him make the most of the talents he was born with."

Seamus knew he sounded like one of those endless propaganda programs spewed out of the radio, but it was true. Michael had a passion for running, and it wasn't his concern if his trainers had Nazi armbands across their biceps. The training facilities were excellent. The National Socialists had taken over all the sporting bodies in Germany last year with the aim of "raising national morale and creating a strong, confident workforce." They were also determined to use the Olympic Games in Berlin next year to showcase the glory of their regime. Michael was doing what everyone in Germany did these days—negotiating his way through the pitfalls of Hitler's Reich and trying to make the best life he could. The Nazis could control the training methods and the propaganda behind sport, but they couldn't manipulate the passion Seamus's son, and so many others, had for it.

"I have two younger brothers in the Hitler Youth, and a younger sister in the League of German Girls." Petra smiled. "I hear about it all the time, not to mention how lucky we all are to have been blessed with Adolf Hitler as our beloved Führer."

From her tone when she spoke about the "dear leader," Seamus suspected she was being a little sarcastic. He was careful not to react. A portrait of the beloved Führer sat on the wall above the bar. It was either an expression of the beliefs of the owner of the bar, or else a cynical ploy to curry favor among the bully boys who ruled the streets. Either way, Hitler was there, watching them.

The bartender, a bald man with an impressive twirled mustache, arrived at the table with four beers. Clayton raised a toast. "Here's to Michael Ritter representing Germany at the Olympics next year, when they come to this city. We'll all be there cheering you on."

The four *clinked* glasses. Clayton reached into his pocket and took out his cigarettes, lighting one up. Not many in the bar were smoking. The National Socialists discouraged it and were known to make things difficult for those who chose to do so in public. As a foreign journalist working for a newspaper based in New York, Clayton was immune to their judgments—on that much, at least.

Several young men in SA uniforms had just entered and were standing by the bar talking as they ordered beers. One of them turned his head at the sound of Clayton saying Michael's name, then made his way over to the table. He was tall—well over six feet—with massive bulging shoulders beneath his brown uniform.

"Michael? I thought that was you," he said, tapping him on the shoulder.

"Rainer, good to see you." Michael offered the young Stormtrooper a firm handshake. "Everyone, this is Rainer. He's in my Hitler Youth corps."

The Stormtrooper smiled around the table, but Petra and Clayton looked down at their drinks. The young man shrugged and returned his attention to Michael.

"You want to come and have a drink with us? You know some of the boys."

"No, thanks. I'm here with my father and his friends. I don't think we'll be staying long."

Rainer nodded. "Ok. We'll be over here if you change your mind." He walked back to his group and whispered something to them at the bar.

"Now, tell me more about your training." Clayton clearly had no intention of inquiring about Rainer and the insanity of what the country had become. This wasn't the time for such loose talk, not in public. "Your coaches are appointed by the DRL?"

"Who?" Petra asked.

"The official sports governing body," Michael answered. "No Deutscher Reichsbund für Leibesübungen, no coaches, no training facilities, and no Olympic Games."

"Yes, we all know the National Socialists are controlling sports in Germany now." Clayton rolled his eyes, then glanced over his shoulder at the SA men standing at the bar.

Michael talked about his trainers and the routine he went through before and after school each day. Clayton and Petra seemed to hang on each word, and Seamus felt the same swell of pride in his chest he always did when his son spoke like this. It wasn't so much how good Michael was—although he was outstanding and could beat anyone in the city on a short track. It was the passion and dedication he had for his sport that made Seamus so proud—the look in Michael's eyes as he peered down the empty track.

"I'm surprised your father allows you to take a drink," Petra said.

"He says I need to blow off some steam sometimes. We come out for one or two drinks every so often."

"Supervised drinks are the best kind," Seamus said.

"What do you do, Herr Ritter?" Petra asked.

"Seamus, please. I run a metalworks with my cousin in Nollendorfkiez. We moved over from America back in '32, when I inherited the factory from my uncle. I knew nothing about the business at the time, so I've been learning as fast as I can ever since. What about yourself, Petra?"

"I'm a film actress. Just bit parts. I'm trying to work my way up to something bigger."

"My wife is the same. She was in *Master of the World* last year. The movie with the robots? She played a robot in that."

"She had to point herself out. We couldn't recognize her with the fake metal outfit on," Michael said, and they all laughed.

"Is she working on anything right now?"

"She is. A movie called *The Dark Moon*. It's about Germans in western Russia after the war. She plays one of the women in the town."

"I'd like to speak to her, if I may. I wonder if there might be any roles left unfilled?"

"Of course. She's always happy to help out a fellow actress after all the struggles she's had herself. You must come to dinner with Clayton."

"I'd appreciate that very much," Petra said. "I'm desperate for anything right now. It's been a difficult time in the film industry these last few years."

"I thought the National Socialists were wild about cinema?" Clayton seemed genuinely surprised.

Petra dropped her voice and leaned in so no one else could hear her. "But a lot of the most talented filmmakers left Germany after Hitler ascended to power. Many actors and directors have been banned by the Reich Chamber of Film the Nazis set up to control the industry. All the Jewish directors have gone. Fewer actors and directors mean the ones left are demanding more money. Then production costs go up and fewer films are made."

Michael, distracted, finished his beer. The boys from the SA were still at the bar. "One more, Father?"

"You can have a soda." Seamus approached the bar to order more drinks. The Stormtroopers didn't shift to let him through, and the man behind the bar seemed disinclined to bring the drinks to their table this time. He had to reach through the crowd of SA men to grab the glasses one by one.

"Not the politest bunch," he said as he brought the beers and soda to the table.

"I'm sorry," Michael said.

"It's not your fault. Nothing to do with you at all, Michael." He turned to his friend. "How is your business, Clayton?"

"As you know, my friend, it's an interesting time to be a reporter in Berlin. You mind if we step outside for a minute?" Clayton asked Michael. "Your father and I are going to get some air."

"No problem at all." Michael glanced over at Petra.

"You behave yourself," Seamus said as he got out of his seat. "And look after the lady."

"I will," his son said, unable to conceal his excitement at being left alone with the gorgeous woman.

Clayton led his friend outside. It was still warm on the now-quiet street, illuminated by bright light from the streetlamps. A couple sauntered past, hand in hand. The young journalist looked around and walked around the corner into an alleyway. Satisfied that they had the solitude they needed to talk, he drew a packet of cigarettes from his pocket and offered one to Seamus. A few seconds later, they were both smoking. The alley was dark. Seamus could only see his friend's face when he dragged on the cigarette, and then only in hellish red.

"I'm lucky to be here. When Hitler grabbed power, Berlin suddenly became the center of the news universe. My bosses back in New York had no idea what they were getting me into. This has become the most prestigious assignment any journalist could ever ask for. I don't know how to push it. My boss—"

"Guido Enderis?" Seamus asked.

"Yeah, you remember him. Sometimes I think he's more concerned with appeasing Hitler and his goons than reporting the truth of what they're doing to this country. The Nazis are suspicious of us already—I've gotten used to visits from the Gestapo, and even late-night calls to my apartment, just to harass me. Enderis tends to err on the side of being sympathetic to the Nazis a little too much, however. I mean, I don't want to end up like Linda, but that doesn't excuse us from our obligation to report the truth as we see it."

Seamus thought of Linda Murphy, Berlin correspondent for the *Chicago Daily News*. She was deported by the Nazis in September of '33 for printing one story too many disparaging Hitler.

"Have you heard from her?"

"Yeah, she wrote last week—still spouting the same lines about the Jews and how they need to get out of Germany while they still can."

Seamus's thoughts turned to his wife and stepdaughter, as they always did when the Jews were mentioned. Lisa was still coming to terms with the Jewish heritage her mother had tried to hide from her...and that she still kept secret. Few people knew: only him, her father, Maureen. The other children didn't know. Heck, little five-year-old Hannah didn't even know she had Jewish blood herself."

"You think she's right?" Seamus asked.

"I don't know, my friend. It seems a little hard to imagine. The Jews themselves don't even believe it. I was at dinner a few months ago with a bunch of Jewish bankers who donated to the Nazis where they were most in need."

"Why on earth would they do that?"

"They were told it would be a way of protecting themselves a little bit, and they believed it. I mean, bankers have been buying influence for generations. Why couldn't they?"

"So Enderis won't print your stories?" Seamus asked.

"Not if he thinks they'll offend our gracious hosts here in the Reich. I tried to report about an American who got beaten up by Brownshirts for not giving the Hitler salute last week. He wasn't interested."

"You think he has an agenda?"

"No." Clayton threw down his cigarette. "He's just overly aware of the fact that we're seen as a Jewish-owned paper, and doesn't want us to get thrown out of the country. He's no Nazi puppet, not like the Americans who write for Jew-hating rags like *Der Stürmer* and the government-controlled newspapers. But I feel like I'm spinning my wheels here sometimes, and no one back home knows or cares."

Seamus finished his cigarette and the two men went back inside.

"One last round?" Clayton asked as they reached the table. "Come on, it's on me."

"Special occasion?" Seamus asked. "In that case, get my son one more beer."

Michael laughed as his father sat back down.

3

Monday, May 27

Seamus was ten minutes early, but wasn't surprised to see Helga already waiting for him outside the Kaiserhof Hotel, on the exact spot where Bruno Kurth had approached him two years before. Wilhelmplatz was awash with people and cars, and a tram passed by just as he was about to cross, leaving him standing across the street from her for several seconds. She greeted him with a handshake and led him inside.

The large luxury hotel was beside the Reich Chancellery, right in the middle of the government quarter—a handy meeting place when meeting a high-ranking Nazi official. Helga made sure to wear a Nazi pin on the lapel of her gray dress. This one might even have been tinted gold. Seamus resisted the urge to make a comment about it.

"Is our friend here yet?" he asked.

"No. Let's go inside. We can take a seat in the lobby while we wait."

His cousin turned and walked into the beautiful hotel. The

front desk was decorated with ornate gold leaf, and a vast marble staircase stood beyond it, covered in red carpet. Men and women dressed like they were going to the opera stood around, though it was lunchtime on a Monday. The two business partners sat in plush leather armchairs, which shone in the light that streamed in from the windows above them.

Seamus found himself unable to think of anything to say. He couldn't believe she'd talked him into meeting a Nazi official to discuss the future of the factory. He lit a cigarette. A waiter approached the table to interrupt the awkward silence, and both ordered drinks. He decided to break his own rule and ordered a beer—he'd need it to listen to a Nazi for the next hour or so. She ordered club soda and sat back in the armchair.

"Don't look so angry. This is a wonderful opportunity," she said through the cloud of smoke between them.

"What opportunity is that?"

"A chance to overhaul the business, to secure our future—and to make millions for us both."

The waiter came back with the drinks. Silence prevailed until he left.

"I just don't want to pervert the mission of your father's factory."

"And what mission might that be?"

"To serve the community he built around it."

"The mission of Ritter Metalworks, like any good business, is to make money. That's what we're here to discuss. We're not a charitable organization."

Seamus was just about to answer when a figure appeared beside them in full gray military uniform. Seamus stood up as the man clicked his black boots together. He gave a Hitler salute, to which Helga also stood to reciprocate. It pained him every time, but he probably did it five or six times a week now.

"I am Oberstleutnant Fritz Spiegel."

"Seamus Ritter, and this is my cousin and business partner, Helga Ritter."

"A pleasure," Spiegel said with a friendly smile. "Shall we proceed to lunch? After you," he said to Helga.

Spiegel was pale, with sandy-brown hair and a clean-shaven handsome face. He carried a leather suitcase, and almost seemed too young to have attained such a senior rank. Seamus strode behind the other two, thinking Helga would probably fall in love with him over lunch. *They could bond over their shared love of the Führer, and goose-step hand in hand along the banks of the Spree at dusk.*

The Nazi officer gave his name to the hostess at the restaurant, and she showed them to a table by the window. Seamus took a second to glance out the window before he sat down.

"Quite the view."

"I love working around here. Never a dull moment," Spiegel said.

"And the proximity to the Führer must be quite thrilling," Helga said.

Here we go, Seamus thought.

"It's quite the thrill. I've seen him in the hallways of the chancellery several times, but haven't had occasion to converse with him one-on-one just yet."

"Perhaps you'll get a chance soon," Seamus added before taking a sip of the beer he brought with him from the lobby.

"Thank you for meeting with us," Helga said. "I should tell you, Seamus, that the Oberstleutnant and I spoke on the telephone last week to set up this meeting."

"Yes, I'm looking forward to detailing all the exciting opportunities that lay ahead."

"In producing weapons?" Seamus asked.

"Of course." Spiegel picked up the menu on the table. He glanced over it a few seconds before putting it back down.

Helga said, "I'm trying to move forward and get in on the gold rush that's ripe to begin in Germany in the next year."

"She's right, Herr Ritter. The opportunities in the Reich for those willing to position themselves in the right sectors will be astonishing. We are embarking on a golden age. I had a meeting with my boss, Herr Göring, last week, where we went through budgets for next year. The government is planning to spend 2.7 billion Reichsmarks in the next twelve months on rearmament, and then doubling that the year after."

"That's billion...with a 'B,' Seamus," Helga said and lit up another cigarette. "We'll never see another opportunity like it for the rest of our lives." She shook the match out and threw it in the ashtray.

"You have some concerns?" Spiegel asked Seamus.

The look in the Nazi officer's eyes made him uncomfortable. If Spiegel detected any liberal sentiment in him, he could order him to be arrested. Seamus needed to choose his words with care.

"What do we know about producing arms?"

"A few weeks' training will bring the workers up to speed," Helga said. "They're experts already. We need only to redirect their skills and our machinery to this more lucrative industry."

Both pairs of eyes seemed to be burning a hole in him. The waiter returned just in time to give him a little breathing room. Helga ordered first. Seamus got the same as his cousin and excused himself to go to the bathroom.

An SS man was at the sink washing his hands. Seamus nodded a greeting and stood beside him, looking at his reflection in the mirror. Would it really be so bad to produce some bombs or bullets for the German Army? The country wasn't at war. Perhaps Hitler was building the military as a deterrent—a fail-safe against another colossal disaster like the Great War. He thought back to it for a few seconds: the mud, the rats, the fallen trees, and the dead. The SS man finished washing up and dried his hands on the white towels folded in the basket between them. A man like him, who'd likely never fired a shot in anger, probably thought war would be a glorious adventure, an extraordinary rite of passage. It was anything but those things.

Lying to himself about Hitler's intentions wasn't going to ease his decision. Hitler and the Nazis were set on conquest. It was only a matter of time until the bullets and shells Helga was angling for them to produce were used on other human beings. But would the factory survive without these lucrative government contracts? The insurance money would cover the rebuild, but not the lost revenue. The capital they'd squirreled away over the last few months was going to run out in a few weeks. What use was it for his workers to lose their jobs because of his principles? Perhaps he needed to set them aside and embrace economic reality. He tried to picture Uncle Helmut's face in the mirror. He never would have agreed with his daughter's politics, but perhaps with her pragmatic approach to the business. The loyalty to the workers, which Helmut cherished, began and ended with providing them with employment. And that included the twenty-three Jews who worked for him, his friend Gert Bernheim among them.

Helga argued that orders were falling off because he insisted on keeping his Jewish workforce. Perhaps it was true. The Nazis were realizing their obsession of marginalizing the Jews from society, little by little.

Perhaps if he were making armaments, that would change, because that would prove his workers' loyalty to the government. Were his principles worth more than allowing his workers the chance to earn a wage and raise their children?

He turned on the faucet and splashed cold water on his face. The SS man was gone. Seamus stood there another moment before drying himself off and returning to the table.

Spiegel and Helga were looking through some papers the

Nazi officer had taken from his briefcase and glanced up at Seamus as he took his seat once more.

"You're not in a position to produce planes or tanks," Spiegel said.

"Best leave that to the likes of Otto Milch," Seamus said and finished off his beer. He caught the waiter's eye and ordered another.

Spiegel didn't respond, instead handing the paper in his hand to the American. It was a list of upcoming government contracts.

"These are some of the projects for later this year," he said. "And this is only the beginning."

The sheet detailed plans to produce millions of shells, bullets, grenades, and steel helmets. A dark sense of dread crept over Seamus as he beheld it. *No use asking this bureaucrat why they're arming for a war that hasn't started yet.*

Helga seemed to be trying to contain her excitement, but her eyes were dancing. Seamus wondered what exactly she'd do with all the money. She never spent a Reichspfennig.

"We'll have to make the decision to refit the factory to produce these goods soon, before the rebuild begins."

"I think you'll find it a most lucrative venture," Spiegel said.

The food came and Seamus handed the piece of paper back to Spiegel. "Interesting. I'll certainly consider the option," he said before cutting into his steak.

The lunch lasted another thirty minutes. Seamus remained noncommittal, much to his cousin's frustration.

"I need to get back to the chancellery," Spiegel said. "I'll leave you to talk. It was a pleasure to speak to you both, and I hope to hear from you in due course."

Seamus and his cousin both stood to shake the Nazi officer's hand, and then he was gone. They both sat back down.

"What do you think?" Seamus already knew the answer.

"We'd be fools not to do this. It will secure the future of the company. Government contracts? Billions of Reichsmarks in the next two years alone? It's a dream."

"You think your father would have approved?"

Helga smiled and shook her head. "You think my father was some kind of an angel? A saint? You knew him how long? Two months?"

"He brought me over to secure his legacy."

"And you want to do that by running us out of business? My father was a businessman, and he made decisions based upon what was best for the bottom line, not on what the latest liberal pipe dream happened to be."

Seamus looked around to make sure no one was listening. Getting a reputation as a liberal in a place like this could be costly. "Can you keep your voice down?"

She stared back at him without answering.

"I wasn't lying when I told Spiegel I was considering it."

His cousin leaned forward, speaking in a whisper this time. "Seamus, I know producing bullets to protect the Reich doesn't fit in with your rosy American worldview, but the Führer will do what's necessary to protect us from the threat from the East. The Russians mean to destroy us. We can play our part in preserving this nation."

"Or starting a war?" Seamus asked so only she could hear. "The National Socialists have been talking about expanding since the twenties. You think they're going to change their minds now that they're in power?"

"Either way, someone is going to produce these weapons. You don't think business owners all over the country are going to jump at this chance to join a new gold rush? The window to take advantage is closing."

"What if I were to agree?" His cousin's eyes widened. "Would you call off the dogs of the Trustee Council?"

The Nazi government, as part of a systematic assailment of every facet of German culture, organized Trustee Councils in every business. The members were elected from among the workforce, from a Nazi-approved list. Most workers neglected to vote, but that meant nothing. The slow seepage of scum flowing to the top continued unabated. The councilors flexed their muscles by bullying the Jewish and Communist-leaning workers, and Seamus spent much of his time these days keeping the various factions away from each other's throats. His promise to his uncle to protect all of his workers like they were his own family weighed heavily on him, but that didn't check his determination to uphold it.

"Would the Jewish and foreign workers be safe to do their jobs in peace?"

"Of course," she said. "The notion that those employees are under threat somehow is—"

"—the next step in the Nazis' plan." Seamus finished the sentence for her.

Helga waited a few seconds. "I'll speak to Benz and the others and we will maintain the current status quo, whereby our most stringent nationalistic workers are separated from the Jews and the Communists. Would that make you happier than the millions of Reichsmarks that are going to fill our emptying coffers if we agree to manufacture armaments?"

Seamus reached into his pocket for a cigarette. He offered one to Helga. She accepted, and seconds later, they were both smoking. Seamus wasn't convinced yet and wanted to speak to Lisa about it again, but securing the company's future with the holy grail of government contracts was hard to resist. He hoped Helga was right, and Hitler was only stockpiling arms to guard against the threat of Stalin, but his instincts told him otherwise.

"I'll make a decision in the next week or so."

"I look forward to hearing from you," she said and stood up.

Seamus also stood up and shook her hand. "Until then."

He sat back down and ordered another beer.

4

Monday, June 3

Maureen Ritter stared out of the lecture hall window at the sunlit square outside Humboldt Berlin University. It was two years since she stood with Thomas on the far side of that square to witness the maniacal book burning. Cheered on by hundreds of Brownshirts, SS, and casual supporters alike, students set massive piles of banned books aflame just outside the lecture hall she was sitting in right now. The surreal sight of wild-eyed students dancing around the fires—like the Red Indians in the comics her little brother Conor read—had never left her. She still recognized some of the faces she saw that night around campus, and even in the classrooms.

The university was an extension of what school became in her last year—a breeding ground for Nazi beliefs. Soon after the book burning, the new government appointed a former Brownshirt as head of the prestigious university. The new man was given free rein to introduce whatever courses he saw fit...as long as they conformed with Nazi ideology, of course. He duly introduced more than twenty courses of study of the cutting-edge field of racial science. All the Jewish students, and even the Jewish professors who'd once been the country's mainstays of education, were banned from university life—not just here, but throughout the country.

Maureen and her fellow students laughed at the fact that every lecturer appointed now to the university had to complete a six-week course at a National Socialist Lecturers Alliance training camp. It was ridiculous to imagine their overweight anatomy lecturer completing a period that included fitness and military drills. It was so absurd that they had to laugh. But Maureen wanted to be a doctor, and what other choice did she have but to go to university? Was she going to let the Nazis and their ridiculous marching drills and these boring courses about racial purity stop her from fulfilling her ambitions? They'd be gone soon enough. Every right-thinking person told her that, but somehow, she'd begun to doubt their assertions. They weren't going to leave until they were forced to go, and anyone who spoke up in public was either brave to the point of insanity or literally insane.

Karen Weber, the only other girl in the class of more than eighty, smiled as she sat down beside Maureen. Karen was blond and blue-eyed, and shorter than her, but pretty. Her father was a surgeon and didn't have a son, so she went to medical school to please him. Her mother was a veterinarian, but animals didn't interest Karen. Maureen didn't need to hold the seat for her—the two girls always sat alone. Their class, and the university as a whole, was dominated by fraternities, and the whiff of testosterone hung heavy in the hallways and classrooms alike. The heads of the university departments did little to counteract the comments and wolf whistles the few female students received daily. On the contrary, they almost seemed to encourage such behavior. It was as if putting the few women on campus in their place would send a message to others to stay away, and that the best place for them was in the home, cooking and cleaning and raising children.

Horst Müller, a physician's son who came from a few streets away from her father's house in Charlottenburg, puckered up his pink lips and made a loud kissing noise before blowing it toward the two girls, sitting in the front row. The other boys with him laughed.

Karen almost stood up to shout at them before Maureen clutched her arm. "Don't bother," she said. "Best to just pretend they're not here."

"You're right," Karen said, relaxing back into her seat. "But my father would shoot them all dead if he saw what they did to us every day."

"Do you think he might like to come in to visit soon?"

They both laughed. The rest of the class was shuffling into the lecture hall and taking their seats. The girls were among the first to arrive, as usual. It wasn't worth it to be late and suffer the looks and the comments from the boys as they walked across the room.

"How is your stepmother's new film role?"

"She's excited about it," Maureen said. "This could be her big break. She's nervous and we haven't seen her much lately, but she's happy."

"Have you visited the studio?"

"We all went last Saturday."

"They work on weekends?"

"Seven days, sometimes."

"What was the set like?"

"Not as glamorous as you might think, but it was still fun. You have to hang around a long time to see anything worthwhile, and we had Hannah with us, but we saw Lisa acting. It was funny."

"Sometimes I think that's the life for me," Karen said.

"An actress with a degree in medicine?"

"I can be two things," she replied with a smile.

"You're right." Maureen smiled back as she reached into her satchel for paper and pencil and laid them out on the desk in front of her. "I'm sure you can be anything you want."

The class quieted as Eugen Fischer, the academic head of the university, emerged from a door to the side of the huge blackboard. A bright Nazi pin shone from his lapel. He stood beneath the portrait of Hitler and the National Socialist flag and opened with a Hitler salute, which everyone in the room reciprocated, including Maureen.

"Thank you for coming to Racial Purity 102 today. I'd like to introduce you to today's distinguished guest, and a personal friend of mine, Dr. Josef Walz."

To Maureen's surprise, her step-grandfather and medical mentor emerged to a round of applause from the class. He was carrying a leather bag, which he placed on the desk before glancing with a slight smile at Maureen. She smiled back, leaning on her elbows, eager to hear what he had to say. Maybe he'd make things more interesting than the usual whiny rubbish about Jews defiling the German blood.

As it turned out, Walz was a persuasive orator. "We are on the cusp of the greatest scientific breakthrough since the invention of the printing press," he thundered after he got started. "Through a combination of scientific research and the political will of the Führer, we will soon be able to eliminate illness and disease, alcoholism, and many other ranges of malfeasance from our society. We can become better as a species through the strict control of genetics, and whom we allow to pass their genes on to the next generation. Through selective breeding, we can become stronger, faster, more intelligent, better human beings. The mistakes of the past can be erased."

Dr. Walz spoke for an hour before wrapping up with the promise of a better future where everyone would be healthy and happy, with healthy and happy children. Swept away by his enthusiasm, every student stood to applaud, Maureen and Karen among them.

Professor Fischer appeared once more to thank the doctor for coming in, and stood with Walz as the students filed up to shake his hand. Maureen had to wait almost ten minutes for her turn. When he was finally free to speak to them, he greeted her with a kiss on the cheek. "How did I do?" he asked.

"You had us all in the palm of your hand," Maureen answered before introducing Karen. "This is my friend, Karen —she wants to be a doctor *and* an actress!"

"Splendid. Have you girls eaten?" asked her grandfather. "Come on, I'll bring both of you to lunch."

∼

To Maureen's pleasure, Josef took them to Horcher's Restaurant on Lutherstrasse, a few blocks south of the Tiergarten. One of Berlin's finest, it was somewhere she'd always wanted to go but could never afford.

"Rumor has it this is Göring's favorite restaurant in the city," Dr. Walz said as they sat down.

"Well, if anyone knows food, it would be him," Maureen said.

Karen burst out laughing as Maureen smiled at the doctor's disapproving look.

The food was sumptuous. They dined on smoked salmon, caviar, turtle soup, and chicken in the style coming to be known as *Kievsky*. Josef even ordered a bottle of champagne, filling their glasses with a generous hand.

"Drink up! My God, this lecturing is thirsty work. And as for all the handshaking and signing autographs that goes with it..."

Maureen was delighted, proud to have such a famous relation buying her the best food to be had in Berlin. And he was so charming and well spoken!

But Karen, perhaps emboldened by the champagne, put down her fork.

"I do have one question though, Dr. Walz. Do you think it's ethical for a doctor to decide who can or cannot have children?"

Walz smiled at her. "Of course, no doctor would make those decisions, Karen. That's for the courts to rule on."

"But don't you think every human being has the right to make a life for themselves, and have children if they choose to do so?"

Worried that lunch would be ruined, Maureen said, "Karen..."

But her grandfather raised his hand to silence her. "No, Maureen. Let your friend speak. I like to be challenged. Karen, let's put this into context. Do people have the right to murder or harm each other?"

"Of course not," Karen said.

"Nor should they. No one has a right to hurt others, correct? Yet there are certain elements of our society who—through little or no fault of their own, may I add—could, through their children, harm future generations. The genes they pass on can only set their offspring down a path that will lead to agony and failure. These people grow up to be the most pathetic elements in our society: the takers, the useless feeders we drain valuable resources to keep alive. Do you think it's so wrong to try to eliminate those poor wretches before they're born, and make our society better and stronger?"

"But in engineering our society, do you not run the risk of overreaching? Maybe eliminating much of the diversity which makes us special as a nation, and a species as a whole?"

"We have the government and many of the greatest minds in science guiding us. None of us are perfect, and we never will be, but I'm trying to make this world better. I need brilliant young minds to join us on our quest. Maureen volunteers at my clinic two weekends a month. She doesn't have the experience to assist in my studies of eugenics, but someday, I hope she will. Would you like to come and have a look around our facility and see the type of work we do?"

"Oh, I would..." Karen seemed to be warming to him.

~

Afternoon lectures were the usual mix of vital information and Nazi ideology, made all the easier by the champagne the girls had with lunch. Those who graduated just two years before would never believe what her generation of students had to face. Still, Maureen clung to the idea that the world she was living in could not be as menacing and ominous as all the signs and circumstances indicated. She held to the notion that she could still fashion a happy and rewarding life for herself, and that the fundamentals necessary for that life could never be entirely destroyed by the Nazis, or anyone else.

The proof of this was in her own family, in her circle of friends, and in Thomas, her boyfriend of two years. Some things still existed that the Nazis could never touch. The sheer momentum of living kept her spirits high and her optimism intact. She wanted to believe in the good in life; she wanted to believe in happiness and health for all, although she was determined not to delude herself. If she did only what was true and good, surely others would do the same.

The day ended, and Maureen said goodbye to her friend.

"What would we do without each other?" she asked.

Karen hugged her. "I ask myself that every day. Are you meeting Thomas?"

Maureen nodded. "At the Potsdamer Café." She slung her bag over her shoulder.

"Even meeting there is going to be a comedown from that

incredible lunch we had. Tell that handsome boy I said hello," Karen said as she hurried off.

Thomas was studying engineering at Humboldt Berlin University, but Maureen rarely saw him as they were in separate buildings. She didn't mind. It meant she could focus on her studies, and it made seeing each other all the more special.

He was standing outside the café as she approached, looking dashing and debonair in a gray suit and matching hat. He took his hat from his head as she came and kissed her on the lips.

"How did your morning's lecture go? Who was the surprise guest?" Thomas asked and put his hands on her shoulders.

"Can you believe it was my step-grandfather?"

"Dr. Walz? Seems like his career is really taking off. How was it?"

"Interesting," she said. "Some of the concepts are a little extreme, but he's definitely committed to the greater good. I mean, everyone in the medical community is attracted to eugenics these days—it's just important to apply it with humanity, as he advocates. He even had Karen convinced, and you know she's suspicious about the whole thing."

"Do you ever see him putting any of those concepts into action at the clinic?"

"No. I only deal with the regular patients, colds and flu, warts and bunions—that sort of thing. He keeps his research separate."

"Secret?"

A middle-aged woman emerged from the café. They waited until she passed to begin again.

"Not secret! Just... He doesn't give me a list of what he does every day, if that's what you mean. Are we going inside?" She pointed to the door.

"Maybe not. I'm going to meet some people. I'd like you to come along."

"Who?"

"Just some friends."

Maureen looked at him for a second or two. Apparently this wasn't something they could discuss in a public setting. As if to underscore that notion, two men in black SS uniforms walked past them into the café, closing the door behind them with an aggressive *bang*.

"Ok, where are we going?"

"It's not far."

His fingers curled around hers and they walked together. The evening was still warm, and he took his jacket off and slung it over his shoulder.

"How's your father?" he asked. "Still stressed?"

"Wouldn't you be? He's frustrated. The factory is slowly going out of business because he still employs Jewish and foreign workers. Aunt Helga is pressing him to go into the armaments business."

"Bullets and bombs for the Nazis?" he asked out loud.

They both cringed and looked around to make sure no one heard. A few seconds later, when she was sure no one had, Maureen spoke again.

"It's not ideal. He's trying to resist it as much as he can."

Thomas led her through a crowd of commuters crossing the street. Most had their jackets and hats off, basking in the warm evening sun. A tram was pulling up just as they reached the station.

"Where are we going?"

"Sprengelstrasse in Sprengelkiez."

"Isn't it quicker to get the U-Bahn at this time on a Monday?"

"You're not a foreigner anymore," he said with a smile. "You're a true Berliner now."

She laughed. "Stick with me—I'll show you around."

The U-Bahn station was a few minutes further and just as

crowded as the tram stop, but the train arrived in less than a minute. They squeezed in among the rush-hour commuters and found a spot to hang on before the train began moving. Thomas was six inches taller than her and looked down with a contented smile. All manner of people surrounded them—businessmen, housewives and children, SA men, and another SS man in full black uniform with his helmet under his arm.

The ride up to Sprengelkiez, a little north of the university, took about ten minutes. As she swayed on her feet, clinging to a strap, Maureen thought again about Josef's lecture. It was sometimes hard to reconcile the kind man who visited the house every Sunday with the renowned doctor on the cutting edge of a new science. Sometimes she wondered how much any of them really knew him—even Lisa, his biological daughter.

One thing was clear, however: Josef wasn't a bully—he was an open man with a calm demeanor. He had no problem with Karen asking questions that some might have considered rude. He was convinced his work was just and right, and that he was striving for a better world.

Like Karen, she herself sometimes wondered if sterilization was a step too far, even for people with deformities or illnesses, or who were alcoholics or criminals. She'd spoken with her step-grandfather about it before, but he convinced her that the science was evolving, and soon, the need for sterilizations and other drastic measures would end. He had a way of persuading everyone around him that the depth of his study into the matter gave him an insight they could never achieve, and that ordinary people had to trust learned members of society such as him. Maybe they should. He was a good man, and the children loved him. Hannah called him *Opa* now. He almost cried the first time she said it.

The train arrived at Leopoldplatz station, and they squeezed through the throng of bodies and onto the platform.

Thomas took her hand again as they walked up the stairs and into the magical golden light of early evening.

Together, they strolled down Luxembourger Strasse and, a few minutes later, turned onto Sprengelstrasse, a street she'd never been on before. Thomas threw away the butt of his cigarette and turned to her as they reached an impressive-looking apartment building opposite a well-tended park.

"I don't know the people inside well, but I think you might feel comfortable among them. Just remember that everything that goes on behind these doors stays between us."

"What are you getting me into?"

"You'll see," he said with a knowing smile.

He rang the bell. Thirty seconds later, a man in his forties with a thick black beard answered the door.

"Good to see you again," the man said to Thomas while staring at Maureen.

"This is my girlfriend, Maureen."

The man relaxed and offered her a hand. "Delighted to make your acquaintance. I've heard a lot about you. You're from America?"

"Yes. We moved here in '32."

"I'm Herman Roth, and this is my place." He stood back to let them in. "Let's talk upstairs. The others are waiting for us in the living room."

They followed Roth up several flights of stairs to an apartment on the top floor. He turned to them as they reached the door, saying to Thomas, "You told her we can't talk about what goes in in here?"

"Yes. She understands."

Maureen began to feel nervous and suddenly had the urge to run back down the stairs, but Thomas took her hand and they proceeded inside. The sound of Debussy's "Clair de Lune" lilted through the air—at low volume.

"I thought this music was banned?" she asked wonderingly.

"It is," Thomas said.

"Because Debussy married a Jew," Herman said, leading them down the hallway into a living room. The sound of conversation mixed in with the music. Seven men and three women were sitting at a large round table with dozens of books and records littered over the surface. All stood up with broad smiles on their faces as the new people arrived.

"Ladies and gentlemen," Herman announced, "Thomas has brought a new member to join our group tonight. This is Maureen Ritter, all the way from America."

"Welcome to the Subversives," one of the women said.

"I'm sorry, what—"

Herman answered her question before she finished it. "This is a free space—a place where independently minded people can come and speak the truth as they see it without fear of recrimination. But most of all, we celebrate the culture that is being stolen from us."

Maureen looked down at the books on the table. All the banned classics from Heine to DH Lawrence to James Joyce and Stefan Zweig were there. The records were jazz and swing, and composers like Mahler, Mendelson, and Stravinsky—also all banned by the Reich Chamber of Music.

"It's wonderful to be here," she said.

The three women were older than her, ranging between twenty-five and about forty, the men from nineteen to sixty or seventy.

And there was a familiar face… "Herr Schultz?"

Her old teacher came around the table to embrace her. "Maureen Ritter. It's wonderful you're with us. I was so excited when Thomas mentioned he wanted to bring you along."

"It's been so long. We all wondered what happened to you. One day you were still in school, and the next you were gone."

"I made the grave mistake of trusting the principal. The Gestapo visited in the middle of the night and took me away. I spent the next few months in various prison camps undergoing a period of 'reeducation,' or at least that's what they refer to it as."

"I'm so sorry."

"I got out last year, but I'll never teach again. Thankfully, my wife still has her job and my children have all flown the coop."

Thomas touched her shoulder. "Herr Schultz was the person who seconded your entry into the group after I suggested it."

"I never forgot that independent spirit of yours," he said. "I knew you'd fit in."

One of the men danced over to the record player in the corner. "Any requests?" he asked Maureen.

"Something lively," she said, with a rush of excitement. "Benny Goodman?"

"Coming right up. This one's called 'The King Porter Stomp.'"

Soon the room was softly awash with the big band sound she'd hardly heard these last few years. It felt like home.

"Where did you get this?" she marveled. It was as if she'd been underwater these past eighteen months, and now, finally, here with these people, she could breathe once more.

The man in charge of the record player held up a blank record sleeve. "There's always a way," he said with a smile.

One of the women produced some beer; another man, a bottle of whiskey; and Herman emerged from the kitchen a few seconds later with a pot of coffee. He gestured to Maureen to sit beside him at the table, and she took a beer as it was passed around. Soon everyone at the table had a drink in front of them. The jazz music was still playing behind them, albeit at a level that wouldn't alert any neighbors.

Herman Roth held up his hand for silence. "I'd like to formally introduce Maureen Ritter to the group. She's a medical student in Berlin University. One of only three women in the class?"

"One of two."

"Tell us a little about yourself."

Maureen spent the next few minutes telling the group about her family and how they came to be in Berlin.

"It's different than New York, I'll bet," said a man in his forties at the end of the table.

"It is now. More so since the National Socialists took over. What do you do here? Sit around and drink while listening to music?"

Several people in the group laughed before Herman started to speak. "Let's talk about music, shall we, and what's happened to it since Hitler and his cronies arrived? Maureen, I'm sure you're aware of this already, but I'll recap. Two years ago, our friend, Joseph Goebbels, founded the Reich Chamber of Music as part of the Reich Chamber of Culture. As you know, the Nazis are completely up front with the mission of these organizations they set up within a few short months of coming to power. They're trying to take over every facet of German cultural life and promote the Aryan art that suits their ideals. But we have someone in the room with personal experience of Nazi bullyboys exerting pressure on artists."

A man at the end of the table with gray hair and a matching mustache spoke up. "Maureen, welcome to the group. My name is Leon Gellert. I'm a composer...at least, I used to be until a couple of years ago. My last major work was boycotted by the Nazis. Brownshirts stood outside the opera house and refused to let anyone inside, and then I was forced out of the Reich Chamber of Music the last year. If you're not in it, you can't be a paid musician in Germany today. Every musical performer in the country operates through it, and hence, Goebbels controls all music performed in every town and city in the land."

His face glum, he stopped to take a sip of whiskey. "It's brilliant, really, how they've managed to take over the industry I loved in such a short time."

"Why are you still living here?" Maureen asked. "Why don't you just leave?"

"The problem is, the authorities have imposed a massive tax on all the wealth of Jews who emigrate. If we leave, we pay an enormous price to do so. Also, I have children still in school, although soon they will be college age and the universities won't accept them because they're Jews. I keep hoping I'll wake up one day and this nightmare will be over."

The man beside Leon patted him on the shoulder. The composer tried to smile, but a pained expression formed on his face instead.

"We should have listened to the Nazis when they told us everything would change," one of the women said. "Welcome, Maureen—my name is Gilda Stein. My husband was murdered by SA men on the street earlier this year. He was walking home from work when he bumped into a Stormtrooper by accident. A fight developed and six of them beat him to death. No charges were brought. The police dismissed it as an accident."

"I'm so sorry." A lull settled over the room before Maureen spoke again. "You said we should have listened?"

"Yes," Gilda continued. "The Nazis told us for years what they were planning to do, but we dismissed it as ridiculous or empty threats, or simply lies. But we were wrong—they meant every word. Hitler is keeping the twisted promises he made, with the exception of those to the working classes, of course. The promise of a new society has come to be: Germany has changed almost beyond recognition since he became Führer. And what's next? They've already announced rearmament. He told us about his plans to expand the Reich beyond our current borders and to take back what the Treaty of Versailles took from us. This road can only lead to war, and on a scale we've never known before."

Gilda stopped to light a cigarette, while the people around the table waited in silence for her to continue. After she had inhaled deeply, she reached for a book and held it up. "How many of you have read this?"

A collective groan rose from around the table at the sight of German best seller *My Kampf*.

"I wouldn't throw that to my dog to play with," one of the men said.

"I've read it," Herman said.

"So have I," said Herr Schultz. "It's a blueprint to Hitler's future plans. He's kept to it like a roadmap so far."

Gilda took a few seconds to search for a particular page. "In his Eastern Policy, he outlines his vision for something he refers to as *living space*—the idea that the great German people need more land to feed the people. He's not interested in restoring the prewar borders that Versailles took from us. Getting those territories back is only the beginning. He and his minions are convinced that we need far more territory to feed our burgeoning population."

"The onus will be on women to provide these babies, and to encourage us to stay home, we're being cut off from higher education and many jobs," Maureen said, agreeing.

It felt alarming, almost unnatural, to express her views out loud. The sentiments she'd heard spoken around this table already were enough to land them all in Gestapo headquarters on Prinz-Albrecht-Strasse.

"Exactly." Gilda put the book down. "We're to stay at home, make dinner, clean, and raise the next generation of strong Aryans to fight the next war. Hitler flat out rejects things like birth control and emigration as ways of controlling the German population. His argument is that military conquest, particularly to the east, is the only way to achieve the 'living space' that German people need to reach their true potential as masters of Europe, and the world as a whole."

"Hitler isn't as stupid as we all wish he was," Leon said. "It's the same as what he said in that book about the Jews. We all assume we're safe because he's been in power two years and hasn't invaded anywhere, nor expelled the Jews from the country yet, but these things go slowly. Reordering a society, rearming the military, and disenfranchising whole swathes of our society take time. I wish he'd tried to do it all at once. If he invaded Poland today, the French and British, and perhaps the Soviets, would crush him, and as Heinrich said, we'd be done with him and the Nazis forever. But he's a clever swine, and patient, too. He's going to build until he thinks the time is right. Then he'll strike out for the 'living space' he's made the central tenet of his foreign policy. His revolution isn't an immediate event. It's drop after drop of water that wears through the stone over time. He's all the more dangerous for that. I wish he was an impatient fool, but he's very much the opposite."

"What would happen to the people living in the territories Hitler wants to expand into? The Poles, the Czechs and the Russians? Would they be annexed into the Reich?" Thomas asked. He turned to Herr Schultz. "You said you were 'reeducated.' Would the Nazis attempt the same with the people in Eastern Europe?"

"Never," Herr Schultz said. "The only reason I was given a second chance was because of the Germanic blood in my veins. Hitler would never stoop to 'pollute' the German gene pool with foreign blood."

"He has no desire to make those people German," Gilda said. "According to the Nazis, they're subhuman, and don't deserve the same rights as us, the chosen race."

"So what's to happen to the people living there if the Nazis invade?" Thomas asked.

"In his writings, Hitler mentions that they should either be sealed off to avoid the corruption of our race, or else removed," Gilda said.

"What does he mean by *removed*?" Maureen asked.

"He didn't specify, but I can hazard a guess. I don't think mass murder is beyond the Nazis."

"Nonsense," one of the other men said. "The British and the French would never allow it—they'd jump on Hitler and crush him in days. Perhaps that's the best we can hope for, and all this insanity would end."

"You think the Western powers would come to the aid of the Czechs or the Poles, Heinrich?" Herr Shultz asked.

Heinrich took a mouthful of his whiskey before he answered. "The German Army is in no position to wage war."

"Not at this moment, maybe, but rearmament has begun," Gilda said.

"My father owns a metalworks factory. His business partner, my aunt, has been pressuring him to shift the business—to begin the process of changing over to manufacturing weapons. Most of his competitors are already moving that way."

"He's considering doing such a thing—to arm the Nazis?" Herman asked.

"Not the Nazis—the Wehrmacht," she replied.

"It amounts to the same thing. Hitler had every member of the military swear an oath of allegiance to him as Supreme Leader of the Reich last year when he merged the offices of Chancellor and President," Herr Schultz said. "It might have been the smartest thing he's done yet. After Hindenburg died, he became the supreme leader of both the government and the armed forces. The army officers would have to break their oath to him to overthrow the government."

"You father is voluntarily doing this? Is he under pressure from the government?" Gilda asked.

"Who isn't these days?" Herman said.

"I don't know everything about his business." Maureen could feel the weight of each person's stare now. She didn't want to displease them, but wasn't going to lie down and take whatever they had to say about her father.

"The pressure is coming from his customer base. My father maintains a diverse workforce, with Jews and Russians among them. His clients are going elsewhere, sometimes even paying more to support German workers."

"The effect of the relentless propaganda we're all subject to on a daily basis," Thomas said and took his girlfriend's hand.

"The tripe that Goebbels and his minions spew from the Ministry of Propaganda is one thing, but the systematic rearmament of the armed forces at Hitler's control, and the flouting of international law, is another," Leon Gellert said.

"Are you content with your father's decision to become a war profiteer?" Gilda asked.

Maureen bristled at those words and took a breath before she spoke again. "He's not a war profiteer. We're not engaged in any armed conflict at the moment, and he hasn't even made the decision to go ahead with the proposal yet. My father doesn't tell me everything, but I can see the stress and indecision in him. This isn't something he wants to do. Not at all."

"Do you think you can persuade him not to?" Gilda asked.

"To what end?" Thomas said. "If he doesn't take the government contracts, someone else will. He's just trying to preserve his business and give the Jews and foreigners a place to earn a living."

"If everyone maintained that attitude—"

Thomas cut Gilda off. "What's the point in living in a fantasy world? The Nazis wouldn't exist without the backing of big business—they were bankrupt when they came to power. If Papen and Hindenburg weren't so concerned about keeping the Left out of power and had delayed a few more months, the National Socialists would have imploded and we wouldn't be dealing with this scourge. And if the so-called *captains of industry* in this country hadn't bailed them out, they wouldn't have had the money to fight the next election."

Thomas's grip on Maureen's hand was almost hurting her now. "You think big business isn't going to cash in now? If Maureen's father doesn't take these contracts, someone who doesn't support Jews and Russians and Slavs in the workforce will."

"At least it won't be Maureen's father profiting from warmongering," Gilda said. Each word came with serrated edges.

"All right! That's enough!" Herman said. "We're not here to pick on anyone, let alone a new member. I think we can all agree that rearming the Wehrmacht isn't something any of us want, and from the sounds of it, Maureen's father's hands could be tied."

"Nothing's decided yet," Maureen said.

"I'm sorry," Gilda said. "I get carried away sometimes."

"Can you keep us abreast of any further details about your father's business?" Herr Schultz asked.

"Of course."

"I hope you don't think any less of us," Gilda said. "This is the only place we can have arguments like this."

"Not one bit." A rush of exhilaration ran through Maureen's veins. She nodded to Gilda, who reciprocated, and the meeting continued.

5

Wednesday, June 5

Lisa grasped her five-year-old daughter's hand as they strode into the school together. Hannah was in the outfit she'd picked out the night before, and she insisted her mother do her hair in pigtails with bright pink bows for the occasion. Lisa wore a white sundress with blue flowers, and a new hat to match. Floods of children ran through the doors in front of them. Several said hello to Hannah, and she answered back with a bright smile.

Herr Hagen, the director of the movie she was working on, wasn't happy when she told him she'd be late, but he'd get over it. It wasn't as if she was the star, or even had more than a few lines to utter. This day had been marked on the calendar for weeks now, and Lisa wasn't going to let Hannah down.

The teacher, Frau Bauer, had told Hannah how much she was looking forward to having her mother—"the famous actress"—come in to read to her class. Lisa laughed at the notion that she was famous anywhere beyond her own house, but her daughter's enthusiasm was delightful.

Frau Bauer was inside the door waiting for them and greeted Lisa with a warm handshake. She looked barely old enough to be a teacher, and Lisa guessed she wasn't more than eighteen or nineteen. Her dark-blond hair was curled tight to her head and her pretty blue eyes sparkled as she spoke.

"We're so pleased to have you here today. Come with me. Class is beginning soon—we don't have a moment to waste."

Lisa followed the young teacher down the hallway, peeking into the classrooms as they went. The children were well dressed and orderly and sat in neat rows as the teachers addressed them. Frau Bauer led Lisa and her daughter into her room, where the children were waiting. A portrait of Adolf Hitler hung above the blackboard, along with the omnipresent Nazi flag. Lisa caught her breath and tears welled in her eyes—Nazi emblems in a class of kindergarten children!

Yet, she'd already heard what happened to the schools after the Nazis took control. She knew about the Nazi flags, and the portraits of the Führer hoisted in each classroom. She knew too about the school libraries and how they'd been cleansed of subversive literature: any book, whether fact or fiction, which expressed a liberal idea or suggested that the people themselves, rather than Hitler, should have charge of their destiny.

Maureen and Michael told her that such books were replaced by those glorifying militarism and nationalism, emphasizing the heroic NSDAP— Nationalsozialistische Deutsche Arbeiterpartei, or Nazi Party—for rescuing Germany from the abyss democracy had dragged it into. Many of these books were thrown together and exhibited the type of grammar and spelling expected of the younger students reading them, rather than that of published authors. The Nazis jettisoned the outworn notion of objectivity, and the vast majority of teachers accepted it. All had joined the National Socialist Teachers' League—either that or lose their livelihoods. Maureen had told Lisa about one of her teachers who had resisted the call back in

'34, a kindly old man called Herr Schultz who implored the students to think for themselves...until one of them told their parents, and he was removed.

Frau Bauer clasped her hands and the boys and girls rose from their seats, jutting out their right arms as one.

"Heil Hitler," the teacher and the children said in almost perfect unison.

"Children," Frau Bauer said with a smile. "We have a very special guest with us this morning."

Hannah was beaming at her mother from her desk, never prouder. Lisa stood in front of the room with every boy and girl in the room gazing at her.

"This is Frau Ritter, Hannah's mother, and she's come in this morning to talk to us. Isn't that wonderful, children?"

"Good morning, Frau Ritter!" the kids chanted in unison.

"Hello boys and girls," Lisa said. "I'm so pleased to be here, and to finally meet all of Hannah's friends. Now, if any of you want to ask me anything about films..."

Several kids put up their hands, and Frau Bauer pointed to a little boy with freckles and pale-green eyes who stood up. "Are you famous?"

Lisa laughed. "No, I'm not famous. Nobody stops me walking down the street, but I have worked with some famous people. Have you heard of Walter Janssen or Hilde Hildebrand?"

The children looked back at her as if she were speaking Chinese.

"Well, they're more famous than I am."

"So, you're famous?" the same little boy asked.

"That's quite enough, Albert," Frau Bauer said. The teacher patted Lisa on the shoulder. "Hannah's told me all about your films. I saw *Master of the World* last year. It was incredible."

Lisa thought to tell her that she only played a robot in the film, but decided not to let Hannah down.

"You're pretty," a little boy with brown hair and gray pants said from a table at the front of the room.

"Why, thank you."

"Gunther, that's quite enough. You know we don't call out in class."

Gunther dropped his head, dejected. Lisa wanted to tell him it was all right, but knew not to undermine the teacher's authority in front of the pupils.

Several of the children raised their hands again, but this time the teacher ignored them—she was busy pulling out a typeset manuscript from a large envelope.

"Now, children," said Frau Bauer. "As an extra special treat — You remember the book I told you about, the one I was writing myself? Well, I have a copy of it here with me today!" She held up a manuscript. "And seeing that we have a famous actress with us, I thought we might ask her to read it to you. Would you like that?"

The children seemed unable to contain their enthusiasm. Several looked like they might burst from sheer excitement. Hannah's cheeks were red, her smile so wide it looked like it might hurt.

"Do you think that would be all right, Frau Ritter?" Frau Bauer asked, dimpling coyly at Lisa. "I'm sorry I didn't warn you about this before, but the publisher only sent the proofed copy to me last night. It's set to be published next year, so I'm very excited about it, and I'd love to hear it read aloud by someone who can do it justice."

"Of course," Lisa said, wondering what she'd gotten herself into. "Congratulations on being a soon-to-be published author."

The teacher handed her the small ream of paper, bound by a ribbon. "I wrote it with kindergarten in mind, so hopefully children all over Germany will soon be reading it. Now, Frau

Ritter, take this chair. Children, gather around Frau Ritter in a circle!"

Lisa sat down, surrounded by the eager swarm of boys and girls. Hannah was right at the front, gazing up at her with adoring eyes. Glancing down at the manuscript, Lisa's heart sank as she read the title. Hannah didn't even know she had Jewish blood herself yet.

Trust No Fox on his Green Heath and No Jew on his Oath.

"Frau Bauer, are you sure this is appropriate for the children?"

"Of course," Frau Bauer said as if it was the most obvious answer in the world. "It's specifically for boys and girls their age."

Lisa glanced around, trying to stall for time or find a reason not to do this. But what? The children were waiting for her, and Frau Bauer was staring at her with ever more suspicious eyes. The bag hanging on the back of the teacher's chair had a picture of the Führer crocheted on the exterior. How could she refuse to read? People had been denounced and reported to the Gestapo for less.

Hannah was still smiling, still gazing up at her with innocent eyes. Running out of here would arouse suspicion. If the Nazis found out that she and Hannah had Jewish blood themselves… She gulped down a breath. She was an actress, so she would act. Today her role would be that of the anti-Semitic Nazi supporter.

Hannah would understand.

She flicked over the page and began to read. "The father of the Jews is the Devil." She stopped and looked at Frau Bauer, who nodded at her to continue with a broad smile on her face.

"At the creation of the world, the Lord God conceived the races: red Indians, Negroes, and Chinese, and the Jews too—the rotten crew. And we were also on the scene, we Germans amidst this motley medley. He gave them all a piece of earth to work with with the sweat of their brow. But the Jew went on strike at once, for the Devil rode him from the first. Cheating—not working—was his aim. For lying, he got first prize in less than no time from the Father of Lies. Then he wrote them in the Talmud."

She paused, and Hannah and the other children sat in silence. Frau Bauer was ecstatic.

"I can't believe I have a professional actress reading my book to the class!" she cried happily. "Please read more!"

Lisa flicked through the pages of the manuscript. She was on page two of fifteen. "It's quite long," she said, "and I have to be at the film studios soon. Perhaps just one more page?"

Frau Bauer was clearly disappointed. "Of course. I understand you're busy. Here, let me find the best bit..." She took the book, then handed it back. "Read from here to the end."

Lisa smiled at the children and put the same intonation into her voice that she would as if she were reading them a bedtime story.

"It's going to be fine in the schools at last, for all the Jews must leave. For big and small, it's all alike. Anger and rage do not avail, nor utmost Jewish whine nor wail. Away with all the Jewish breed. 'Tis the German teacher we desire, who leads the way to cleverness, wanders and plays with us, but yet keeps us children in good order. German teachers make jokes with us and laugh, so going to school is quite a joy."

As soon as she'd finished, she handed the book back to Frau Bauer. Even her hands felt dirty from touching it. "This is being published, you said?"

"Next year. My parents are so proud," beamed Frau Bauer.

"Congratulations. Could I read from another book before I leave? Hannah requested a story about Babar the elephant. I saw one book on the shelf as I came in."

"You're not in too much of a rush? I thought you had to go?"

"I realize now I can spare a few more minutes."

She picked out Babar the elephant's book from the bookcase. "I'll just read a short passage from this before I leave."

The kindergarten students parted to let her sit down again, and she began to read once more, not waiting for the teacher's permission this time.

Ten minutes later, she closed the book. The children were enraptured, the filth of the teacher's book forgotten—or at least she hoped so.

Frau Bauer stood up as the students began an impromptu round of applause. Several asked for Lisa's autograph, which she wrote on the inside cover of their notebooks. Hannah stood by as the boys and girls lined up to hug her goodbye. Lisa's eyes were wet as the last child embraced her. She glared at the photograph of Hitler on the wall and then at the teacher, whose back was toward her as she herded the pupils to their seats.

"Can I speak to Hannah outside for a moment?" she asked.

"Of course," Frau Bauer said cheerfully, but she looked anxious as she followed Lisa and Hannah to the door. "Thank you so much for coming in today," she said to Lisa. "Just one thing I wanted to ask, I'm worried... You didn't enjoy my book?"

"It wasn't that," Lisa spluttered. "It was just...quite long. Hannah had requested the Babar book before I came. Your book was creative, and the language was effective. I'm sure it'll cause a splash next year when it lands."

The young Nazi seemed satisfied with this answer and her face brightened. "It was a pleasure to meet you, and thank you for raising such a wonderful daughter."

"Thank you for having me."

The teacher went back into the classroom, clapping her hands to bring the children to attention.

Lisa led her daughter a few steps away from the door and got down on her haunches to look into her eyes. What could she say to her at this moment? How did she know Hannah wouldn't go straight back inside and tell the teacher?

"I love you, my sweet."

"I love you, Mother."

"I want you to stay true to the person you are in here." Lisa touched Hannah's dress, right over heart. "No matter what anyone says or reads to you, or anything like that. Stay just as you are right now."

Hannah nodded and smiled, but Lisa knew this little speech meant more to her than to her child. Hannah was only five years old and didn't even know she had Jewish blood, or that the filth the teacher wrote was about her.

Lisa hugged her daughter one more time and brought her back to the classroom. Frau Bauer was pointing to the letters of the alphabet on the blackboard and turned to wave goodbye. Lisa returned the gesture and hurried down the hallway toward the front door.

It was a warm sunny morning, and she held back her grief as she walked to the car, aware that someone might be watching. Only once she was behind the wheel with her head in her hands did she let the tears come. Who would Hannah become? What was this twisted rhetoric doing to her, and to all the other children's minds?

She reached for her cigarettes in her bag with shaking hands. Her tears dried as she sat behind the wheel, gazing at the window to her daughter's classroom. Was it time to leave Germany? To leave everything she'd ever known to move to America with Seamus?

"He doesn't even want to go himself," she said out loud. "Go to work, Lisa."

She started the car and backed out of the school parking lot. It felt wrong to leave Hannah behind, but she knew she had little other choice.

∼

The 25-minute drive to the studio in Potsdam, southwest of Berlin, gave her a chance to clear her mind. The school year was almost over. Hannah would soon have a new teacher, and hopefully this next one would not be such an ardent Nazi. Perhaps Hitler and his cronies would be gone by then, anyway. The country had to come to its senses sooner or later. A few words from the right generals and the army could sweep him out of power. The international community was also watching. This whole nightmare could be over soon, and some kind of normalcy would return, whether that be a return to the days of democracy, or even the Kaiser. She said this to herself enough times on the drive that she almost started to believe it.

A familiar feeling of dread overtook her as she drove along the highway through the Grunewald Forest, southwest of the city. Images of the night she and Seamus buried her abuser, Ernst Milch, back in '32, infested her mind. His face appeared in front of her, and she shook her head to dismiss it. She and her husband rarely spoke of that night. What good would talking about it do? It was best to leave the past behind them—where it belonged. Her eyes darted to the rearview mirror and the empty road behind her. She imagined leaving *everything* behind, driving away with the ones she loved. If only it were that simple.

At least Ernst's father, the powerful industrialist Otto Milch, had stopped talking to the newspapers about finding his son. Ernst was declared dead the previous year, eighteen months after he went missing. Seamus knew Otto Milch, and his stories of the rich man's misdeeds eased her guilt. Somewhat, anyway.

Her eyes settled on the mirror again, but this time she was looking at herself.

"What have you got to feel guilty about? Would you rather it was you buried in that forest? Because that was the only other choice," she said aloud to her reflection. "It was you or him. That bastard tried to kill you."

The rational side of her agreed with her words, but the deep-seated emotional guilt she felt bubbled beneath the surface nonetheless. She never discussed these feelings with Seamus, but they remained. Would they always be there? Would the specter of Ernst Milch, the man who tried to murder her, haunt her forever?

She sighed with relief as the highway emerged from the cocoon of the Grunewald Forest. The sun was shining, and she rolled down the window. The air rushing into the car invigorated her, and she focused her mind on the part she had to play that day in the new film.

Because of Babar the elephant, she was running nearly quarter of an hour late, and it was almost ten in the morning when she arrived at the film studios. The guard at the gate recognized her and nodded as she bade him good morning. She parked and hurried inside.

The studio was busy, as always, and nobody seemed to notice her tardiness. The director, Alfred Hagen, was facing off with the film's female star, Lotte Kraus, shouting and gesticulating with his hands. He was tall and slim with a short gray beard. She was brown-haired, with sallow skin, and was dressed as a peasant, as were the rest of the cast, except for those tasked with playing the dastardly Soviet soldiers. They stood off to the side, laughing and joking, with their rifles slung over their shoulders. The set dresser was finalizing some details on the realistic-looking backdrop behind them as the cameras shifted into place.

Relieved not to be yelled at over her timekeeping, Lisa rushed down to costumes.

The wardrobe supervisor, a large man with a monocle named Frank List, greeted her as she arrived. "How was your daughter's school?"

It was hard to know exactly how to answer that question. "It was eye-opening." She wanted to say more, but didn't know how much she could trust him. He was likely not a Nazi sympathizer, but why take the chance when a few misplaced words could have the Gestapo at her door within days? It wasn't worth it. Best to talk about something else.

"Sorry I'm late. Did I miss much?" she asked.

"No," he said. "Lots of posturing and gesturing on the part of Herr Hagen, but as far as actual shooting? No—nothing."

Lisa found her peasant outfit on the rail. Less than five minutes later, she emerged from the changing rooms as the German-speaking villager she was playing. List was gone, and she scuttled over to where her fellow peasants were standing, to wait for shooting to begin.

The day wore on. Lisa was still standing by, waiting to be called. Her main scene was meant to be shot that afternoon, but it wasn't looking promising. Hagen argued with Lotte Kraus, the lead actress, all afternoon. He had a reputation for being difficult and seemed determined to prove it. Lotte was the same.

Lisa and the other supporting actors stayed silent, drinking from the coffee mugs in their hands as Hagen pursued Lotte across the set. "A wooden doll could play Ursula better than you!"

She turned to spit at him, red-faced, "I'm doing my best! It's not my fault the script is so bad! Did an illiterate child write it?"

"If you were any good, you'd make it work."

Lotte ripped off the headscarf wrapped around her hair and threw it at the older man. "That's it. I'm finished—I'm done. If you think I'm no good, take your role and shove it. I won't work with you again."

He caught the scarf in one hand. "Get off my set, you drunken nobody!"

Enraged, the actress stormed off, too incensed even to remove the rest of her peasant outfit. Lisa heard the sound of a car door slamming and an engine starting.

"What do we do now?" asked Ferdinand Nusbaum, the leading actor, a star of the Berlin stage. "Do we even have a movie anymore?"

Wim Lang, the producer of *The Dark Moon*, ran after her. He returned inside a minute, looking dejected. Lang was in his sixties, but this was the first movie he'd produced alone, and it showed. He approached Hagen. The two men gesticulated for a minute or two as the entire cast looked on. They couldn't have a picture without Lotte. She was the star who was to carry the whole production on her back. It was all too familiar to Lisa—she'd been on set for several films that collapsed before, and never gotten paid for any of them.

She watched in silence with the rest of the cast, trying to listen in to the conversation between the two men. Hagen seemed to be suggesting that they wind up production and cut their losses. Lang, the calmer of the pair, put his hand on his shoulder and told him that the production had to continue.

"We have a great script," Lang said. "And who says we need Lotte Kraus? We'll find our own star. Who do we have on set? We must have someone here who could slot into the role."

Hagen took a few seconds to ponder the idea. "Ok, but we hold auditions today—otherwise, I walk."

"Let's do it right now."

A ripple of excitement extended over the set, to which Lisa wasn't immune. Could she fill Lotte Kraus's shoes and play Ursula? Before she had a chance to contemplate such a coup, Hagen approached where she was sitting with several of the other female cast members.

"Can you learn the lines?" he asked.

Ilse Weber, a twenty-five-year-old actress Lisa met on the first day of shooting, put her hand on her chest. "Me?"

"Yes, you. What's your name?"

Ilse responded.

"And the one beside? What's your name?" The director was pointing at her.

"Lisa Ritter."

"You have a good look for this role. How fast can you learn the lines?"

"As fast as you need."

"That's what I want to hear. Come with me, and any other ladies who want to audition for the part of Ursula. Right now!" he shouted.

Ilse, Lisa, and three other women all lined up on the set. The background was a sunset over a field of wheat.

"We'll do the death scene. Ferdinand!"

The actor who played the husband murdered by the Soviet soldiers hustled over and stood beside the director.

"Get in position," Hagen said.

A stagehand ran over with a copy of the script for each of the actresses. Lisa refused it. She knew the lines already after watching them shoot the scene for hours the previous day, and had learned every syllable by heart.

"No makeup," Hagen roared as the makeup artist ran over. "We're doing this now. No shooting."

The cameramen joined the rest of the crew to watch.

Ilse held the script as she bent down to Ferdinand's character. The actor writhed in agony, nursing a fatal bayonet wound to the stomach. Ilse was good, but nervous. She didn't stumble or make any mistakes, but it was obvious the director remained unimpressed as she finished the lines. She stood back to let the next actress try out.

Lisa was last, and stood waiting as the others went. Lang was next to Hagen, but it was plain who would make the final decision on the role. The director's facial expression didn't change through any of the auditions. He maintained his look of quiet disgust throughout.

Then it was Lisa's turn.

"No script?" Hagen asked as she took her place.

"No."

The director looked at her for a second, as if to tell her that she was equally as useless as all the others, before raising his hand to bid her to begin.

Lisa was calm, much more so than she thought she'd be. She'd dreamed of this moment so many times, and now it was happening. She softened her voice, dulling the melodrama the others had injected into the scene, and played the role as a damaged woman with few options remaining. The image of Ernst Milch's bloodied face came into her mind and she kept it there, used it. She thought of burying his body in those dark woods, and the horror that infested her that night.

The scene was over in less than a minute. Hagen's face was unchanged. He bade the actresses to go back and sit down as he paced over to the producer. The two men whispered for a minute or two before Hagen strode over to where the five women who auditioned were sitting together.

"Lisa, the role of Ursula is yours."

Lisa stood up, her heart soaring. The other actresses patted her on the back, and she went with Hagen. Ferdinand greeted her with a handshake.

"Someone get this woman a script. She's our new Ursula," Hagen called out.

Lisa couldn't keep the smile from her face. Was this how wishes came true, because someone else got fired?

6

Saturday, June 8

The party Seamus insisted upon having to celebrate his "beautiful wife's ascension to stardom" was organized and set for that Saturday night in the house. On such short notice, luminaries such as the US ambassador and his wife had to respectfully decline the invitation, but that didn't dull Seamus's determination to celebrate her new starring role. On Thursday, he took the afternoon off work to make phone calls, and came home that night satisfied that the party would be fit to celebrate her achievement.

Lisa appreciated his sincerity in observing what was far and away the most prominent role of her career to date, but was more focused on keeping her head above water on set. She had gone from having six lines in the entire movie to having a dozen or more every day. But she'd always been able to remember things. The new lines remained in her mind, and she could reach back and take them as needed. It was hard to say Hagen was impressed by her talents, but Thursday and Friday passed without him getting into a screaming match with her. Ferdinand, her costar, assured her that this was quite the achievement.

Filming ended in the late afternoon on Saturday, and Lisa was home just as dinner was served. Maureen took it upon herself to cook on the nights when her stepmother was late home—if she was around herself. On the other occasions, Seamus blundered through. No one had complained yet, though Conor, in particular, seemed to miss Lisa's cooking. Dinner that evening was light fare, as food was being served at the party. Trays of hors d'oeuvres were already laid out on tables in the dining room, along with bottles of wine, beer, and champagne. Lisa resisted the idea of getting the party catered, and also of employing servers for the night. Seamus was disappointed but agreed.

The guests began arriving at eight, and within an hour, the house was packed with men and women in their finery. The sight of Seamus talking to Hagen—and Lang, the producer—in the corner set alarm bells off in Lisa's mind. She tried to walk past and leave them to their conversation, but her feet wouldn't cooperate with her mind's intentions. Hagen was wearing a blue cravat over a white shirt, with a gray blazer. Lang was wearing a blue pinstriped suit, like the American gangsters in Conor and Michael's books.

"Here she is," Seamus said as Lisa appeared beside him. "The new rising star of German cinema."

Neither man gave the response he seemed to be fishing for, drinking their champagne in silence instead.

"I'm honored you gave me this chance," Lisa said.

Hagen didn't want to have this conversation—she knew that much about him already.

"Are you a native Berliner, Herr Hagen?" she asked.

"Yes. From this area, actually. I still live close by."

Lisa stayed, monitoring the conversation for another ten minutes while the four of them made small talk about the city and America. She had no doubt her husband had the sincerest intentions, but didn't consider Lang, and Hagen in particular, to be open to his forms of charm. When the time came to move on, she took Seamus's hand and led him across the crowded room to where Maureen, Thomas, and his parents were standing. Lisa's father was across the room, lapping up compliments from some neighbors.

"I'll need an autograph soon," Thomas's father, Joachim Reus, said.

"For me?" Lisa laughed. "But you might need it for him." She pointed at Ferdinand Nusbaum, standing with his wife and chatting with some of the other cast members.

"It was good of them to come on such short notice," Maureen said.

"I haven't known many actors to refuse an invitation to a party," Lisa said. "Particularly one with free alcohol."

Clayton strutted over with a glamorous blond lady on his arm. Seamus seemed to know her and greeted her with a kiss on the cheek.

"Lisa, I have someone I want you to meet. This is Petra Wagner—an actress, just like yourself," the journalist said.

"Pleased to meet you," Petra said with a beautiful smile. "And congratulations on everything you've achieved."

"I'm still trying to get my head around it all," Lisa answered. "That lot over there keep my feet on the ground." She pointed at Conor and Hannah. The two children were at the hors d'oeuvre table, picking up various canapés and putting them back on the trays after taking a bite.

"I'll deal with them," Maureen said and left the group.

"So, have you much acting experience?" Lisa asked.

"Some. I've done a few plays, and bit parts in movies. Actually, I was wondering if there were any roles available in your movie?"

Lisa saw herself in the young woman. Going to a party to

meet people and try to pick up roles? She would have done the same just days before.

"Come with me," Lisa said and took Petra by the hand. The two women walked over to where Hagen and Lang were standing.

"Gentlemen, this is a new friend of mine, Petra Wagner. She's an actress and wants to audition for the role I just vacated."

Hagen looked at her with the same contempt he reserved for any human being, but Lang seemed taken with the starlet. He spoke first—before the director could spew his usual negativity.

"You should come to the set on Monday. We haven't filled the part yet. I'm sure we could find a place for you."

"You'll need to audition first," Hagen said.

"Of course," Petra said with a coquettish smile.

∼

The party wore on. Without the aid of hired servers, Seamus found himself running around all night, and had only had a few drinks even as midnight approached. The children were in bed. Only Michael and Maureen were still up. His two oldest were adept at mixing with the guests, many of whom were fascinated by his journey to next year's Olympics and her experiences in the male-dominated world of studying medicine in university. Lisa was magnificent as always, and even made a short speech when he called the room to order by banging on the side of his glass with a butter knife.

He strolled over to the drinks table and drained a bottle of champagne into an elegant glass his uncle had left him. Gert and Lil Bernheim stood a few steps away and greeted him with warm smiles as he *clinked* glasses.

"Got yourself a drink at last?" Lil asked. "It's easier going to parties rather than throwing them."

Her husband extended an arm around her waist.

"Pity we can't play the music we want," he said. "I could go for some Duke Ellington or Tommy Dorsey about now."

"Yeah," Seamus responded. "They're always there, aren't they?"

"Who?" Lil asked.

"The Nazis. I haven't heard one person mention them all night, but their claws seem to reach into every situation."

"Speaking of Nazis, where is your cousin?" Lil asked.

Gert glowered at her, but Seamus laughed. "She's home sick. This isn't her type of thing, anyway."

The three kept talking until the sound of the telephone ringing from the foyer interrupted them. *Who can that be at this time on a Saturday night?* Seamus thought as he excused himself to go and answer it. Few people had gone home, and he had to push through the throng of people to get to the phone. He picked up the receiver and held it to his ear.

"Shemoose Ritter?" the voice on the line asked. He ignored the pronunciation of his first name, used to it by now.

"This is Captain Ansel Ressler of the Berlin Fire Brigade—there's been an incident at your factory. We were called about an hour ago and have been fighting the fire ever since."

Seamus felt like he'd been drenched with a bucket of ice-cold water. "A fire? What's the damage? Where's Alofs, the nightwatchman?"

"We found him unconscious in his hut, but he's in stable condition in the hospital now. He claims someone hit him in the back of the head with a baton. We don't know."

"Is he ok?"

"Just a little beaten up. I'm sure he'll be fine in the morning."

"What's the damage?"

"The fire is extensive. It's too early to judge what damage it might have done."

"I'm coming down there," Seamus said and put down the phone.

He ran back through the crowd to where Bernheim was standing. "The factory is on fire. Come on, we have to go."

Before his friend had a chance to answer, Seamus bustled through the crowd of people to find his wife. She was standing with her father and a few others. Her face melted as Seamus told her.

"I have to get there."

Lisa couldn't leave all these people alone in their house. "Go," she said. "I'll deal with everyone here."

"I can help," Dr. Walz said. "I'll start clearing the guests out."

Seamus didn't hesitate any longer, and he and Bernheim ran for the front door and to his car.

Neither spoke much for the fifteen minutes it took to arrive at Ritter Metalworks. They didn't know any details, so there was nothing to say. Dark thoughts filled every corner of Seamus's mind as they sped through the city streets.

The orange glow against the night sky was visible from several blocks away.

"Our very own Reichstag fire," Seamus said.

The gates were unlocked and several fire trucks were in the parking lot, their hoses drawn as the firefighters pumped water on the blaze. The windows along the outside wall were blackened and smashed, and flames danced inside the factory. It seemed like the entire west side of the building was in the process of being razed.

Seamus pulled up and jumped out of the car. Sparks flitted among the smoke billowing into the night sky, looking like the fireflies he used to chase as a child on warm summer nights by the river. The police were marshaling the small crowd that had gathered to watch.

Seamus ran to see if he knew any of them, the light of the fire flickering across their faces. Somehow he expected to see some of the workers, but the people in the crowd were strangers who'd stopped to behold the spectacle.

Uncle Helmut's life's work going up in a cloud of smoke. He moved forward, walking toward the burning building until a member of the police put a hand on his chest. He was in his late thirties, with bushy red eyebrows.

"Where do you think you're going?"

"It's my factory," Seamus said. "I own the place, with my cousin."

"Nothing to be done now, except let the fire brigade do their job. Please step back with the rest of the crowd."

Seamus slinked back to where Bernheim was standing. The only sounds were the crackling of the flames and the shattering of glass, the water gushing from the hoses, and the firefighters shouting to one another.

Seamus thought of the 324 workers he employed. The government had fixed their wages during the trough of the Depression, and he knew that few had enough aside to ride out the weeks and months it would take to rebuild. He and Helga could surmount this wave, but what of them?

"Helga's over there," Bernheim said. He pointed into the darkness. Seamus could make out the figure of his cousin, her silhouette illuminated by the glow of the flames. He jogged over to her, she took his hand. He had never seen her cry before, but rivulets of silver shone on her gaunt cheeks.

"I'm just glad my father isn't alive to see this."

"Who did it?"

"I have no idea."

"What's the damage?"

She turned to look at him. The orange flames glittered in her eyes.

"Absolute."

7

Sunday, June 9

The first rays of a brilliant dawn sun woke Seamus from a fitful sleep. It took a few seconds to figure out where he was, before the memories of the night before descended on him like an anvil. Lisa came to get him and persuaded him to go home after watching the factory go up in flames for an hour or so. With little point in watching the inferno consume the place all night, he agreed. Bernheim and Helga retreated to their homes at the same time, with the promise that they would meet in the morning to decide what on earth they were to do next.

His clothes smelled of smoke, the house silent as he rose from the couch. The detritus of the party to celebrate Lisa surrounded him. The trays were empty and most of the glasses were cleared away, but the odor of cigarette smoke, wine, and stale beer remained, now combined with the factory fire's smoke. His shoes were on the rug, and he slipped them on. The cushions sagged beneath his weight as he sank back down. He put his head in his hands, an image of his uncle filling his vision.

How could this have happened? The inquiries they pursued the night before hadn't provided any clues. The fire brigade captain had no idea—he was more focused on containing the blaze than trying to figure out how it had started. Asking the firefighters and the police who were securing the scene didn't offer any further insight. No one knew anything.

Someone out there does, and it's my job to find out who and what.

He called the hospital to ask for Alofs, the nightwatchman. After a few minutes, a nurse came on the line, who told him that he would be discharged in hours. Seamus asked to pass on a message to meet him at the factory after he was released and hung up.

He made himself a weak cup of coffee in the kitchen before buttering a slice of bread. The knock on the front door he was expecting came as he finished the bread, and he rubbed crumbs off his hands before jogging to the door. Bernheim stood with hat in hand and black rings beneath his eyes.

"Do I look as bad as you?" Seamus said.

"Let me check." Bernheim stepped inside and looked at himself in the mirror hanging in the foyer. "Pretty much," he answered and followed Seamus into the kitchen.

Seamus offered his friend a coffee, and neither man spoke for the few seconds it took for Seamus to boil the kettle to a whistle once again. He poured the drink and brought it to the table, where he took a seat opposite his factory manager.

"Did you take a trip to the factory—or what's left of it, at least—before you came over?" Seamus asked.

"No, I thought I'd wait to take a look with you. I can't bear the thought of seeing it in the daylight."

"Alofs is fine. I left a message with a nurse for him to meet us at the factory later."

"Hopefully he'll have some answers." Bernheim wrapped his hands around his coffee cup, warming them.

"Will the insurance company come out today?"

"Not on a Sunday. I haven't called them yet. They don't answer the phones at midnight on a Saturday night either. I'll try them first thing tomorrow."

"I'm sure they'll have caught wind of it by then. It'll probably be in the papers."

"Any thoughts on who did this?" Bernheim sipped his coffee and placed it back down, looking drawn and pale. If Seamus hadn't known better, he would have thought the man was sick.

"You mean any new thoughts since I last saw you about five hours ago? No." Seamus pushed out a deep breath that seemed to catch in his throat. "I had no idea last night, and have even less of a clue now."

"Helga swears up and down that she went over the safety protocols before she left on Friday."

"She's nothing if not fastidious. I can't see her overlooking something, and besides, someone took the trouble to knock Alofs out."

"Alofs is a Nazi sympathizer. Maybe his friends in the Brownshirts did it. We wouldn't be the first business sympathetic to Jews that they've hit."

"It wouldn't surprise me at all," the manager said. "I'm just thinking out loud here, but Helga clearly wasn't happy with the direction the factory was going in. What if she had something to do with this?"

Silence filled the air around them like water. Seamus thought back to meeting his cousin last night. If she was hiding something, she was a caliber of actress that Lisa and her friends could only dream of becoming. The shock was plain to see in her eyes, and her tears seemed real enough. Her hands were shaking as she stood there, and her skin was cold and clammy to the touch. It seemed almost inconceivable that she was putting on an act—the factory was all she had left of her father, and it was gone now.

"Why would she?" Seamus asked. "She hasn't mentioned a word about the Jews and the Communists in the factory in months. The Nazis control the unions, the wages, and have their ridiculous council in the factory. You really think she'd burn down her father's metalworks to make a point to us? What would she have to gain?"

"The insurance money?"

"She has more than she could ever spend. What would she need more money for? And besides, I get half the insurance money, but Helmut was clever enough to stipulate in his will that it only be spent on rebuilding the premises."

"The old man didn't trust you as much as you thought, eh?"

"He covered his bases, like any businessman." Bernheim looked puzzled. "It's a baseball term."

"What do I know about that sport?"

"I meant, he didn't take any chances."

"Apparently not."

Bernheim reached into his pocket for a cigarette. Seamus refused when he offered him one, but pushed over an ashtray. Gray smoke from the party lingered in the air.

"So, if she didn't do it, who else could have, apart from the Nazis?" Bernheim asked.

"What about our old friend Otto Milch?" Seamus responded. "We haven't heard from him in a while, but he wasn't above undercutting Ritter Metalworks to force us out of business two years ago."

"You really think he'd stoop to industrial espionage? I don't see it," Bernheim said. "We're a mosquito on his back—no real threat to him and his business. Besides, rumor has it that he's preparing to devote most of his activities to rearmament. We're not even in direct competition with him anymore—that's why we haven't heard from him. He's moved on and doesn't care about us."

Lisa appeared at the door behind them in her dressing gown. "Early morning meeting?" she asked with no mirth in her voice.

"Just trying to work out who did this," Seamus said.

"It doesn't make any sense. Did the nightwatchman say anything?"

"I don't think he saw much, as he was hit from behind. We're meeting him later this morning at the factory," Seamus answered.

"Let's see what the fire marshal says, too," Bernheim said.

A knock on the door signified Helga's arrival, and Lisa returned with Seamus's cousin and business partner. She was dressed in the same tight black dress she always wore. Her hair was tied back tighter than a snare drum, but her pale face had an unhealthy gray hue. Her eyes were puffy and lined with blood vessels, giving her an almost sinister appearance. Seamus was thankful she'd left her gold-tinted Nazi Party member pin at home.

She greeted him with a rare embrace, but stopped short with Bernheim, instead offering him an outstretched hand.

"Are the children awake?" she asked as they walked back into the kitchen.

"No," Lisa said. "But Michael has training in an hour."

"It's probably best if we let him sleep through. He had a late night," Seamus said.

"We should get to the factory," Helga said.

Lisa stood by the sink as the two men got up. Seamus put his arms around her, taking in her scent, the feel of her body against his.

"Have you changed your clothes from last night?" she asked as he drew away.

"No."

"I think you look wonderful, Seamus," Bernheim said.

"You heard the man," Seamus said to his wife. "My deportment isn't the most important thing right now. Tell the children...something. I'll try to see them later. I have no idea how today is going to go."

"They'll understand," Lisa said. The others said their goodbyes.

"We can take my car," Helga said as they walked out into the morning air. The sun was sparkling in a clear blue sky. The light reflecting off the windshield of Helga's Buick Series 40—which she'd imported from America the year before—made it shine like it was covered in diamonds. Seamus sat in the passenger seat, with Bernheim in the back.

"The Trustee Council members will likely be along sometime this morning," Helga said as she pulled out into the leafy western Berlin suburb of Charlottenburg. She knew the place well—she grew up in the house Seamus lived in.

"You can deal with them," Bernheim said.

"They're your people," Seamus said. It wasn't the time to twist the knife, but he couldn't resist. "Did you speak to Benz?"

"Briefly."

"Did he or any of his cronies have any insight into how this happened?"

"Not that he told me."

"There's a shock. The most idiotic people in the workforce have become the most powerful," Seamus said.

"What use is that right now?" she replied. "Those men were voted into their positions by their peers. They deserve our respect."

Bernheim remained silent, as he always did. Jews had little other choice these days.

Seamus bit his tongue also. No use in poking the bear any more than he already had. The council was a fact of life, as much as the Reich Economic Chamber he and every other businessman were forced to join.

They continued in silence for a few seconds before they began to discuss the insurance in place.

"It should cover the cost of refurbishments," Bernheim said.

"It's the workers I'm worried about," Seamus said. "What are they to do while we rebuild? We can't pay them in the interim."

"Can you have a word with some of the other members of the Reich Economic Chamber about taking them on temporarily?" asked Bernheim.

"I will, but I don't hold out a lot of hope for that idea."

Helga's knuckles were white on the steering wheel, but she didn't say a word. No one spoke as they approached the smoldering wreck that the day before had been a working factory. Black smoke hung in the air, almost mocking them like a malevolent spirit. The gates were still open, so they drove through. Helga's face fell, finding the forecourt outside deserted. Helga pulled up and got out in silence. The ground was wet from the night before, and huge puddles lined the charred factory walls. The doors were open. Seamus walked up to peer inside.

The factory floor was a mess of charred machinery. The roof was gone, and the light of morning illuminated a nightmare he never could have envisaged twelve hours before.

"I'm going in," he said and stepped through the door before either of them had a chance to protest. Scenes of the war flashed into his mind. It was the only other time he'd seen destruction to compare to this. He pushed the memories back into the recesses of his mind. The parts of his brain that housed the memories of that time weren't places he relished visiting, and wouldn't benefit him in the situation.

Charred wooden beams crunched under his weight as he negotiated his way to the stairs that led up to his office. The metal stairway was stained black, but looked sturdy. He weighed the idea of taking it up to his office before deciding it was worth the minor risk.

The metal banisters were warm to the touch, so he kept to the middle, making sure each footfall was secure as he ascended.

Bernheim was on the floor behind him and called out, "Are you sure that's safe?"

"Seems fine. It's all metal."

"If you're sure," his friend answered. "Just be careful."

Seamus didn't respond and kept on until he reached the landing at the top of the stairs. From his lofty position, he could see the complete picture of the devastation the fire had wrought. Rubble and black debris lay six inches thick on every part of the floor, the machines twisted and mutilated beyond repair. The windows were all gone. The roof... The lunch and locker rooms... Everything that was on the walls... All gone.

The door to his office was on the floor. He continued inside as if he were visiting the scene of a crime. *Perhaps that's what this is,* he thought. His desk was destroyed, collapsed in on itself and lying in a shrunken mess in front of what had once constituted his chair. The papers and files in the bookcases were ash.

The safe sat on the floor in the corner. It was, as everything else, darkened by the fire, but seemed intact. What fire could damage a ton of solid steel? He entered the combination, and it opened to reveal the cash and papers he left inside on Friday evening.

The sound of shoes crunching on debris announced Bernheim's arrival.

"You came up."

"I figured if you didn't die on the way up, I wouldn't either," the manager replied.

"What's your office like?"

"The same."

"Have you noticed anything? Any sign of how this could have started?"

"I don't know what to look for past cans of gasoline lying around, or a written confession. Do you?"

"I hope the fire brigade does."

"They should be along in a few minutes."

"Where's Helga?"

"Outside, waiting for her friends from the council."

Seamus kneeled down and reached into the safe, taking out a leather bag with petty cash in it: a few hundred Reichsmarks. The papers were contracts. The contents of the safe were everything in his office that survived the inferno. Business had improved these last few years under the Nazis...for those who adhered to their stringent guidelines. Seamus thought back to the Chamber of Commerce meeting he attended a few weeks after Hitler became Chancellor. The captains of industry were right: the rich had gotten richer under National Socialism, with corporate profits soaring. Otto Milch, Gustav Krupp, and the other titans of the German business world had been vindicated in the investment they made in the Nazi State. If they'd sold their souls, at least they got a good price.

Seamus was richer now too—more so than he'd ever been—but the workers still struggled. Unable to raise their wages due to regulations set down by the Reich Economic Chamber, he and Bernheim took to finagling the books to give bonuses and dividends, but the regulators were cracking down on that too.

"Do you have any contracts at home? Anything valuable saved?"

"One or two. Not a lot," Bernheim answered.

Seamus walked to where his desk used to stand: nothing left but charred wood and ash. Uncle Helmut sat there for thirty years, and it was gone now, just as he was. Everything he built went in one night.

"Benz and his cronies are going to try to use this to push out the workers they don't approve of."

"Including me, I suppose," Bernheim said.

"I won't let that happen."

"I don't doubt your sincerity, but your hands might be tied."

Seamus walked to the window and picked up the decanter he kept on the table below it. The table was gone and the whiskey had spilled out and dried, but the decanter itself had survived somehow. He opened the leather case he was still holding and put it inside, along with the contracts and the cash. Without another word, the two men left the office. Seamus followed the factory manager down to his office, where they surveyed the damage together.

"I don't understand how the fire got up here," Seamus said. "The stairs and the floor are metal."

"The roof, I suppose."

Seamus paced down to Helga's office, where the situation was the same—devastation. Her personal safe was intact in the corner and seemed to have sustained minimal damage.

"They couldn't get into the safes," Seamus said. "Everything else was destroyed."

Bernheim didn't answer. "I wonder if there's enough left of the doors to check if they were forced," Seamus continued.

He left his cousin's office and descended the stairs. Anger rose within him. *Who did this? What else were they trying to destroy in burning the factory down?* The two men shuffled through the debris on the factory floor.

The sound of Helga's voice interrupted them, and they stood up in unison. A car pulled up and two men got out. Seamus and Bernheim saw them shaking hands with Helga as they approached.

The men were in their late forties or early fifties. Helga introduced them.

"This is Roland Frick of the Berlin Police."

"Pleased to meet you," Frick said and offered a meaty hand to the two men. He was red-faced and sported a thick salt-and-pepper beard.

"And you spoke to Captain Ansel Ressler of the Fire Brigade last night."

Ressler greeted them. He was several inches taller than Seamus and had a black mustache and a sallow complexion. He was in his uniform, complete with the Nazi pin on his lapel.

"Have you had a chance to inspect the property yet, Captain Ressler?" Seamus asked.

"Not in any significant detail."

"We were just inside. We noticed some strange signs."

"I would warn against jumping to any conclusions before we've had a chance to look the place over properly. Leave the inspection to the professionals."

Ressler pulled on his cigarette and motioned toward the building. The two men left without another word.

A car roared through the gates toward them, and Seamus grimaced as he recognized Benz and two other members of the Trustee Council: Artur Borst and Hilmar Kopper.

"That's all we need right now. Benz and his circus."

The Nazi government, as part of their system of assailing every facet of German culture, organized Trustee Councils in every business, elected from among the workforce from a Nazi-approved list. Most workers neglected to vote, but that meant nothing. The slow seepage of scum to the top continued unabated. They flexed their muscles by bullying the Jewish and Communist-leaning workers, and Seamus spent much of his time these days keeping the various factions away from each other's throats. His promise to his uncle to protect all of his workers like they were his own family weighed heavily on him, but that didn't check his determination to uphold it.

The Trustee Council had taken to ignoring Bernheim entirely of late. They couldn't abide taking orders from a Jew, and Seamus was powerless to punish them for it. Their influence grew with every decree from the government that supported them. Helga, as a member of the Nazi Party, dealt with them alone, relaying their demands and castigations to Seamus. Gunther Benz, a fourth-year metal polisher—who, before the Nazis' ascent to power, had been a junior staff member with a reputation for drinking too much—was the primary spokesman for the council.

The most idiotic and lazy people in the workforce had become the most powerful. But there was nothing to be done about it. The council was a fact of life now, as much as the Reich Economic Chamber.

The car pulled up beside them. The doors flew open, and the three employees of Ritter Metalworks—all sporting not just swastikas on their lapels but Nazi armbands across their biceps—leapt out. Seamus wanted to ask what occasion they'd dressed up for, but held his tongue.

"Have there been any arrests made yet?" Benz asked.

His black slicked-back hair was freshly combed over his pale, pockmarked face. He was hardly the picture of Aryan health. Borst was taller, with broad shoulders and a thick brown beard.

Kopper was bald, and at almost sixty, had worked for Uncle Helmut for twenty years before Seamus and Helga took over. Seamus recalled meeting him before the Nazi seizure of German life. He was pleasant and polite then. No more.

"The fire brigade captain and a police detective are inside—" Seamus began.

"Where were you last night?" interrupted Benz, pointing a finger at Bernheim. The two other men stood behind each shoulder as he spoke.

"At a party in Herr Ritter's," Bernheim said.

"Any witnesses to that?" Borst asked over Benz's shoulder.

"Dozens."

"What about the other Jews?" Kopper asked.

"Stop this!" Seamus said. "There's no one I trust more than Herr Bernheim, and unless you have evidence to the contrary, stop throwing around accusations."

"It seems like whoever set this fire knew what they were doing," Benz said. "Seems like someone with insider knowledge."

"We've been warning you about the Jews and the Communists in there for months," Kopper said.

"Years!" Borst added.

"You're suggesting that the workers did this?"

"The Jews," Benz said. "The vipers you took in to suckle at your teat."

"We have twenty-three Jewish workers," Bernheim said. He sounded tired. "Why on earth would they want to burn down their place of employment?"

"Why did the Communists burn down the Reichstag? The same Bolshevist-Jewish conspiracy is at work here as tried to destroy our elected National Socialist government," Benz said.

Seamus looked at him for a second without answering. *It must be exhausting to live like this.*

"The fire captain warned us about jumping to any conclusions," Seamus answered. "It's only natural to look to lash out at someone—"

"We've had enough," Benz said. "This incident proves the dangers we loyal Germans face every time we come to work."

"What are you talking about?" Bernheim asked.

Benz's face contorted into a twisted mask of hate. He pointed his finger as he spat the words. "I'm talking about the Jews, the leftists, and the other enemies of the German people we're forced to share our workspaces with."

"You have no contact with our Jewish or foreign workers," Seamus said. He'd separated the hardcore Nazis from the rest of the employees the year before, after the Night of the Long

Knives, when Hitler consolidated his power by eliminating his enemies within. Benz and the others became unbearable after that. The act of segregating them saved hundreds of wasted man-hours.

"Let's wait to see what the fire captain says," Seamus said. It was evident that engaging with these men was useless, and nothing productive would come from the conversation. "If there's nothing else, gentlemen." He turned to leave.

"This is an opportunity," Benz said.

Seamus stopped. "For what exactly?"

"For a fresh start for Ritter. This is the chance we've been waiting for to cleanse our workforce."

"You mean blame the fire on the workers who don't share your political views and fire them en masse, don't you?"

"And hire good, honest German workers—men committed to the glorious, bloodless revolution happening in the Reich every day."

"You know I won't do that," Seamus said, staring into Benz's brown eyes.

"We'll see what the German Labor Front has to say about it," the man answered with a sly smile.

Seamus walked away, bringing Bernheim with him. He waited until they were far enough away from the three Nazis to open his mouth. "What was Benz like before all this?"

"Painful in different ways," Gert answered. "The Nazis have given the dregs of our society free rein to impose their idiocy on the rest of us. And now Benz and his cronies are going to try to use this to push the workers they don't approve of out."

They joined Helga outside the main door.

A few minutes passed before Flick and Ressler emerged from the burned-out factory and came to report to Seamus and Helga. Benz and his cronies were still lurking by the car. The policeman and the fire captain were only inside the building for thirty minutes or so, and Seamus wondered how much they could garner between them in such a short time.

"Were you able to find anything?" Helga asked.

"Some things," Ressler said. "But nothing conclusive."

"Did you find the source of the fire?" Bernheim asked.

"It could have been the faulty wiring by the machines at the back. It's hard to say."

"By the machine presses? I checked those wires myself two weeks ago," Helga said. "I didn't find any problem."

"I could repeat what I said earlier," the fire captain said. "Listen, I don't think anyone is best served by drawing out this process. I'll write to the insurance company and you'll get your check. A long, drawn-out investigation is only going to delay that process."

"You're not going to continue the investigation?" Seamus asked. "The nightwatchman was knocked out and had to go to hospital."

"Was he knocked out, or did he fall over drunk? I found an empty bottle of whiskey in his hut," Frick said. "Maybe he was too embarrassed to admit it and faked being injured."

"That's ridiculous," Seamus said.

"I understand you want to try to understand this calamitous event, and you want to assure yourself that once whoever is responsible is behind bars your property will be safe again, but let me assure you, even if this was deliberate, it's more likely kids playing with matches than anything else," Ressler said.

"So, you do think it was arson?" Bernheim asked.

"Not necessarily. I'm saying that even if it was, the grand conspiracy that people seek rarely exists."

"What do you think?" Seamus asked the policeman.

"I didn't see any sign of forced entry. No one observed any suspicious activity before the fire. Have you received any threats?"

"Not as such," Seamus said.

The Golden Age

"In these situations, I watch the owners. You and your cousin own the factory 50/50?"

"Yes," Helga said. "But my father's will stipulated that any insurance monies received be used to rebuild the factory."

Frick nodded and reached into his pocket for a notebook. He opened it up and took a pencil in his hand. Seamus noticed that the pages were blank. "You're American?"

"Yes," Seamus answered.

"You didn't want to burn the place out, get the insurance money, and disappear back to Kansas?"

Seamus almost told the man he wasn't from Kansas, but stopped himself. "My business partner just informed you that any insurance monies don't go directly to us, but to an intermediary who will hold the funds to be used solely for rebuilding the factory."

"And you can prove that?"

"I'll have our lawyer call you in the morning," Helga said.

"That rules out that, I suppose." He put a line through the words he'd just written. "Any disgruntled employees? Any enemies?"

Seamus wasn't quite sure how to answer that question and hesitated. Helga jumped in.

"Plenty of shady characters in our workforce," she said.

"I heard about your plethora of Jews and leftists," Frick said and wrote something down on his notepad.

"Now, hold on just a minute," Seamus said. "We have no evidence of any wrongdoing on the part of any of our employees."

"No real evidence of any wrongdoing by anyone," Ressler added.

"Do you believe the Jews in your ranks might have had reason to burn the factory down?" Frick asked Helga.

"It's certainly a possibility," she answered.

"What are you talking about?" Seamus asked.

Bernheim stepped back. The bones of his jawline were sticking out, but he didn't say a word.

"You see?" Ressler said. "If we do start a detailed investigation, we may have to ask a lot of uncomfortable questions—particularly of the Jews among your workforce."

Seamus turned to his cousin, but she didn't return his gaze and it remained fixed on the fire captain.

"The first thing we look for—apart from evidence of gasoline or other accelerants—is a sign of forced entry. We found neither. It seems this could drag on for weeks, or you could drop the entire matter and declare it an accident. You could start rebuilding next week."

Were these men lazy or corrupt, or both? Seamus felt his anger rising but knew he had to control it. He took a deep breath. Helga still hadn't looked at him since she'd raised the possibility of blaming this on the Jews. It was difficult to see Bernheim working with her after this, but he'd said that before several times and somehow, they always managed to trundle on. Perhaps the problem this time would be whether he himself could work with her anymore, but what choice did he have? Return to America with nothing but the money he'd saved and relinquish control to her? That wasn't a choice at all.

"It seems the sensible option is to declare it an accident and get on with our lives," she said.

"Herr Ritter? Is that your opinion?" Frick asked.

Seamus turned to Bernheim, even though it was his decision to make. The factory manager nodded to him with a pained expression. He still hesitated. This wasn't an accident. He knew that much, but what was there to gain from an investigation the police didn't want, that Helga and even Bernheim didn't want? Would Helga and Benz and the other Nazis use an investigation to weed out the Jewish and leftist workers? Was there anything he could do for them even if the fire was declared accidental?

"Ok, have it your way—we'll call it an accident and start rebuilding. At least we can get our people back to work as soon as possible."

"I think you'll look back on this as the right decision," Ressler said.

Seamus felt as if he'd been violated.

"I'll write up the reports and speak to the insurance company. I don't foresee any problems in getting the check," Frick said.

The two men offered handshakes to each of them and said their goodbyes. The three watched as they walked past the members of the Trustee Council and got into their car.

"I didn't mean to imply you could have done this," Helga said to Bernheim.

"No, just my kind," he answered.

"I said what I thought was right for the well-being of the business, as I always will. This is our chance to restructure and rebuild better than before. This awful tragedy could be a blessing in disguise."

"I'll speak to you next week," Seamus said, though he could think of little he wanted to do less at that moment.

Helga said goodbye. She left, passing where Benz and his acolytes were lurking, and stopped to talk to them for a few minutes.

"You think she had something to do with this now?" Bernheim asked.

"I'm not dismissing any possibility. I know someone did this, and if the police aren't going to look into it, we're going to have to. If there's someone willing to go to these lengths to destroy us, we need to find out who."

The two men turned around and walked back into the smoldering hulk that had been their place of work the day before.

Alofs arrived just before eleven. The portly middle-aged

single man was a remnant of Uncle Helmut's policy of giving jobs to those in need despite their abilities, and Seamus wasn't expecting much insight.

"So, you didn't see anyone?" Seamus asked the nightwatchman standing in front of him.

"No. I was facing the other way and felt something strike me in the back of the head. The next thing I remember, the fire engines were spraying water on the flames."

"Were you drinking? The police found an empty bottle in your hut," Gert asked.

Alofs hesitated before answering, like a schoolboy caught in the act. "It's a lonely job, sitting there for hours with nothing going on."

"And the one time something did happen, you were too drunk to react."

"Leave it, Gert. No use in getting into this." Seamus turned to the other man. "You appreciate that I have to let you go now."

The nightwatchman had nothing else to say and left in silence.

8

Monday, June 10

Maureen had never met Thomas for breakfast before. She was wary both of how she looked first thing on a Monday morning after such a stressful weekend, and her boyfriend's intentions. She had a busy day ahead. Two of Dr. Walz's nurses were out sick with summer flu. Her morning lectures were optional, so she had agreed to come into the clinic to help out.

They met outside a café they both knew on Dorotheenstrasse, near the university. His wide smile upon seeing her set some of her fears to rest.

"What time are you due at the clinic?" Thomas asked.

"Not until nine."

"It's not even seven thirty. We'll have time for a leisurely breakfast to start the week."

They took a table by the window and ordered coffee.

"Why did you want to meet at this time?" she asked after the waitress left.

The sharp tone of her voice seemed to knock him back. "I

just wanted to see how you were. It can't have been an easy weekend. Anything new? What did the nightwatchman say?"

"Just when everything seemed to be falling into place..." Maureen replied. "The nightwatchman was useless—drunk on the job and not any help. The police are going to close the investigation already. My father's stressed to the breaking point."

Thomas ordered potato pancakes. Maureen asked for bread rolls with sausage on the side.

She was spreading jam on one of her rolls when he asked, "What's the matter? You don't seem yourself. I know the fire is on your mind, but is there something else?"

"I'm just wondering who might have done it." She took a bite of her bread.

"The police will find out, I'm sure."

"It just seems like a coincidence that you brought me to that meeting last Monday and my father's factory went up in flames that weekend."

"What are you talking about?" he asked.

"What better way to strike a blow against rearmament than by burning down a factory about to begin producing bombs and bullets?"

It was hard to know if she truly believed the words coming out of her mouth, but she said them anyway.

"You think they—" He cut himself off to look around. No one else was listening. "You can't seriously think any of them had anything to do with this? My father is one of that group."

"I just hope for their sakes they didn't do it. My father will find out, even if the police don't bother to try."

"Think about what you're saying here. Those people would never do that. Particularly to someone like your father."

"How well do you really know them?"

"They would never stoop to the likes of that."

"They didn't seem too keen on the possibility of my father producing arms. The rancor was there. I felt it."

Thomas threw down his napkin. "I understand the pressure you must be under—"

"You have no idea," she said. "And if you think I'm coming to another meeting with those—" She looked around and whispered "—lunatics, think again."

She got up. Her chair fell over, but she didn't reach to get it. "I've had quite enough of this 'leisurely breakfast,' thank you."

"Don't leave like this."

"I need to get to the clinic."

"You'll be an hour early."

"I'd rather wait alone."

He slumped back in his seat. "I'm going tonight. I'll wait for you on the corner if you change your mind." His voice was even once more, devoid of the anger and surprise it was filled with seconds before.

"Don't hold your breath."

She strode out of the café and onto the street, dodging the early morning commuters until she reached the U-Bahn station. The anger simmering within her almost brought her to tears as she boarded the train. All that her father worked so hard for these last years—gone in one night. Did she really believe the Subversives had something to do with it? Probably not. It was more likely random Brownshirts targeting Jewish friendly businesses. Thomas deserved an apology, and she'd give it to him later. She realized a truth she'd never confronted before—how protective of her father she'd become.

The journey to Reuterkiez took about twenty-five minutes —more than enough time to cool down from her fight with Thomas. It wasn't the first one they'd ever had, but she'd never stormed out of a public place like that. A sickly embarrassment brought itself to bear on her as she emerged onto the street.

The clinic wasn't going to be open for another forty-five

minutes, but as Maureen rounded the corner onto Hobrechtstrasse, she saw a woman knocking on the door. All thoughts of breakfast were dismissed as the woman turned to her.

"Am I too early?" The strange woman's clothes were clean but plain—the mark of a poor person trying to conceal their circumstances. She looked about thirty and was pretty, with long chestnut-brown hair and sad, dark eyes. "My name Gisela Meyer. I'm here to see Dr. Josef Walz."

"The doctor won't be long," Maureen reassured her. "I work here too. He's my stepmother's father." She felt proud of her relationship to this benevolent man, who cared so much for the poor. "Don't look so anxious, Frau Meyer. He'll take good care of you."

Maureen drew her set of keys from her pocket and opened the door. She knew she shouldn't let the woman inside yet, but she looked nervous. Frightened even.

"We don't open until nine, but you can wait inside if you like."

"Oh, you are kind." The woman's lip quivered and a tear ran down her cheek.

Maureen brought her into the office and the woman took a seat in the waiting area.

"I'm sorry..."

"Don't be sorry... Can I help? What's the matter?" The woman seemed healthy, unlike their usual patients.

"It's not easy to talk about..."

Maureen got her a glass of water and sat opposite her. This woman needed help. "Talking can make things easier."

Gisela took a gulp of water. It seemed to settle her and she began to speak.

"Five years ago, I had a son. The doctors told us Carsten was born with a fault in his spine. It didn't develop properly in the womb. My husband wouldn't accept the diagnosis and visited every doctor he could find, but they all said the same thing.

Carsten grew weaker as time went on, and died before his third birthday."

"I'm so sorry." Maureen moved down on her haunches and took the crying woman's hand.

"I was brought before the Hereditary Health Court and they ruled that Carsten died because of a genetic fault I passed on to him, and that I have to be sterilized. That's why I'm here."

Maureen gripped Gisela's hand tighter, trying to hold back the tears.

"All my poor husband wanted in this world was a child of his own, and I couldn't give him that. Now he's left me."

"It's not your fault."

"I'll never have children now," she said. "I'll be alone for the rest of my life."

Maureen felt her heart turn to stone in her chest. She remembered the doctor taking her and Karen to lunch after his lecture, and talking of his vision for his nation. A snarling anger arose within her. Who were the Nazis to tell this woman she could never have children again?

"Do you have documentation to show the doctor?"

"This..." Gisella took a letter from her bag. It was an order from the Hereditary Health Court stamped with the Imperial Eagle. She was to begin procedures to be rendered infertile as soon as Dr. Walz examined her. Maureen handed it back.

"Do you have anywhere you could go? Any family abroad?"

"I have a cousin in Copenhagen."

"Go there."

"I can't afford the fare. The trains and buses are so expensive."

Maureen reached into her purse and drew out five Reichsmarks. "How much will you need?"

"I would say 100, or more."

"Meet me on the corner of Luxembourger Strasse and Sprengelstrasse at nine tonight. Make sure you have your bags packed and you're ready to leave. Do you know where that is?"

"Yes," Gisela answered. "Why are you doing this for me?"

"Because I can't just sit back and let it happen. Are you going to be there?"

"Yes."

"Ok. Get out of here before the doctor arrives, and tell no one we met."

The woman seemed to understand the urgency of the situation and got out of her seat. She turned to Maureen at the door. "Thank you."

"Don't thank me yet. Just be there later, ready to leave."

Gisela nodded and shut the door behind her.

Maureen sat down in the waiting room alone. A thousand thoughts swirled around in her mind as she realized what she'd just done.

The door opened and a voice brought her back into the moment.

"Good morning, Maureen," the doctor said. "You here long?"

She took a deep breath, trying to calm the nerves jingling around inside her like beads in a baby's rattle.

"Just a few minutes. I got the early train. I never usually make it."

"Good to see such dedication in a young person," he said with a smile. "The medical profession needs people like you."

Maureen watched as he hung his keys on a hook on the wall behind the front desk. "How is your father?"

"Stressed."

"I can only imagine. I enjoyed meeting your friend the other day," Dr. Walz said as he put down his bag.

"She said the same about you."

He headed into his office, calling over his shoulder, "I can't believe you're the only two ladies in the entire class, in this day and age!"

"It's not easy. Sometimes it seems like no one wants us there."

"The National Socialists have set the women's movement back generations, but I'm sure they'll soften their stance in time."

"I wish I had your confidence." Maureen washed her hands in the sink outside the doctor's office. "I heard it was very different just a few years ago."

"It was." The doctor reappeared and stood against the wall with his arms folded. The clinic wasn't due to open for another twenty minutes, but the other nurse would be arriving at any moment. "It seemed like things were opening up for women in the medical field, and a lot of other places too, but the Nazis are old-fashioned."

Old-fashioned is one way of putting it. "It's frustrating. Karen and I have to be the best just to keep up with the rest of the class. They jump all over us if we get something wrong."

"They're trying to justify their bigoted attitudes. I know it's hard, Maureen, but I'm confident you'll prove them all wrong someday. Console yourself with the fact that when you're running the Charité Hospital, you can fire them all."

"And hire the best women doctors in Germany, or America?"

"You'll be a huge success wherever you end up, my dear."

The front door opened and the head nurse appeared with a cheery "Good morning!"

"Good morning, Nurse Gunnel," said the doctor as he disappeared back into his office to ready himself for the day.

Nurse Gunnel was in her early fifties, with graying hair and a square face accented by red cheeks. Maureen had been scared of her at first, but had grown to love the older woman. Now the two made small talk about Maureen's week in university, and

Nurse Gunnel told a story about her neighbor's cat breaking into her apartment the night before. Maureen tried to focus on what the older woman was saying but her mind was still a maelstrom, and she had to laugh at the end on purpose.

Her job, as always, was to shadow her step-grandfather and help out with administrative duties. She also covered the desk and took calls when Frau Gunnel or one of the other nurses wasn't available.

The docket was full that day, as it always was now that the office was open just three days a week. The rest of Dr. Walz's time was dedicated to his research and, she supposed, the operations the State mandated him to carry out, though he never spoke of them.

The first patient was a regular—a poverty-stricken middle-aged man called Jens Norman, and Maureen proceeded to help him through the door. He smiled and took her hand, bearing most of his weight on the cane in his left hand. "Good morning, Maureen."

"Same to you, Herr Norman. How's your back treating you?"

"Like the wife," he answered. "No, that's unfair. Better than the wife."

After Jens, the morning passed with a steady stream of predominantly poor patients. Many were homeless. She had grown used to the smell over time, trying instead to focus on the human being. It was all too easy to fall into the trap of dehumanizing people because of how they looked, or how they made you feel. That was something the Nazis did every day, and she was damned if she was going to be like them.

She couldn't get Gisela out of her mind—it was almost impossible to focus on anything else at times. Perhaps the woman could disappear more easily if her file did the same. Where did the doctor keep his eugenics files? She realized she had to see them, not just so Gisela could escape, but also to know what was happening. Surely the court made a mistake. The people they sent for sterilization were criminals or unfit to be in normal society, weren't they? She had never met any of them before. This was the first time she'd ever worked here on any other day than Saturday.

For her own peace of mind, she had to find out. She didn't know for sure where the files were, but could hazard a decent guess. It was just a question of getting an opportunity to find them. Her hands were shaking, so she shoved them into her pockets.

How would he react if he caught her? Was this a betrayal of his trust? *He's been so good to me from the first moment we met. What will Lisa say?*

Her shift was due to end at one, but she found Nurse Gunnel and explained that she'd like to stay on until the clinic closed at four. Gunnel looked at her as if she were joking. "You're staying on? Don't you have university this afternoon?"

"I'd like to help out."

"Ok. We can always use you."

Lunchtime came and the doctor emerged from his office with his hat on. The next batch of patients was due in an hour and the waiting room was empty. Maureen was behind the front desk going over some paperwork.

"I'm meeting a friend for lunch in Hackenthal's," Dr. Walz said. "I'll be back in an hour."

Maureen looked up from her paperwork. "Enjoy yourself. We'll take care of the place while you're gone."

The doctor stopped. "Are you all right, Maureen? Your skin is gray, and you look like you're running a fever."

"I'm fine. I was out with friends last night. I might have overindulged a little."

"Time is the only cure for that particular ailment," he said with a smile. "How is Thomas?"

"Very well."

"She wants to stay on until we close this evening," Nurse Gunnel said. "Hangover and all."

"That work ethic will get you far," he said and walked out. The restaurant he was having lunch in was two blocks away. It was difficult to see him coming back before the hour was up. His office would be free, and her access to his files unbarred.

Only one problem remained—the head nurse standing beside her.

"Are you having lunch in the office?" Maureen asked.

"As I always do."

The older nurse was a creature of habit. She had ham sandwiches on white bread at her desk for lunch every day and then tidied off the crumbs in time for the subsequent patients at two o'clock. *How do I get her out of here?*

"Do you ever go out for lunch?" Maureen asked. "I've been coming here for two years now, and I can't remember you ever doing anything other than eating at the desk."

"I'm happy to work through. The paperwork piles up if I don't keep on top of it, particularly with all the extra work Dr. Walz does these days." She reached down into her bag. "You reminded me of how hungry I was," she said with a smile.

The sandwiches she took out were wrapped in paper, and she was just about to take a bite when Maureen interrupted her.

"Let me take you out to lunch!"

The nurse hesitated. "I've already made my sandwiches."

"We can give them away this afternoon." Maureen picked up the schedule. "Ernest Klammer is coming in at three. He's always starving, poor man—I'm sure he'd be glad to take them."

"I don't know. Look at all this," she said and motioned to the papers on the desk.

"I'm staying late today. I'll help out. Let me take you to lunch. You've been so kind to me since I started here."

Her words were sincere, and she had been meaning to take Gunnel out for some time.

"Look at how I'm dressed."

"We'll go next door. They won't care. It's a casual place."

The restaurant next door was dark, with sawdust on the floor. Maureen was pretty sure most of the meat they served was horse, or cats they found in the alley, but the plan she was formulating in her mind depended on them going there.

"I've never been, in all the years I've worked here."

"Never? In eight years? Come on, it's great. I've been many times. My treat."

The truth was she went once with Thomas and swore it was the last time.

The old nurse smiled at her. "You're paying? No—I can't let a student pay my way. I'll go, but we split the bill."

"Ok," Maureen said. "Let's go."

Maureen led her colleague out the front door to the restaurant beside the office. Round wooden tables sat in neat rows, but that was where the order ended. The frosted windows blocked out much of the light from outside, lending the illusion that it was dusk outside and not a sunny afternoon in June. The walls were covered in wood paneling, and photos of the Kaiser and the Führer sat alongside Bavarian landscapes and sunsets over Lake Wannsee.

The patrons were more the types they'd expect to see inside the clinic itself. She and Gunnel were the only females, and several men stared at them as they sat down. A sour, meaty smell hung in the air. Maureen turned to her companion and smiled. "Isn't it great?"

"You want to eat here?"

"Wait until you try the sausage. This is a true, old-fashioned Berlin restaurant. You don't get many places like this anymore, or so people tell me."

Gunnel looked like she'd tasted something awful and

hadn't even tried the food yet. The menu was written in chalk on a board on the wall above the bar.

A man in a dirty white shirt with a bushy red mustache arrived at the table. "What can I get you ladies?"

Maureen took the initiative, not waiting for Gunnel to walk out. It was likely the first and last time she'd ever go out for lunch. "I'll have the sausage and potatoes, and a beer too."

Gunnel took a few seconds. The waiter stared at her and seemed just about to say something when she decided to get the same as Maureen. The waiter turned around without another word and disappeared behind a swinging door.

"You like this place?" Gunnel asked.

"Oh, yeah. I just wish it was closer to the university so I could bring my friends here. Thomas and I come here quite often."

Gunnel seemed to settle and lit up a cigarette as they waited. The waiter came back with their beers a minute later, and they both drank from the smudged glasses.

"At least the beer's good," Gunnel said.

She continued talking, telling a story about her son's teacher that Maureen had already heard at least twice. Concealing the consternation within her wasn't easy.

"Excuse me a moment. I need to use the bathroom."

The nurse nodded and lit up another cigarette. Maureen didn't want to leave her alone in this dump, but Gisela was more important.

She walked down a dark hallway toward the sign for the bathroom. A door at the end piqued her attention. She had considered climbing out the washroom window, but this would be preferable. Making sure no one was around, she tried the handle and daylight flooded in. The alley behind the restaurant led around the side and separated it from the clinic next door. The trash cans were overflowing, and she had to hold her breath.

The image of Gunnel sitting alone in the restaurant was in her mind as she went, and she hurried up the alley to the street. The key to the front door was in her pocket, and she used it to get back in. *How much time do I have before Gunnel gets suspicious? Three minutes? Five?*

The doctor's office was deathly silent as she shut the door behind her. The only sounds were of the traffic outside and her breathing. The doctor's keys were still where he'd left them, and she ran around the front desk and grabbed them off the hook. The bunch of metal was heavy in her hand. His office door was open, but the filing cabinet was locked.

Which key is it? How many are there? Fifteen? The ridiculousness of what she was doing hit her like a fist. She didn't even know what she was looking for, let alone where to find it. Gunnel was probably wondering where she was. Her feet caught on the thin carpet as she turned for the door. What about her promise to Gisela? This small act of rebellion could ease her getaway. She raised the keys and plunged one into the filing cabinet. It didn't work, so she tried another, and then another. The fifth key unlocked the drawer, and she pulled it open.

How long did she have? Seconds? The drawer was full of files, each two inches or thicker. Her hands were shaking as she reached in to pull out a folder. It was a list of patients and the medications they were on. She recognized some of the names and realized this wasn't what she was looking for. The clock on the wall told her she'd already been gone about seven minutes. She had about three more before Gunnel was going to start asking questions.

The keys jangled in her hand as she locked the drawer once more. Deciding to try one more, she took a likely-looking key and slid it into the lock. It worked, and the drawer opened to reveal much the same as the first. She ran her finger along until she saw the word *Sterilizations*. The file was three inches thick and had lists of names at the back, perhaps 300 or so. She found the name—Meyer, Gisela—and removed the Health Court's letter. She closed the drawer and was just about to lock it again when the sound of the front door opening turned her heart to ice. She withdrew the key and listened as someone came into the office.

"Gunnel?" Dr. Walz called out. "Maureen?"

What on earth was he doing back so soon? The keys were in her hand, and she had no way out of the office. What would he do if he found her in here with the paper she stole? The closet was deep enough to hide inside, and so she climbed into it. She stuffed the sheet in her brassiere. The door shut behind her just as the doctor came in. Maureen held her breath, unable to believe what she was doing. The gap between the doors was just wide enough to afford her a view of the office. The doctor walked to his desk and picked up the phone. He asked the operator to put him through to a number and waited. Maureen didn't dare breathe and felt her lungs burning. A few seconds passed before Lisa's father started speaking.

"My Führer," he said. "So good to hear from you again." He paused for a few seconds. She could hear the voice on the other end of the line, but couldn't make out the words. "Yes, the plans for the Babelsberg Experiment are progressing. I understand this is a sensitive matter, and I'm honored to be chosen to conduct such a vital study." He stopped again to listen. "Any waste will be disposed of on-site." He listened for a few more seconds. "I'll keep you informed of any more details as they arise. I understand this is of utmost importance to you."

The doctor said goodbye and hung up the phone. Maureen watched him as he smiled to himself before walking out of the office. The sound of the front door opening and closing followed. Almost a full minute passed before she was confident enough to step out of the closet.

Balancing the urge to run back to the table next door, where

Gunnel was no doubt wondering where she was, and the fear coursing through her, she tiptoed toward the doctor's office door. The clinic was quiet once more. He must have come back to make the call and then returned to lunch. Perhaps he was with a government official who told him the Führer was expecting his call. With no time to dwell on her thoughts, she slipped the bunch of keys back on their hook and made for the front door.

Her hands were sweaty, and she had to make a conscious effort to slow her breathing before she jogged down the alley that separated the doctor's office from the restaurant. A rat scurried across in front of her, disappearing behind a beaten-up old trash can. Maureen stopped for a few seconds before realizing she hadn't time to be scared and kept on. The back door creaked as she pushed it open. She hurried to the bathroom to wipe the sweat off her brow before taking a few deep breaths and returning to the table.

Her sausage and fried potatoes were sitting on the table, getting cold. Gunnel's plate was clean. She looked at the younger women with a mix of curiosity and pity on her face.

"I'm sorry," Maureen said as she took her seat.

"I was beginning to wonder if you'd run off home."

Maureen thought to make up some kind of a story, but then realized the woman wasn't going to ask any more questions. "You like the food?"

"It's better than I thought it'd be."

Maureen picked up the knife and fork on the table and cut into the sausage. It was hard to believe what had just happened. Her breaths were still roaring in and out of her lungs.

"Are you all right?" Gunnel asked.

"I'm feeling a little off."

She put a piece of sausage in her mouth and discovered the nurse was right—it was good. The questions bubbling to the surface of her consciousness were too much to keep in. *Be careful*, she said to herself.

"Does the doctor have any business in Babelsberg?"

Gunnel reached for her pack of cigarettes, her face stony. "I have no idea. Why do you ask?"

"I overheard something in the office. I might have been mistaken."

"I think you were."

Maureen ignored the stony replies. "Do different types of patients come in depending on the day?" Gunnel looked at her. "The patients seem to have aliments I don't deal with on Saturdays here."

"Certain things are dealt with in the office on Mondays and Tuesdays that don't come up on other days, but that's not your concern. The doctor's private meetings with his patients are none of our business."

"Of course not."

Gunnel reached for her purse and took out a few coins.

"Oh, no," Maureen said.

"We agreed to split the bill." She put the money on the table and stood up. "And don't come back in if you're not feeling well. Go home and get some rest."

"Perhaps that would be best."

"See you next week," the nurse said and left.

Maureen continued eating. The adrenaline fading from her system had been replaced by ravenous hunger. She finished the food on her plate in three minutes before sitting back to drink her beer.

Gunnel's reaction to her questions about Babelsberg and the different types of patients bounced around inside her mind. Asking her was a mistake. Perhaps the nurse was involved in whatever top-secret experiment the doctor was undertaking. Or maybe she just didn't know. She sat in the restaurant alone for a few minutes, trying to process what happened. A phone call with the Führer. It was amazing that Lisa's father was in such close contact with the man millions considered to be a demigod living among them.

Maureen could boast to almost everyone in college, if she were so inclined, and most would listen in incredulity to her close links to the Führer himself. The truth, which she'd never utter in public, was that the kindly doctor who'd taken her under his wing was on speaking terms with that pint-sized despot. It embarrassed her. Dr. Walz assured her and Lisa that he was using Hitler, as the Führer was using him, and that the breakthroughs he produced would be worth it in the end. His work was everything to him, and he was consumed by his mission to eradicate the genetic errors he saw around him every day. Still, his association with Hitler sullied him in Maureen's eyes, and she had little doubt that future generations would see things in a similar vein.

9

Monday, June 10

Maureen stood alone on the corner of Universitätsstrasse. Her suspicions about the Subversives setting the fire at her father's factory had faded over the course of the day, but she still wanted to bring them up during the meeting—among other things. The early evening sun cast long shadows and filled the air with a golden haze. The thumping of her heart was allayed by the sight of Thomas approaching.

The paper she took from Lisa's father's office was in her bag. It felt like contraband—and the Gestapo would come barreling down the street after her at any moment. How did she feel about the doctor now? It was hard to say. They were going to his lake house that weekend, where she'd see him again. Since discovering he had a daughter, the doctor was taking more time off, and since he started working in tandem with the National Socialist government, he was seeing fewer regular patients. His work on engineering future generations was becoming an obsession—at least, that's what it seemed from the outside. He didn't talk about the details of what he did with her or anyone else, just in vague terms about improving society and how the Nazis were wrong a lot, but right about this one thing. He had a way of making everyone believe in him.

The conversation she heard between the doctor and the Führer played in her mind again. *The Babelsberg Experiment. A vital study. Any waste will be disposed of on-site.* What did it mean? One thing was for sure: it must have been significant if Hitler himself was taking the time to call about it. Rumor was that the Führer was lazy and took meetings only for a few hours in the afternoons. The pressure on his aides must have been terrific. For him to take time out of his day to call the doctor about something must have meant it was of vital importance to him personally, or the Reich, or both.

Thomas greeted her with a kiss on the lips. He looked every inch the handsome young man in his white shirt and blue slacks. Maureen realized she was sweating as she held him.

"Surprise," she said.

"I didn't expect to see you here."

"I'm sorry about earlier."

"Are you all right?" He pulled back. The concern in his eyes spread through his face.

"I have news. A lot of it. I'll share at the meeting," she whispered.

He nodded his head, a serious yet contented smile on his face. "Well, then, let's get going."

"Will your father be joining us tonight?"

"Yes. He'll be at the apartment," he replied, but left it at that.

He tried to take her by the hand but she shrugged him off, all too aware now of how wet her palms were. They walked across the street together, through the rush-hour traffic and onto Friedrichstrasse. They talked about college and their classmates, things they usually would have been happy to go over on a sunny Monday evening in the city, but not what either of them were dying to speak of at that moment. But talking about the Subversives on the street would be tantamount to a betrayal. She hadn't even told her family about them. No one could know.

Maureen remembered being told by her teachers to report her parents if they said anything suspicious. In America, a group like the Subversives could likely meet in a local bar to discuss their ideas, but here, in Hitler's Reich, they were an underground operation—branded enemies of the people. Maureen wasn't under any illusion. Membership of such a group was an offense punishable by being sent to one of the new concentration camps people spoke of in hushed tones. As if to reinforce her thoughts, a squad of Brownshirts marched down the street in front of them, singing songs about the evils of Jews and how Hitler was Germany's savior.

Maureen wasn't comfortable until they stepped off the train at Leopoldplatz station and emerged on Luxembourger Strasse.

"Did you have much trouble getting the list?" Thomas asked at last.

"Yes."

"You don't think—"

"No, I don't. Everything's fine."

"Just wait a minute." Thomas stopped outside a café and reached into his pocket for a pack of cigarettes. He lit one up and put one foot against the wall. "You see anyone?"

Maureen scanned the faces of the people on the street, looking for someone from the U-Bahn, or even from Universitätsstrasse. They stayed long enough for him to finish his cigarette before making the silent agreement that the coast was clear and they hadn't been followed.

A few minutes later, they turned onto Sprengelstrasse, and the sight of the apartment building brought Maureen's heart rate back down. She wanted to turn to Thomas and admit that this all excited her, but didn't want to sound childish, or as if she wasn't taking it seriously enough. Some things weren't meant to be shared aloud.

Thomas rang the bell and Herman answered. He greeted them with his familiar smile and brought them up the stairs. Duke Ellington was playing on the phonograph as they pushed the door open. Once again, they were last to arrive, and the others stood up to shake hands, Thomas's father among them. He hugged Maureen and then his son in turn. Gilda Stein stayed in her seat, waving to them with quiet grace before they sat down.

Maureen started talking before she sat down. This wasn't a place for baseless accusations, but she could judge the mood.

"Someone set a fire in my father's factory on Saturday night."

A collective gasp swelled the air in Herman's apartment. She studied each face around the table and found no cause for question or concern in any of them. She spoke for several more minutes, detailing everything about the fire she could remember. No one reacted with anything other than shock and sympathy. Several offered help in any way they could. Satisfied, Maureen let the subject drop.

The conversation turned to Hitler's disdain for the arts—a group specialty. Leon Gellert, the composer the Nazis had forced into early retirement because he was a Jew, spoke for several minutes about his experiences.

Maureen stayed quiet for almost an hour, only chiming in with comments on what the others said before Gilda Stein asked her a question.

"What is life like here for you, Maureen, as compared to back home?"

Maureen took a sip of the beer Herman poured for her before answering. She knew what they wanted to hear, but opted for the whole truth as she saw it.

"I have to say, day-to-day life here isn't worse or better than in America. The things we discuss here aren't common for most people. Not a lot of people have been through what happened to Gilda when her husband was murdered. We're a group of people who have been affected by the Nazis more than most, but Berlin is still an incredible city. The nightclubs and bars and cafés are open. People can go to the movies and buy a beer afterward, and they can walk along the street without too much fear of crime. My family is far better off now than we ever were in America. Even with everything the Nazis do, there is a great life to be lived here."

"Would you move home to America if given the chance?" Leon asked.

"And leave this man?" Maureen put her hand on Thomas's. "Absolutely!"

The group laughed, and she turned to her boyfriend and shook her head.

"I don't know…I really don't. The Nazis are a scourge and must be stopped, but they're an undercurrent. I know we see their flags and swastikas everywhere, and you can't speak ill of them anywhere except among your most trusted confidants, but there are people like us everywhere."

"It's refreshing to hear that," Thomas's father, Herr Reus said. "But just because only some people's lives have been destroyed by the Nazis doesn't make them any less evil. They've warped our nation almost beyond recognition in just over two years."

"I agree. I don't think anyone would deny the transformative effect they've had on society, but for a lot of people, their lives are better, not worse."

"Or at least they think their lives are better, Maureen," Herr Schultz—Lisa's old teacher, forced out for not complying with the Nazis' view on education—said.

"Yes. Most of my father's workforce was pleased with the calming effect the new government has had on industry…

Before the fire, anyway. My father makes a lot more money than he used to. Yet, the workers' wages are stagnant and unions are illegal. Even my father has lost his economic freedoms, being forced into cartels and not able to control his prices. Most of his workers don't see the cost of the economic revival because all they can remember is the hard times of '30 and '31."

"During the depths of the Depression," Thomas said.

Maureen nodded. "Yes, and when they hear the messages on our radios and read the tripe in our newspapers every day about how the National Socialists are our only protection against the evils of the world, like Communists and Jews, they believe them. The Nazis were clever enough to tap into the latent hatred of the Jews bubbling just below the surface of our society."

"None of this would be possible without that," Gilda said.

"Perhaps the people will change their minds once the inevitability of war comes to pass," Maureen said. "But by that stage, it might even be too late."

Gilda raised an eyebrow. "And you still wouldn't want to leave, having said all that?"

"Would you?" Maureen asked.

"I don't know. I've never left Germany. Where would I go?"

"Maybe the Nazis will disappear next year. How do we know what the future will bring?" Maureen sighed. "All I know is the past and the present. Our past in America was hard, and our lives here are better. It's hard to see beyond that."

"Well said," Herman responded. "This country is worth fighting for. Sometimes we have to remind ourselves of that. Thank you for helping us see it, Maureen."

"I went into my step-grandfather's clinic to work this morning, and I met someone outside before the office opened."

She detailed meeting Gisela. All twelve around the table sat in silence as she spoke.

Maureen took several minutes, recalling both Gisela's story

and that of how she got the paper, prompted by a dozen questions from the group. Once those subjects were dealt with, she moved on to what she overheard.

"He picked up the phone," she said, "and it was the Führer on the other end of the line. He mentioned something about an experiment in Babelsberg... Said it was of utmost importance."

"It must have been if Hitler himself was talking about it," Gilda said. "Did he say what it was about?"

"No, but he said he would dispose of any waste on-site. It was all too cryptic."

"What if it's to do with sterilizations?" Leon asked. "It must be. What else would they be talking about?"

"I don't know."

"Is there any way of finding out, Maureen?" Herman asked.

"To what end? I wouldn't be able to stop it."

"We could expose it—perhaps stop their plans before they bring them to fruition. If the general public knew about it—"

"And how would we get this information to them, Herman?" Gilda cut him off. "What newspapers would print the story? They're all in Hitler's pocket."

"The foreign press might be able to print it," Maureen said.

"And how would we get the news to them, even if you were somehow able to find it?"

"I have a way," Maureen answered. "My father's best friend is a reporter for the *New York Times* bureau in Berlin. Surely he'd be able to report it, and then the world will stop this happening."

"I told you she'd make a good addition to the group," Thomas said, and several people around the table clapped.

"One more thing," Maureen said as the applause died. "I'm meeting Gisela outside in an hour. She needs money to get out of the country, to go to her cousin in Denmark, where she will have a chance to bear children someday. I thought we, as a group, could help her."

Gisela was as good as her word and was waiting on the corner of Luxembourger Strasse with a tattered old suitcase beside her.

Maureen didn't speak, just reached into her pocket and gave her the 246 Reichsmarks thrown onto the table in Herman's apartment.

Gisela's eyes shone bright with tears. "Why are you doing this for me?"

"Because you needed help."

"Thank you so much," she said and embraced Maureen.

"Just get going." Maureen pushed her off. "Don't stop until you reach Copenhagen."

Gisela nodded, drying the tears on her cheeks. "I'll never forget you," she said and left.

10

Wednesday, June 12

Lisa rested the script in her lap and gazed across the film studio, where they were just about to call her for the big scene. The film was set in an area of western Russia inhabited by German speakers. Lisa played the heroine, Ursula, who led her fellow villagers to freedom in Germany after her husband was killed by the dastardly Russians. Ferdinand, playing her husband, was in makeup, having blood applied in preparation for his death scene. Hagen was circling the set like a wildcat. The pent-up energy lit his eyes and seemingly made him incapable of speaking in a normal tone of voice.

Petra Wagner sat on the other side of the set with several other villagers. Having passed her audition on Sunday, Petra had been on set since Monday morning and was readying herself for the few lines she had in the film.

"Lisa, are you ready?" Hagen roared across the set.

"Yes!" She jumped up. The script fell to the floor, but she didn't wait to pick it up. It wasn't prudent to keep this man waiting. Her heart was thumping as she jogged across to her position. Ferdinand ran up beside her to lie on the floor. He brought a hand to his head and let his eyes droop, and a loud groaning sound came from his mouth. She leaned down and took his head, cradling it. The landscape of western Russia came into her mind. She tried to surround herself with it and the grief that losing her husband would engender within her.

The camera crew was ready, and Herr Hagen was in place. Someone shouted, "Action!"

Lisa stared down into Ferdinand's face. A true professional, he had slipped easily into character, grimacing in pain, kicking out his legs.

Lisa wiped the hair back from his face. "What have they done to you, my dear?"

He spluttered and coughed. "The Russians," he said. "They came for our crops, and shot us down like dogs when we resisted. Peter and Hans are gone... I couldn't save them. I hid after they left. I never thought I'd see your beautiful face again. Are you here with me, darling?" He stared up at her, his eyes glazed and blank.

At once, the image of Ernst Milch and his dead stare entered her mind. For the first time, she allowed the memory to rest in her consciousness so she could use its horror. She shuddered and tears welled in her own eyes; her body tightened as she cradled her "husband."

"Don't talk anymore," she sobbed. "Hush now. I'm going to bring the doctor for you."

"It's too late for that."

"No!" She maintained her focus on the grisly image of Milch in her mind.

"It's up to you now," gasped the actor. "It's up to you to lead the village."

"No, you're going to survive this. We need you now more than ever."

"I see the strength in you. Lead them. Deliver them from the tyranny of Soviet rule so our children can grow up free."

He closed his eyes and let his head drop back. Her face was burning as hot tears flowed down her cheeks. She pressed her cheek to the actor's face, feeling the fake blood smear on her skin, thinking of the real blood that once had covered her. She prayed for Hagen to end the scene, but he didn't. He let the cameras roll for the longest fifteen seconds of her life before he finally yelled out.

She exhaled and stood up, shaking.

"That was great," Ferdinand said, fake blood running down the sides of his mouth.

Hagen came running over, and Lisa braced herself for criticism—but for once, he didn't curse or throw anything.

"It was good. It worked, but can you take a little longer next time, say goodbye, maybe? Makeup, get over here." The makeup artist appeared and wiped the two actors clean, applying the requisite fake blood to Ferdinand once more.

Hagen made them shoot the scene three more times, and each time she summoned the horror from her past until she was so weak with emotion she could barely stand.

At last came the order to take a break.

In the pause, Petra came over and sat beside her. Lisa barely knew Clayton's girlfriend and only got her the role as a favor, but Petra's work ethic had impressed everyone around her in the short time she'd been here.

"That was incredible," the young woman said with a smile. She put her hand on Lisa's knee. "I felt the whole scene. I could have closed my eyes and been in the same place. It was all in your voice."

"Thanks," Lisa said. "I'm just trying to stay afloat."

"Isn't that what you do when you're thrown in the deep end?"

Lisa was about to reply when the doors to the studio were

flung open and a small man in a brown suit with a Nazi armband entered. Lisa knew without looking that he was a dignitary of some sort—no one who wasn't could have gained such easy access to the film set.

"Who's this?" Petra whispered.

Lisa thought she recognized him; she knew a lot of powerful, posturing men from her days as a dancer. "I could be wrong, but I think we're being honored by the presence of the head of Reich Chamber of Culture, Joseph Goebbels."

Both women fell silent as Goebbels marched up to Hagen. The director greeted him with a smile and a handshake. It didn't pay to greet the man who controlled every aspect of German cultural life any other way.

Lang walked over to greet the small man with slicked-back hair and a noticeable limp. None of the actors approached him. Everyone on set was a member of the Reich Chamber of Film —otherwise, they couldn't have been here. Nonmembers were locked out of the industry. Despite their membership in the guild, few actors seemed to believe in the goals of Goebbels's creation. Most of them were just trying to make a living, and if that had to be in a movie about ethnic Germans being subjugated by evil Russian soldiers, then so be it.

Lisa and Petra watched in silence for a couple of minutes, waiting for the outcome of the meeting happening in front of them. One thing was sure: this wasn't a social call. Goebbels was here for a reason. No one on set was talking except for the Reich Minister for Propaganda. Hagen and Lang were listening to him, nodding their heads.

Minutes passed before Hagen turned and gestured to both Lisa and Petra to come forward and meet the great man. With no other choice, the two actresses got off the bench and approached the group of men. Goebbels's eyes slithered all over them as Hagen introduced the actresses.

"Herr Reich Minister, this is Lisa Ritter, a new star in the making. She's playing the role of Ursula, the leader of the peasant revolt against the Soviet forces."

Goebbels took her hand and kissed it. Lisa mustered all of her acting skills in pretending that she enjoyed the experience.

"And the young starlet who joined us this week, this is Petra Wagner."

"Like the Führer's favorite composer," Goebbels said and subjected her hand to a kiss.

"The Reich minister would like to observe us on set with a view to improving the script, if necessary," Hagen said.

Lisa wondered how the director really felt about a politician coming to usurp his vision of what essentially was already clunky anti-Soviet propaganda. Hagen had been a great director during the Weimar era, but now had to jump through the same hoops as everyone else. It was a choice between doing their bidding or finding another way to make a living.

"Let's try that last scene again," Hagen shouted. "Everyone in their places. Makeup!"

Petra started to follow Lisa, but the Reich minister caught her by the arm and the young woman had little choice but to stand and converse with him. She was still standing beside him when Lisa took her position on the set with Ferdinand's head in her hands. The actor winked at her just as they were about to begin, and to her amused annoyance, it was all she could do to keep from bursting out laughing.

Everyone was in place once more, except now the head of the entire German movie industry was watching too. They went through the scene again. Somehow, having Goebbels watching made it even easier to summon the dead face of Ernst Milch, and Lisa groaned and wept more than ever. Hagen almost smiled as he yelled, "Cut!"

Goebbels stood with his arms crossed. Everyone waited for him to speak. He stepped forward, leaving Petra alone at last.

"Excellent. The execution is flawless," Goebbels said. "But I think we need some changes to the script." He approached the actors, stopping a few feet short of where Lisa was still crouched down over Ferdinand, his fake blood smeared across her face. "What if we introduce a Jewish moneylender? The villagers could be divided by the evil influence of the Jews among them, who betray them to the Bolshevist authorities. We could still retain the intense realism of the film while issuing a stark warning to the populace about the dangers the Jews present."

Goebbels stopped talking and stared directly at Lisa; he seemed to expect her to fill the silence that ensued. Her heart sank like a stone.

"You want me to ad-lib the lines right now, as part of this scene?"

"Are you capable of that?"

All eyes were on her, including Hagen, who nodded his head behind Goebbels's back.

She fumbled for the words for a few seconds. "I can try," she said at last.

"Set it up again," shouted the director.

"Just think of the last propaganda bulletin you heard," Ferdinand whispered to her as soon as they were freshly made-up and ready. Lisa nodded and glanced at Hagen. Goebbels was standing beside him, his arm around Petra. His head barely reached her shoulder. The cameras started rolling again, and Lisa jumped into character.

"What have they done to you, my dear?"

"The Jews joined with the Soviet soldiers. They turned against us," Ferdinand said.

"Just as we always knew they would. Those vipers lived among us for years, waiting for their chance to strike."

"They came for our crops and shot us down like dogs in the fields our forefathers sowed for generations."

"We won't bow to the evil forces of the Jewish Bolshevist

conspiracy," she said. It felt so ridiculous—no one watching the film could take it seriously, but Goebbels was smiling and nodding his head. "I, as a trueborn pure-blooded German, will lead my people, not only against the tyranny of the Soviet hordes, but against the Jewish vermin that support them," she said.

Ferdinand died in her arms for the tenth time that day, and Hagen yelled for filming to end.

Goebbels stepped out of the shadows behind the director, clapping his hands. "Bravo!" he cried. The other members of the crew joined in until everyone was applauding her.

Goebbels put a hand on Hagen's shoulder. "Get me a copy of the script and I'll have some of my people alter it to reflect the new direction of the film. This production will be an important landmark in the reawakening of the German people. It will be your greatest triumph."

As the powerless director mumbled his thanks, Goebbels strode over to Lisa and embraced her. She stood as still as a statue, sickened by the words that had just come out of her mouth.

"And you, my dear," he murmured in her ear, "are going to be a star."

"Thank you, Herr Reich Minister," she managed.

"Great things are in the air," he said and returned to Hagen once more. The two men spoke for a minute, not even bothering to call the scriptwriter over before the Reich Minister for Propaganda limped off the set.

With no script to work off, and on the expectation that the story they were working on would change almost beyond recognition overnight, Hagen called shooting for the day. The mood on set was solemn, and Lisa felt used and empty as she changed back into her street clothes.

Petra came into her changing room with a smile on her face.

"Goebbels? On set? Who could have imagined? This film is going to be huge!"

Lisa continued putting on her blouse.

"I know the story's taken a rather unsavory direction, but what if he attended the premiere? What if Hitler came?" Petra asked.

"We'd make the newspapers," Lisa said with no enthusiasm.

"Our film would be on the front page of every paper. Your face would be everywhere."

Lisa considered the prospect of becoming what she'd always striven to be because of this movie. She tidied her hair.

Petra frowned at her in the mirror. "If you don't make this film, someone else will."

"I know, but at least it wouldn't be me pulling the trigger."

"Standing up for your principles won't halt anything but your own career. You told me that this is the break you've been working toward your entire life."

Lisa sighed, picked up a brush, and ran it through her hair. "The Reich minister seemed to take a liking to you."

"Men," Petra said with an air of disgust. "They're all the same."

"Not all are like him. Are you still seeing Clayton?"

Petra laughed. "You'd have as much luck pinning him down as a leaf in a gale-force wind. He's a nice man, but let's just say he intends to enjoy his time in Berlin to the fullest."

A knock on the door interrupted their conversation, and Hagen entered with his hat in hand and an uncharacteristically doleful look on his face.

"We're suspending shooting for a few days until the new script comes in. I just spoke to Herr Goebbels on the telephone. He promised me we'll have it in a week or two. His best people are working on it." He wiped his hands down his cheeks. "God knows what they'll come up with. We'll all be goose-stepping around the set."

Lisa was taken aback by the honest anger in his voice. It wasn't safe or easy to talk like this in public. She wasn't going to make the same mistake, despite her misgivings about the scene she'd just played. Being arrested would mean exposing her past, and if the authorities determined she was a Jew, her career was over. She wouldn't care so much about that except for the fact that if they discovered she was Jewish, they'd know Hannah was the same.

Hagen didn't move, just stared.

"Is there something else?" Lisa asked.

"The Reich minister is requesting the pleasure of the company of both of you ladies at the Reich Chancellery on Friday of next week."

Lisa dropped the brush in her hand, but Petra sprang up from the armchair in which she'd been reclining. "He wants both of us to come?" she asked.

"To have tea with him and the Führer."

"With Hitler? Oh, I can't, I'm not important enough..." Lisa scrambled for an excuse.

Hagen continued to stare at her, almost coldly. "This isn't the type of engagement one can refuse, Lisa. The truth is, we need their approval for funding. I'm certain we won't get it unless you both attend."

"But what am I going to say to...the Führer?" she asked desperately.

"The adjutant said they wanted to speak to you about the film. They both know you're a married woman, so you don't have to worry about your honor."

"But Petra?"

"I can look after myself," said the statuesque blonde with a tiny smile.

Lisa wondered if that was true. Goebbels would be delighted to work with the beautiful young actress. Rumor had it that he took his pick of the young starlets coming through the system, and he would probably invite Petra to his country house for a private consultation soon. She didn't judge her friend for what she might be willing to do in a world where men made the rules and passed women around like playthings. Goebbels was such a man—to take advantage of his position in that way. After all, what woman would look at him twice if he weren't one of the most powerful men in the Reich? Sometimes she wondered if that were the real reason men like him rose to power—to make up for their inadequacies. Hitler was not like that, however. The mission of changing Germany seemed to be the end goal for him.

"The invitations will be delivered to your homes," Hagen said. "Bring them with you, and show them to the guard at the gate."

Lisa stood up to leave the changing room, but Hagen seized her by the arm. "I understand this might make you feel uncomfortable, Lisa, but we need you to smile and say the right things. This film is over if you don't, and all of these people will be out of a job."

"I'll be there with you," Petra reassured her. "We can get through it. We've been dealing with unwanted male attention our whole adult lives."

"Yes," Lisa said. "Yes, of course. Until Friday of next week, Petra."

She walked off the now almost-empty film set and got into her car. She slammed the steering wheel and screamed. How did she know the SS didn't check into the background of everyone Hitler invited to tea? Her father met with Hitler and the other members of his inner circle at the Reich Chancellery. But Josef Walz was as determined as she that the Jewish heritage of his long-lost daughter be kept a secret. It was doubtful that he would have retained the government sponsorship for his research if they found out his daughter and grandchild were Jews. He had almost as much to lose as she did.

And she had a lot to lose. If she were discovered to be a Jew, her career was over. If she walked off the set and refused to portray the anti-Semitic filth of the writers at the Reich Ministry for Enlightenment and Propaganda, she would be blackballed and would never work again. Keeping her mouth shut and reading the lines could lead to success she never dreamed of. What price was her integrity worth? If she refused, her past might be investigated, and that would put not only herself, but her own daughter at the most terrible risk.

Her hands were tied.

Several minutes passed before she started the engine. She tried to console herself with the fact that, having finished early, she would be home before Hannah's bedtime for the first time in days.

~

Thursday, June 13

Seamus wiped the sweat from his brow and leaned his shovel against the wall. The official cleanup efforts had begun, and the dozen or so hired laborers had been there since Monday morning. It was still impossible to stand by and do nothing. He arrived intending to oversee the cleanup, but couldn't resist rolling up his sleeves and digging a shovel into the debris. Gert Bernheim was the same, but had the good sense to wear appropriate clothing. He and Seamus had come every day since the fire, usually with the help of ten to fifteen workers. Those employees were almost always the Jews and the foreigners—the ones with the most to lose.

Seamus picked up his shovel once more and looked over at Andrei Salnikov, the Russian foreman of the metal polishing section. He was working alongside three Jews: Leonard Greenberg, Judith Starobin, and Robert Greenfield. Several other factory employees were upstairs cleaning out the offices. None spoke as they dumped charred debris into dumpsters in the parking lot, outside the hulk that had been the factory.

Seamus walked over to Bernheim, whose face was a bright shade of puce. The sun was high in a cloudless sky, and with the roof entirely gone, it beat down on them with relentless efficiency.

"Time for a break, Gert."

The manager looked up and nodded his head. The factory floor was almost cleared now, and it was just a matter of removing any broken machinery. A lot of it was still salvageable, but needed to be cleaned up before being used again. Bernheim took a seat on a bench in the shade as Seamus summoned the other volunteers to do the same. The hired laborers were on their own schedule, and Seamus left them to their own devices. The Ritter employees sat in the shade, drinking bottles of soda and eating sandwiches that Seamus brought along.

The conversation was light. Judith told the story of her interview for the job with Helmut ten years before.

"So you didn't notice you had baby vomit on your hat until Helmut pointed it out?" Seamus asked.

"Bright-white baby vomit. So much it almost glowed in the dark."

They sat another half hour or so before Seamus insisted the workers go home. "The job's almost done. The laborers have everything in hand. I appreciate everything you've done—I won't forget it."

"We know that," Judith said.

Each person shook his hand before leaving. Ten minutes later, only he and Bernheim remained.

"You got any new ideas about who did this, Gert?" Seamus wiped his face clean with a towel.

"God only knows."

"You think anyone in there saw anything?" He pointed to an apartment building looming over the fence. The top floor overlooked the factory courtyard. "I wonder, did the police already interview them?"

"I don't think the police bothered to interview anyone. Writing it off as an attack on a Jewish factory was easier."

"You want to go talk to the residents ourselves?"

Bernheim got up, the sweat dried from his face. "Yes, I do."

The men took a few minutes to put their shirts and suit jackets back on. Seamus beat the dust from his trousers and wiped down his shoes and the two men began to walk together.

"Have you spoken to Helga?" Gert asked.

"Yesterday. She mentioned rearmament again. It'll be decision time soon."

"The old question: Do we make pots and pans or bullets and shells?"

"She's not backing down."

"I can see her point. That's where the money is going to be in the next few years."

"Feeding the Nazi war machine?"

"If we don't do it, someone else will. Your old friend Otto Milch has been transitioning to becoming an arms manufacturer for months now."

Seamus protested, "People are still going to need gates and railings and knives and forks."

"But the contracts the government is going to hand out for weapons will be huge. We don't have the scale to produce tanks or planes, like Milch does, but we could do a nice business producing the smaller items. We'll need to completely change everything about the factory, if we do. And now is the time to do it, with the insurance money from this fire."

They walked through the factory gates together. "I can't believe you're saying this, Gert. Of all people! The Nazis are hurtling toward another war. I can't help get them there."

"I'm just playing devil's advocate, my friend. The way I want things to be and the way they actually are, are usually miles apart."

"You'd actually consider making bullets for Nazi guns?"

"I don't want to lose my job. I don't know if I could get another. Why do you think the Eastern Europeans and the Jews are the ones in here helping us shift rubble every day? They're the ones who won't find work if we close down. Without you and this factory, they have nothing."

"We can make it without churning out weapons. We were doing just fine before this fire."

"Our competitors are going to jump on our bones. I've been on the phone every day, trying to court our clients."

"So have I. Milch and the other vultures are picking us clean."

"Perhaps we could devote a percentage of our business to rearmament? One good government contract would see us through. But that's up to you and Helga to decide, as co-owners."

"I value your opinion. Thanks, my friend," Seamus said.

They arrived at the gate of the apartment building beside the factory. Seamus opened it and led his friend inside.

"I'll think about it. Good enough?"

"For now, but we don't have much time."

The conversation stopped as they reached the door of the apartment building.

"No point in talking to anyone on the ground floor," Seamus said as he pushed through the door into the foyer.

"Up we go, then," Bernheim said, pointing toward the stairs.

The two men ascended together in silence. The stairwell was hot and sticky, and both took off their jackets. Three doors waited on the second of the two stories in the block. Only one faced the factory. It was possible someone from the other flats might have seen something, but if anyone was likely to have any information, it was the occupant of the one overlooking the place, so they decided that door was first.

Seamus rapped on it with the knuckle on his middle finger.

The sound of rumblings inside came first, then footsteps, and then the door opened. An elderly man peered around at them with a suspicious look on his face.

"Hello, sir. I'm Seamus Ritter, and this is my colleague—"

"Hans Friedel," Bernheim said, interrupting him.

Seamus took pause at his friend giving a fake name before continuing. "We're from the factory next door."

"Were you the ones who burned the place down?" he asked in a rasping voice.

Seamus looked at Bernheim and then back at the old man. "Could we come in for a moment?"

"Sure." The old man opened the door and sauntered back into the apartment. The two men followed, down a small hallway and into the living room. An old terrier was lying on a cushion on the floor. It raised its head to look at them before deciding they weren't worth the trouble of getting up.

"Never mind Albert," the man said. "He's tired after his dinner."

The furniture was faded and gray, but the place was impeccably clean. A portrait of the Kaiser sat above the fireplace, and some black and white photographs of what Seamus presumed were his grown-up children. The old man offered them a seat, and they both dropped onto the sofa, inches apart.

"Thank you for having us in your apartment, sir. What's your name?"

"Timo Weiss." The old man sat by the window, his book upturned on the table in front of him. The windowpanes beside him offered a clear view of the factory. The damage was even more startling from a height.

"Pleased to meet you," Bernheim added. "You asked us

outside if we are the ones who burned the factory down. Why did you say that?"

"I was in insurance myself back in the day," he said. "I saw enough fires in factories in my time. It was almost always the owner cashing in."

"That wasn't the case this time," Seamus said. "The police have ruled it an accident. Were you here the night of the fire?"

"I was sitting in my chair with Irmina," he said and pointed to a black and white photo of a woman.

"Your wife?" Seamus asked.

Weiss nodded. "She's gone a few years now, but I keep her close. I didn't see the fire start. I must have been dozing in my chair. What did the nightwatchman tell you?"

"Not a lot. He was knocked unconscious from behind—saw nothing." Seamus was embarrassed at the question, but kept on. "Did the police come to interview you?"

"No one—you're the first. I was wondering when someone would show. You say the police have washed their hands of it?"

"Yes," Seamus said.

"I saw a truck parked out on the street, just a little down from the factory that night. It was about 100 yards away. It's rare to see anyone parked out there at night, so I remember."

"Have you any idea what time you saw this truck?"

Weiss looked out the window and then back at the two men. "I don't know. It must have been about ten because it was dark. I'd finished my dinner and cleaned up after and was out for a walk with Albert. What time did the fire start?"

"About ten thirty. Did you notice anything about the truck? Did you see anyone inside, or a license plate?"

"I was across the street when I saw it—too far away."

"Were there any distinguishing marks on it? Could you identify it again?"

"I think I could," the older man said. "I saw the writing on the truck. It was a delivery van of some sort. The lettering on the side was faded, but I stopped to read it. I was testing my eyes."

"What did it say?" Bernheim asked.

"The name was painted over, but whoever did it forgot to scrub out the address at the bottom of the back door. I saw the words *Wrangelkiez Bakery*."

"A bakery? Why would a delivery van for a bakery in Wrangelkiez be in this part of town on a Saturday night?" Bernheim asked.

"That's what I thought. It was still there when I walked back, but I saw it speed off when I was back in my chair. I didn't think anything of it at the time, but then the fire started."

"And you never thought to approach the police?" Bernheim asked.

"I figured if they weren't coming to see me, I wasn't bothered to go to them."

Seamus thanked the man and waited until they were on the street outside to say his piece. "Do you know Wrangelkiez?"

"Not really."

"You want to take a trip over there? See if we can find this bakery?"

"I don't have anything better to do. It's not like I can go to work."

The two men walked back to Seamus's car together and got in. Seamus pulled out onto the street and started east toward Wrangelkiez.

"So, where are we now?"

"No further along," Bernheim answered. "A suspicious vehicle outside the factory doesn't confirm that it was arson."

"No, but I'd like to know why that truck was there."

The traffic in the city was light, and they got to Wrangelkiez in about twenty-five minutes.

Neither man knew the area well. Seamus figured he had to keep the river on his left as he went, but soon he had to admit defeat. He saw a policeman on the side of the street and pulled the car over.

"Excuse me, Officer. Do you know where Wrangelkiez Bakery is?"

"It's one of my favorites," the policeman said with a smile. "It's on Köpenicker Strasse: two blocks up, on the left."

Seamus thanked him and drove on. They pulled up and parked outside a large bakery with an ornate sign two minutes later. Entering, they spotted a man at the cash register in his late thirties, with jet-black hair and a sparse beard. All manner of bread and cakes sat behind the glass of the counter.

"I'll have to bring something home for the family," Bernheim said.

"Can I speak to the manager, please?" Seamus asked.

"You're speaking to him already."

Seamus introduced himself and his friend. "It's a sensitive matter," he said. "Is there somewhere we could go?"

The manager directed him down to the end of the counter and brought him back through a door that said STAFF ONLY above it.

The man motioned for them to sit at a small round table in what appeared to be the lunchroom.

"Olaf Kurtz," the man said and shook both their hands. "What can I do for you?"

"Do you run a delivery service across the city?" Bernheim asked.

"Yes, we deliver fresh bread every morning. We have fleet of a dozen trucks."

"Have you had any trucks stolen in the last few weeks?" Seamus asked.

"Who are you? Not the police?"

"We run a metalworks factory over in Nollendorfkiez. It's not there anymore because it burned down about a week ago. One of your delivery trucks was seen parked on the street outside just before it went up in flames. The writing on the side was painted out, but a witness identified the address of the bakery."

"And why aren't the police asking me these questions?"

"They wrote it off as an accident. We don't think it was."

Kurtz shook his head. "Gosens," he said under his breath.

"Excuse me?" Seamus said.

"Sebastian Gosens, an old neighbor of mine growing up. Had a hard time, just got out of jail and needed a job. I took him on here as a favor. He drove for me for a few months, but disappeared along with one of our trucks about two weeks back."

"Have you any idea where we can find this Gosens?"

"If I did, I would have dealt with him already myself. The snake stabbed me in the back. Imagine treating someone like that who gave you a job?"

"He just stole the truck and ran? You haven't heard anything of him since?"

"No. I know his family. They haven't seen him—nor do they want to. If you find him, bring him to me. He owes me 500 Reichsmarks for the truck."

"When exactly did he go missing?"

"The morning of the eighth of June. It was a Saturday."

"The same day as the fire," Bernheim said and turned to Seamus.

"You think he'll show up here again?" Seamus asked.

"Not if he knows what's good for him."

Kurtz stood up and explained that he needed to get back to the counter. He walked the two men to the sidewalk outside the bakery. "You let me know if you find him."

"We will," Seamus said. He waited in the car while Bernheim went back inside to buy some cakes for both their families.

"You think this is our man?" Seamus asked when his friend got back into the car.

"I don't know. It's certainly quite the coincidence if it's not. One thing I don't understand is why the police didn't ask the questions we are."

"That is a mystery, my friend." Seamus pulled onto the street. "We need to find this Gosens, but I have no idea where to start."

"I think it's time to employ a professional. I know someone—a private detective, name of Alfred Leder. Not cheap, but he's excellent."

"Why do you know a private detective?"

"A friend had an issue with his wife a few years ago. Leder was a huge help."

"Ok. Contact him and tell him to find our new friend Gosens. I'll pay the money. We need to know whose crosshairs we're in."

Seamus kept on. Bernheim took out one of the cakes and started eating it. He offered it to his friend, but Seamus refused. After a few minutes, he changed his mind and had sugar on his fingers the rest of the drive home.

11

Friday, June 14

Lisa pushed back the covers on the bed she shared with Seamus. It was an hour since dawn, and she had been lying awake for much of the night. Thoughts of her career, the film, the production crew, and her imminent meeting with Hitler and Goebbels kept her up. Her husband was still asleep, and she did her best not to rouse him as she got out of bed. She went into the bathroom and looked in the mirror. Her face was puffy, and large dark rings were settled beneath her eyes. Looking good was imperative. It was the currency she traded on, and had done so since she was a girl, but more so today than almost ever before. Goebbels didn't invite Hagen or Lang to tea with him and Hitler. He invited her and Petra, the other glamorous woman on set.

Their jobs that day would be to look pretty, to accept the script from Goebbels, and to obtain the funding they'd need to finish the picture. It was just like the old days back in the club, dancing on stage for leering men who thought they owned you because they bought a bottle of champagne and invited you to their table.

She pulled back the skin on her face. Would Hitler and Goebbels appreciate her wearing makeup? Would they differentiate between movie actresses and the woman on the street whose job, in their eyes, was to produce healthy children to fight the next war? *Not too much. Just enough to cover the rings under my eyes.*

Trying to thread the needle of appearing to be desirable while not being available was going to be difficult. Goebbels, though he was married with children, had a reputation for being a womanizer. She knew to be wary of him. Hitler was a different story, opaque in the matters of the heart. Rumors abounded of his preferences, from his relationship with his niece to boys or worse, but no one seemed to know for sure. Either way, she wasn't eager to find out. The plan she and Petra formulated when they met the day before was to smile, nod, look pretty, get the script, and leave.

"How are you feeling?" murmured her husband from behind her.

She smiled at him in the mirror. "I feel like an antelope venturing into the lion's den."

He wrapped his arms around her and kissed the skin on her neck. It calmed her. "They have no idea who you are. No one does."

"It seems like a matter of time, and then my career will be over."

"Says who? How are they going to find out when you never even knew you were Jewish yourself until after your mother died?"

"Drawing attention to myself like this won't help."

"What choice do you have?" He let go of her. "Your father coached you on what Hitler's like. He certainly doesn't want his boss to find out that his daughter is a Jew."

"He's safe. I'm almost positive Hitler doesn't know I'm Josef Walz's daughter."

"They'll never suspect you're Jewish. Just go in there and do what you need to do to get what you want."

"I don't even know what I want," she said and picked up her tooth powder and brush. "I dread to see what they've turned the script into. Just uttering those horrible words on set turned my stomach."

"I understand that." Seamus approached the window. "It might not be as bad as you think. Perhaps they might use a more subtle approach than the anti-Semitic garbage the tabloids print every day."

"Would that be any better? Would spreading subtle hatred be preferable to the more obvious kind? Against my own people?"

The sound of the children getting out of bed spread through the house. "I'll get breakfast ready for Hannah," he said.

"No. Let me brush my teeth first and I'll do it."

"Don't worry—Hitler doesn't invite people he perceives as enemies for tea and biscuits. The Gestapo kick down their doors in the middle of the night."

"I just hope one doesn't lead to the other."

Seamus seemed to realize nothing he could say at that moment would offer her the comfort he wanted to afford her and backed off. Lisa brushed her teeth and finished getting ready.

Breakfast with the children was now a rare delight to be cherished. Maureen and Michael were already eating when she arrived with Hannah and ten-year-old Conor. Fiona was still in the bathroom, brushing her long brown hair. Getting her out of there was becoming more difficult by the day.

"You ready for the Führer?" Maureen asked.

"As ready as I'll ever be."

"It's exciting," Conor said. "My teacher was talking about it yesterday in class. She seemed jealous."

"Yes. Handsome Adolf is quite the dish," Maureen said. "Nothing like a short, pale weirdo with a tiny mustache to get the blood racing."

"Don't talk about the Führer like that," Conor said.

A heavy silence descended upon the room. Only the sound of eating filled the air. Lisa knew she had to be the one to speak next.

"Maureen was just joking, Conor," she said.

"No, I wasn't," snapped Maureen.

"My teacher says that people with detrimental opinions of the Führer and his mission to save our country should keep them to themselves," the young boy parroted.

"Different viewpoints are important. People with differing perspectives deserve to be heard, and treated with respect," Lisa said.

"Even if those views put the existence of the Reich in danger, and leave us open to destruction by our enemies in the East?" he replied.

Seamus was standing at the door and walked to the kitchen table. He put his hand on Conor's shoulder. "Who told you this? Your teacher?"

"And my Hitler Youth leader," he said and kept eating.

"I want to talk about this while we're all here," Seamus said.

Michael didn't look up, so his father went to him. The young man had already run five miles that day, just as he did every morning.

"What do you think, Michael?"

"You really want to know?"

"Yes."

"I think Hitler wants to make Germany strong and prosperous again, but sometimes I wish I wasn't reminded of politics everywhere I go. Why do my trainers wear swastikas? I just want to run."

"My teacher says everything's political these days," Fiona said from behind them. Her hair was perfect and tied off with a pink bow. "She went through some statistics from the newspaper with us the other day. Hitler is ending the Depression. Unemployment is plummeting. German workers can afford to feed their families, or buy a stein of beer at the end of the week again."

"Tell them, Father," Maureen said. "Your workers are no richer than they were in the depths of the Depression back in '29. The government has frozen their wages. Only the rich are getting richer."

"It's true," Seamus said.

"My teacher said industry is booming and set to reach heights never seen before," Fiona said. "Hitler is the economic savior this country has been crying out for since the war."

"The wheels of industry are indeed turning again and set to accelerate, but what kind of industry? Hitler and the Nazis are taking this country on the road to war. All the talk among Father's peers is of producing bombs and bullets—strange products in peacetime. I'm just worried about where it's all going to end," Maureen said.

"I'm just trying to keep my factory afloat," Seamus said.

"My Hitler Youth leader and a few of my teachers said we need to be wary of what our parents tell us, and that they might be too old-fashioned to understand the revolution that's taking place in Germany," Michael said.

"And what do you think? Am I naïve? Too set in my ways?" Seamus asked.

"I don't know," he replied. "It's hard when everyone else seems to believe in it."

"Do you believe the songs they make you sing? 'The old must perish, the weak must decay,'" Maureen asked.

"I sing when I have to sing. Everyone I know is in the Hitler Youth or the League of German Girls. I try not to think about their sermons too much. I just want to run faster and make it to the Olympics next year."

"What about Hitler's treatment of the Jews?" Lisa asked.

"We never talk about that," Fiona said.

"It's wrong," Michael said.

"It's monstrous," Maureen said. "Their treatment of anyone who doesn't conform to the standards of their made-up superrace is hideous. I'm amazed you can't see through them. Michael. You're not falling for their lies? Tell me you're not."

"I'm not interested in politics, or the Nazis."

"Yes, but maybe they're interested in you," Maureen said. "Fiona?"

"I don't see anything bad happening, and my teachers talk about how Hitler and the Nazis are improving this country every day."

Seamus put his arm around Fiona. She shrugged him off, not because she was angry—just because she was thirteen.

"I understand the stresses you're all under. I just want to say one thing: no matter what happens, stay true to who you are in here." He put a hand on his chest. "The Nazis can talk and tell us everything they want us to hear, but as long as we're faithful to what's in our hearts, the parts of us that make us who we are will remain. No matter what anyone tells you, know that the people in this room want nothing but the best for you."

"I read a quotation from Goethe the other day," Lisa said. "It said 'Despite all the powers, maintain yourself.' I think that's what your father is trying to say. These crazy times will pass. As long as we maintain ourselves and stay true to the beliefs in our hearts—and not the ones the National Socialists promote in their newspapers or radio broadcasts—then we will have won."

She went over and picked her daughter up. The little girl was heavy now, the flower of her infancy all but faded.

"You're such a pretty girl, but it's time to get off to school. Everyone. Let's get moving."

The children, although it was hard to call them that anymore, got off their seats and left. Maureen hugged her as she passed by.

"Good luck today," she said.

"Yes, let us know how it goes with the most powerful man in Europe this afternoon," Michael said with a smile.

"He'll be eating out of her hand, just like we all do," Seamus said.

"Go get him," Maureen said.

Forty-five minutes later, with the school runs complete and her husband gone to a business meeting, Lisa was alone in the house. With little else to do, she set about choosing her outfit for her meeting with Hitler that afternoon at the Reich Chancellery. At least that was something she could control.

After thirty minutes of back and forth decision-making, she settled on a red sundress with a matching hat. She laid her clothes on the bed, then took a bath. After a quick wash, she applied a hint of makeup—just to hide any blemishes, but not so much as to offend the old-fashioned chauvinistic sensibilities of the Führer. She got changed and was ready much sooner than she needed to be.

The phone rang as she finished up her makeup, and she ran downstairs to pick it up. It was her father.

"I wanted to wish you good luck today," he said. "I've met the man a few times now, and I can say he's a human being just like the rest of us. You'll charm him no end. I'm sure of it."

"Thank you," she said. "Any last-minute tips?"

"Remember not to use the Hitler salute when you see him. My only other advice would be not to engage him on any political matters. I know you're probably thinking you might change his mind on something even a little, but believe me, he's as movable as Mont Blanc."

"I'll resist the temptation. I'm going to do my job and nothing more."

"That's my girl. And Lisa—"

"Yes?" She cut him off, able to read his mind. "I won't mention you."

"Good. Your Jewish blood must remain a secret, for Hannah's sake as much as yours."

"I have to go, Father, or I'll be late."

"Really? Go, go! You can't keep the Führer waiting. Good luck."

"Thank you." She hung up the phone and sat staring at the wall. Was her father ashamed of her for being a Jew? Surely not, or he wouldn't be so loving and kind.

It was still an hour before she was to meet Petra outside the Kaiserhof Hotel beside the Reich Chancellery, but she got in her car and drove into the city.

Her palms were so wet on the steering wheel that she reached into her bag for a handkerchief to dry it off.

Thirty minutes later, she was sitting at the bar in the Kaiserhof, sipping a glass of wine. A young man in a blue suit approached her, but she held up her hand to display the wedding ring on her finger and he backed off without another word.

"Thank goodness you're here," Petra said as she walked in. She was luminous in a blue dress and beret. Both women made sure not to wear high heels—the Führer disapproved of them. It seemed he was quite prone to offense for such a powerful man, particularly from women.

Lisa got up and kissed her friend on the cheek.

"How are you feeling?" Lisa asked.

"Nervous, but honored, if I'm honest. The most powerful man in the world requested to have lunch with us. It's quite a feeling."

Lisa finished her wine. She was more nervous than excited.

"It's an acting job, like any other. I'll do what I need to."

"I know this is strange, and I don't like the Nazis any more than you do, but even if you're not a monarchist, it's still an incredible experience to meet the king."

"Yes, it'll be a day to remember, whatever happens."

"We'll get through this together," Petra said and put her hand on Lisa's.

Comforted by the thought she wasn't alone in this, Lisa's nerves settled.

Before she knew it, it was time to go to the chancellery and the two women left the hotel.

Neither spoke on the short walk. The SS guard on duty at the gate met them with an intense stare and didn't react to Petra's smile as he handed back the invitations. The six guards who checked their papers on the way in were all identical versions of the one at the gate. Nothing about them varied.

"Seems like the Führer is undertaking some refurbishments," Petra said under her breath as they were led past painters and workmen in stained overalls.

An adjutant met them at the bottom of a marble staircase that had signs declaring the paint on the banisters was wet. He was short, with round spectacles and thinning hair. They followed him down another hallway and past yet more guards until they reached a door. He opened it and showed the ladies to a small table, where two trays with fine china teapots and cups and saucers were laid.

"The Führer and the Reich minister will be with you momentarily," the adjutant said and left.

Petra looked out the window, which offered an impressive view of Wilhelmstrasse. "Isn't this incredible?"

"I think we should sit down," Lisa said.

"Of course." Her friend took a seat beside her. "Shall we pour ourselves a cup?"

"No, I don't think we..."

The door opened again. Adolf Hitler, a man she'd seen countless times on movie reels, entered with Goebbels at his heels. The German leader was wearing a gray suit and tie with a white shirt, with the ubiquitous swastika armband across his bicep. His dark hair was brushed back and his pale complexion seemed almost translucent. His hands remained clasped in front of him as the two ladies stood up, and his serious expression didn't change when Petra beamed at him. Discomfort crept up Lisa's spine, but Petra seemed to be having a different experience.

"Thank you for coming in today, Fräuleins," Goebbels said.

"It's an honor," Petra said.

This is an acting job, Lisa told herself and switched over to the role of adoring sycophant.

"It truly is," she said. "My children were so excited for me at breakfast. It was like Christmas morning in the Ritter house."

Hitler's intense stare was unchanged. He seemed to be studying their faces. "The pleasure is ours," he said with no warmth and little emotion in his voice. His speaking voice was different from the authoritative, harsh screaming he employed during his speeches. "You both look vibrant."

"Thank you, my Führer," breathed Petra. Hopefully she was acting, too.

"Shall we?" Goebbels asked and motioned to the chairs at the table. The door opened, and the adjutant reappeared to pour the tea. No one spoke as he filled the cups.

"Thank you," Lisa said when all four cups were filled. The aide left without saying a word.

"I see you're refurbishing the place—just like the country itself," Petra said.

"The previous iteration was a disgrace," Hitler said as he reached for the cup of tea.

"You ladies certainly brighten up the place," Goebbels said with a lecherous smile.

Lisa lowered her eyes as she drank her tea. It was hot and strong.

"The Reich minister was impressed with your performance on set when he visited, Frau Ritter," Hitler said.

"Thank you, my Führer."

"We have been looking for a new film star to showcase our ideas to the nation," Goebbels said. "The medium of film is ripe to propel our people forward to fulfill their potential. In the new script, you'll find your character to be a stronger iteration of the ideal Aryan woman—one unsullied by the Communist and Zionist influences she fights. You are ideal for the role. My man will deliver the improved screenplay as you leave."

"I look forward to seeing it," Lisa said.

"And you, my pretty flower," Goebbels said to Petra. "Your new role will be that of the heroine's younger sister, defiled by a Jewish moneylender but strong enough to rise again. I suggested the role myself. It's an exciting time. I see great things ahead for you both."

"You do? My God, to hear you say that!" Petra seemed as if she was about to burst. "It's the greatest honor of my life."

Hitler seemed unmoved by Petra's childish enthusiasm. "The Reich minister and I have been talking for some time about the importance of having the right role models in film. Much in the same way Hollywood studios have their panel of stars, we intend to do the same."

Petra put her hand on Lisa's leg under the table and squeezed. Her breath was coming in soft pants of excitement.

Hitler inclined his head. "Herr Goebbels has been talking about this for a while."

"You want to have us as part of your panel?" Petra asked, her hand in Lisa's now.

"I intend to visit the set again—several times," Goebbels said. "And if the production goes well, huge possibilities sit on the horizon for you both."

"I can't tell you how overwhelmed I am," Petra said. "Thank you so much."

"This is incredible," Lisa said.

Hitler turned his attention to Lisa. "I believe your husband is American."

"Seamus spent much of his life in America, but his father was German. His uncle left him his metalworks factory when he died. Living in Berlin is like coming home for him."

The answer seemed to please the Führer—his lips even curled into a tiny smile. "That's as it should be. All good Germans should live in the Fatherland."

Lisa kept smiling too, though inside she was terrified. This wasn't something one could refuse. No one could ever say no to the Nazis. If she did well, they'd take her in for countless more propaganda films. She might become a Nazi pinup... And then surely it would be only a matter of time before they found out about her heritage. Fear and disgust made her want to vomit.

"These films would be huge events within the Reich," Goebbels said. "Time permitting, the Führer himself would attend the premieres. Can you imagine the glamour? It must be what you've dreamed of your entire lives."

"Ever since I was a little girl," said Petra. If she was acting, then she certainly was a fine actress. And why shouldn't she be thrilled at the chance of a lifetime?

Hitler stood up and walked to the record player sitting on a table behind them. "Do you like Wagner?" he asked. "I assume you do with a name like yours, Fräulein Wagner." He applied the needle to the record, and *The Ride of the Valkyries* swelled in the air around them. The Führer's mood seemed to improve upon hearing the music; he appeared almost content as he sat back down. Once again, Lisa found it hard to tally the public orator with this removed, socially awkward individual she was having tea with. She almost wouldn't have believed they were the same person if she didn't know better. His polite reserve emboldened her.

"Might I inquire about the funding for the remainder of my current film?" she asked with a bright smile. "My director, Herr Hagen, is keen to know when we can expect the remainder."

Goebbels intervened. "You can tell your Herr Hagen that he'll get his check as soon as he reviews and approves the new script. That's nothing ladies such as yourselves need worry about. Financial worries are not for women. You just need to concentrate on your roles, and in portraying the Aryan ideal we've written for you."

"It feels good to be part of the master race," Petra gushed.

Lisa let go of Petra's hand under the table.

"It's a responsibility, to be sure. We as a people were born to rule," Goebbels said.

"Indeed." Hitler drained his cup and rattled it back onto the saucer. "Racial purity is the bedrock of our society. Without it, all else in the Reich will fail. It is our sincere hope that through the production of this film, and many others, we can demonstrate to the German people their racial superiority and the importance of protecting it."

He stood up, as did Goebbels. Petra and Lisa followed suit.

"Now, if you'll excuse me, I must leave. It was good to make your acquaintance." The Führer left by the same door through which he'd entered.

Goebbels lingered. "You'll have something to boast about to your grandchildren now," he said with a ridiculous laugh that sounded like a hyena.

Lisa inclined her head. "Thank you for the wonderful opportunity, Herr Goebbels."

"This is the best day of my life!" Petra was still beaming.

"Unfortunately, I also must go. It was a pleasure and privilege to meet you beautiful ladies today, and we will meet again, very soon."

He kissed each of their hands and followed Hitler out of the room. Immediately, the other door opened behind them and the adjutant appeared once more. He handed Lisa a large envelope, then led them out to the guard at the front gate. Seconds later, they were on the street.

"Let's go back to the hotel." Petra said, still starry-eyed. "I need champagne!"

Lisa didn't feel the same way. She just hugged the young actress and hid her face in Petra's shoulder.

"I need to get home," she said in a muffled voice. "The children. They'll want to hear how my meeting went. I can't keep them in suspense!"

But Petra grabbed her arms and shook her. "No. Stay to celebrate. This time next year we might not be able to do this anymore. We'll be swamped by autograph hunters."

As the bartender set down a bottle of champagne in an ice bucket, and two flutes, Lisa opened the envelope to find two copies of the amended screenplay. She handed Petra one, then opened the other.

The first page was set in the fields where Lisa's character and the other women of the village were out threshing grain.

The next scene was Petra's character going to the local Jewish moneylender. The Jewish character was described as ancient, with a filthy gray beard, hunched over with a long pointy nose and sharp teeth. When Petra's character was unable to repay the interest on her debt to him, the moneylender violated her.

"Of course," Lisa said. "It didn't take long to get to that."

Petra's eyes were huge, as she realized what a big part she now had. "I've been waiting my whole life for an opportunity like this." She held up the script, gripping on to it with white knuckles. It had a Nazi stamp above the title. "My parents will be so proud."

Lisa's eyes filled with tears. "I look forward to seeing you in your new role."

"I'm all emotional too! I couldn't be more excited!"

They carried on looking through the pages to the point where the Jews in the village ally with the Soviet authorities to subjugate the German-speaking locals and kill Lisa's on-screen husband.

"And this is where my brave character rises up to lead the villagers in their fight against the evil Zionist threat." She couldn't help the sarcasm dripping from every syllable she uttered.

"It's hateful trash," agreed Petra, who seemed sincere. "But if we don't go along with it, they'll throw us out of the Reich Chamber of Film and we'll never work in this country again."

"Not while the Nazis are in power, anyway." Lisa closed the script and pushed it across the table.

"They're not going anywhere... Lisa, what is the matter? Do you really mind that much? I mean, I have close friends who are Jewish. They're great, but even they would understand that we have to do what we have to do to survive... It doesn't affect us, does it?"

"I don't know. It just isn't right."

The bottle of champagne was drained and Petra ordered another. Lisa gulped down the glass her friend poured for her.

Lisa's acting skills were being pushed to their limit. The role of delighted young actress getting her big break was perhaps the hardest she'd ever had to play. Petra was a natural. Lisa listened to her saying the same things over and over about how happy she was and how proud her family was going to be. She longed to tell her what was tearing her apart inside. She never asked for this. Never even knew she was Jewish. What had she done to deserve this treatment? What had anyone done? Would playing the role be more dangerous than not? She longed to speak to Seamus, or to confide in someone who knew who she really was.

Petra finished another glass of champagne. "You know you can play this role, don't you? Everyone starts somewhere."

"It's not that," Lisa answered. The alcohol seemed to be having an effect. She wanted to confide in Petra, though she knew she shouldn't. But what if she had someone on set with her who knew what she was going through? That could make all the difference.

"Is there something you're not telling me?" Petra asked.

Lisa took the glass in her hand and stared into the effervescent liquid.

"Are you friends with Jews? I grew up with—"

"I am a Jew," Lisa whispered. Petra's eyes widened.

A stiletto of regret pierced Lisa's heart. "I shouldn't have said that. It must be the champagne."

"No," Petra said and took her hand. Both women looked around to make sure no one was listening in. No one was paying them the slightest bit of attention, save for two young men at the other end of the bar, too far away to hear what they were saying. "I'm honored that you confided in me."

Lisa paused a few seconds to stare into Petra's blue eyes. She saw kindness in them.

"I didn't even know myself until my mother died in '33. She converted when she was young and never told me. My daughter doesn't know either. Only a handful of people do."

"Don't say another word," Petra said. "I understand. I'll be there to help you on set whenever you need a shoulder to cry on. I won't breathe a word to anyone."

Lisa felt embarrassed in front of the younger woman. "Thanks, Petra. I should go."

"Very well. I'm going to sit here, learning my part. And you get reading those pages. We'll likely be back on set in a few days."

She stood up to embrace Lisa, and whispered, "Don't worry," in her ear.

Lisa's head was swirling as the breath of the warm summer air hit her face. The new screenplay was in her hand, and she stuffed it into her bag as she strode toward her car. She had to get home and prayed Seamus would be there.

His car was in the driveway as she returned. It was just before three o'clock, and the children were still in school. Maureen was in college and wouldn't be home for hours after. Lisa heard her husband on the phone as she pushed through the front door. She pulled out the screenplay, let her bag drop to the floor, and approached him in tears.

He made an excuse and got off the call. "Is everything ok?"

"They changed the script, and it's like an edition of *Der Stürmer* now," she said. "I can't turn it down. I have to protect Hannah and my father. I'm going to have to do it—I have no choice."

"They wrote it about Jews?"

"To suit their agenda. I'm to be a propaganda pawn."

It took her a few minutes to explain everything. It was only when her husband stopped asking questions that she told him what she did in the hotel.

"I let it slip to Petra that I'm a Jew."

He took a few seconds to digest her words before answering. "You think you can trust her?"

"I hope so. It was a moment of weakness. I shouldn't have said anything."

He ran his fingers through his hair. "It's done now. She seems like a decent person. Perhaps it'll be good to have someone on set who understands your motivations." He put his arms around her and kissed her.

They sat and talked until the children came home, but nothing he said made her change her mind about what had to be done. The vise had closed in around her.

12

Saturday, June 15

The doctor bought the house at Wannsee the year before, proclaiming to be happy at last to have something to spend his money on. Lake Wannsee, the most popular bathing spot outside the city, was heaving with Berliners trying to escape the summer heat. Traffic was heavy through the Grunewald Forest all the way down to the water. Josef Walz's house was on the south side. What should have been a twenty-minute drive took almost three times that, and the kids, young and old, were sweaty and irritable as Seamus pulled up to Lisa's father's house.

The gray brick house with its square windows and intentionally important-looking pillars led down fifty yards of manicured lawn to a jetty and the lake below. The beach was only five minutes' walk away. Maureen and Michael's mood lightened as Seamus pulled up. Lisa reached over to him as their five children spilled out the back doors. Each had their own room at the house and always left clothes here to negate the need to pack.

Seamus got their few bags from the back of the car, and with Conor and Michael's help, brought them inside.

The door opened. "Welcome!" Dr. Walz said. "How was the traffic?"

"As bad as you'd expect on a sunny Saturday in June," Seamus said.

He took a moment to greet Maureen, Michael, Fiona, and Conor individually before picking up Hannah to bring her inside.

"How was your meeting yesterday with the Führer?" he asked once the youngsters had scattered to change in their rooms.

"Eye-opening," she said. "His thousands of female admirers would do well to keep their fantasies about him in their minds and not to meet the man behind them. He has the social skills of a wet sponge."

"I've noticed that myself. The public and private personas are often disparate," Dr. Walz replied. "Any update on your investigation into the fire, Seamus?"

"I'm still looking into it." Seamus took the bags upstairs and deposited them in the various rooms.

Twenty minutes later, they were all ready to relax. After some prodding from the adults, Maureen and Michael agreed to take Fiona with them to meet their friends at the beach. Conor and Hannah went down to the jetty and played in the shallow water by the shore. Seamus, his wife, and father-in-law sat under an umbrella a few yards away, watching them. Each had a cold drink in front of them.

"So, tell me more about your meeting with the Führer," Lisa's father asked her. "I still haven't told him we're related, by the way... Like I said, I wouldn't want you to think any of your success was because of me. It's all your own doing."

"I didn't mention it either. I didn't know if you wanted to be thought of as the father of a Nazi pinup."

"Is that what you think is ahead of you?" he asked, amused.

"At best," Lisa replied. "Goebbels got his hands on the script and distorted it to fit his agenda. They wrote in a Jewish moneylender with a hump like a camel and a nose like a vulture."

"Everyone has to play parts in life they'd rather not," her father said. "You're an actress. Act. This is your dream."

"It seems dreams and nightmares are interchangeable these days. Seamus is being offered a contract worth millions, but to make bullets and bombs."

They stopped talking for a moment as Conor ran along the jetty and jumped into the water feet first, emerging a few seconds later with a massive smile.

Then Josef turned to Seamus. "Seriously, a contract worth millions? I'm not a businessman, but I can recognize an amazing opportunity when I see one."

Seamus shrugged. "I don't know if I want to be in the business of arming the Nazis."

"I understand your moral concerns. I know you didn't come to Germany to manufacture arms, but times have changed almost beyond recognition these past two years, and we have to move with them. It's hard for an old man like me to believe the effect Hitler and his Party have had on our society."

"It's your party, Josef," Seamus said and immediately regretted his words.

"You know I'm a member of the Party to enable my work, and nothing more."

"Of course. I apologize."

"I think this is the way forward," Walz said. "And anyway, is it so wrong that our Führer wants our country to be strong once again? Haven't we all had enough of the feeling of other countries pushing us around? The threat from the East is real. Stalin would lay waste to all this if given half a chance."

Hannah came up from the water, dripping wet. Lisa took

the towel on her lap and used it to dry the little girl off in a moment.

"When is lunch?" she asked.

"Not for a few minutes. Go and play."

Her daughter ran back down to the water.

Walz carried on once she left. "Times are changing, Seamus. The new government is business friendly, and about to become even more so. The scourge of democracy is behind us."

"You remember my friend, Hans Litten, the lawyer who got Hitler on the stand in '31? He was taken on the night of the Reichstag fire. They never let him go. He's still rotting in jail—without ever receiving a trial."

"I don't know anything about that," Walz said. "What's that got to do with what we're talking about?"

"These are the people I'd be allying myself with," Seamus spat. "This is what the government does."

Walz asked, "Do you have the desire to leave Germany?"

Seamus was annoyed at himself for letting his anger show. Lisa was silent, her face stern as she stared out at the children playing in the water.

"Seamus?" pressed the doctor. "Do you want to go back to America?"

It was an interesting thought—one that had come into his mind a few times recently. "My children grew up in the States. I haven't forgotten about the place. Lisa and I have spoken about it in the past."

"But only in passing, about moving back," Lisa said. "Would you really want to do that? Michael would have to begin training again. The Olympics is next year. We'd have to find him new coaches, and he'd never make the American team in a few months. You can't do that to him. And what of Maureen and Thomas, and her studies here?"

"And my promise to Uncle Helmut about committing to the long-term future of the factory? I'm well aware."

But Lisa was right. Moving again, after settling here as a family, wasn't the answer. They'd been through so much tumult. The kids had only just forgiven him for leaving them for two years. Perhaps Maureen never had. Still, the thought of leaving the National Socialists, and the SA and the SS and all the hatred they sowed, was a tempting one.

His wife walked down to the water and called the children for lunch. The men sat in silence as she wrapped towels around them and led them back up to the house.

∽

It took them a few minutes to pick out who they were looking for among the sea of towels and umbrellas on the beach. Karen was visiting for the weekend with her own family and had arranged to meet them on the beach along with Thomas and his friend, Dieter.

Maureen and Karen lay down about five or six paces back from the edge of the clear blue water, watching the smaller children play. Michael came and sat with them.

"Fancy seeing you here," Karen said.

Michael grinned. "Karen, good to see you."

He was in his bathing shorts, and Karen seemed to eat him up with her eyes. She watched as he rolled out his towel and took off his shirt to reveal his fit and muscular chest. Maureen shook her head and left them to talk as she brought Fiona down to the water.

Dieter liked Karen, but couldn't compete with Michael, so he went for a beer with Thomas instead.

Maureen and Fiona wallowed in the water until their hands and feet were white and wrinkled. The sun was still hot and the sand even hotter when they hit the shore, and they had to dance back to the safety of their towels. Michael was lying down, and Karen had moved her towel next to his. Maureen had to endure her brother flirting with her friend for the rest of the afternoon. Thankfully, her boyfriend and Dieter came back to keep her and Fiona company.

Afternoon turned into evening, and soon it was time for Dieter and Thomas to drive back.

Thomas took Maureen aside as they were saying their goodbyes. They walked away from the group, and he only began speaking when he was sure no one could hear.

"You think you can do it?"

"I don't know where he has that kind of information," she replied. "He has a study in the house, but I don't know what documents he keeps there."

"Have you ever seen anything relating to Babelsberg in the clinic?"

"Nothing."

"And Babelsberg is only a few minutes away from here by car. It stands to reason he'd keep any documents he had in the lake house."

"I'll see what I can find."

"Just be careful. Do you really know who this man is?" She didn't respond. A young couple holding hands breezed past them. He waited until they were gone to continue. "I know what everyone at the meeting said the other day, but I don't want you to take any risks, ok? If you can't find it, then we'll let it go."

She reached up and kissed him on the mouth. "Thank you, but I'll be fine. I won't get caught." She remembered stealing out of her Aunt Maeve's house in Newark to meet her old boyfriend, Leo, the boy who wanted her to settle down with him. He was probably married now.

The heat of the day was fading and the beach was almost

clear. Dieter called after Thomas, "Come on, we're never going to get home with all the traffic."

"That's my cue." Thomas kissed her one last time. "Don't forget—safety first. You promise? I know how you can get sometimes."

"So do I, but I promise."

Maureen saw Fiona make a motion like she wanted to vomit behind Karen and Michael's backs. They would have to endure their flirtation over dinner, too.

"Come on, let's get going." Maureen had something other than her brother's love life on her mind.

∼

Lisa was in the kitchen preparing chicken and salad for dinner as they returned. Seamus and Dr. Walz were on the back porch with drinks. Both greeted the group of young people with more enthusiasm than she expected.

"How was the beach?" Dr. Walz asked.

"Michael likes Karen," Fiona said.

"Oh, stop it, Fiona!" said Karen, blushing.

"I can neither confirm nor deny those rumors," said Michael.

"I can't hear about this again," Maureen said and went inside.

A streak of shame shot through her as she realized this would be a perfect time to check the study. She went upstairs, her palms moistening with every step she took. The study was beside the main bedroom and overlooked the lake. She pushed the door open with a shaking hand and could hear Michael flirting with Karen through the open window directly above them.

Was now the time to do this? The doctor seemed drunk, and

she could hear him laughing with Seamus. Perhaps she wouldn't get a better chance. She sneaked into the study. The leather-covered desk was clean, with just a neat stack of letters and a cup of pens on top of it. The walls were covered in bookcases, with each full end to end with medical books, some old, some new. She was still in her bathing suit, though it was dry now, and had a towel wrapped around her. She waited in the doorway, listening to the conversation below and the sounds of Lisa working in the kitchen.

After thirty seconds, Maureen realized that dinner might be ready soon, or the doctor might come inside to the bathroom, or Hannah might wander upstairs. The thought of Gisela spurred her on and she dismissed her doubts. The desk seemed like the logical place to look first. The drawer was locked, and she cursed under her breath as it caught. Down on the veranda, Michael said he was going inside to wash up. Dr. Walz asked Karen about her day.

Maureen reached into the cup of pens on the desk looking for a key, but didn't find one. *That would have been too easy.* Was she making too much noise? Could they hear her below? She thought to close the window, but decided it was better to be able to hear them, despite the risk.

With no filing cabinets or safes in the room, it didn't seem like any sensitive documents could be anywhere but the desk. She searched her mind for bunches of keys she might have seen downstairs, but couldn't remember seeing any. Breaking into the desk wouldn't be easy, and would almost guarantee her getting caught. She was just about to give up when she noticed a book out of place on the shelf behind the desk.

The sound of footsteps coming up the stairs paralyzed her and she ducked behind the door, which was a few inches ajar. Getting down on her haunches, she peeked through the gap and breathed a sigh of relief when she saw Michael enter the bathroom and shut the door behind him. The sound of the doctor laughing again calmed her, and she tiptoed to the bookshelf. The out-of-place book was embossed with gold lettering saying *Racial Theory as a Guide to a Better Future*, authored by someone she had never heard of. It was jutting out from the other books by an inch or so, and she reached and pulled it out. A key sat hidden behind it, and she reached up and took it in her hand.

The thought to put it back and come back later when everyone was asleep occurred to her, but sheer curiosity and the desire to get the drawer open drove her on. No one in the house had moved.

The key fit the lock, and she turned it. The drawer opened. Several letters sat piled on top of one another, along with a mishmash of paperclips, fountain pens, and a Nazi Party pin. She picked up the pile of letters. The first was from a patient, thanking him; the second was a job offer from a hospital in Dresden that the doctor would undoubtedly decline. The third letter was from the Reich Chancellery, and the Führer's official stamp and signature at the bottom caught her attention before she read the text. It was only four lines long:

11 JUNE 1935
DR. WALZ,
THE ARRANGEMENTS FOR THE BABELSBERG EXPERIMENTS HAVE BEEN MADE. TEST SUBJECTS WILL BE PROVIDED ON-SITE ON JULY 26, 1935. UTMOST CONFIDENTIALITY IS DEMANDED.
ADOLF HITLER, REICHSFÜHRER

But she heard voices inside the house as she read the last words...and footsteps coming up the stairs. The footfalls grew louder, and Maureen stuffed the letter back into its envelope. Treading a fine line between speed and discretion, she pushed the drawer closed and locked it. The footsteps were coming toward the study. She replaced the key, pushed the book back into place, and made for the window just as the door opened.

"What are you doing in here?" Dr. Walz asked. His tone was friendly, but his words demanded an answer.

Maureen held her hands in front of her to stop them from shaking. "Just admiring the view of the lake. It's so beautiful at this time of night."

"Each time of the day lends it a different majesty," he said.

She turned away from him to the window, afraid to look him in the eyes. She couldn't see him, but sensed him coming to stand beside her. He put a hand on her shoulder.

"You can see the lake from your room," he said.

"I just wanted to see it from a different angle. I hope you don't mind. I don't mean to pry."

"No, not at all. I want you to feel at home here. We are family, after all."

"I should take a shower," she said.

They both turned as Michael emerged from the bathroom. "Seems like it's your turn."

"I'll see you at dinner," Maureen said and walked out.

It took every sinew of self-control within her not to run down the hallway to the bathroom, or turn around. She felt Dr. Walz's eyes on her as she went.

The bathroom door shut with a *bang* behind her, and she collapsed to her haunches against it. How could she have been so stupid? Why didn't she wait? Curiosity had gotten the better of her. The doctor didn't see her at the desk, and she was sure she had put the key back in its place in time. She'd been lucky, but might not be next time.

The text of Hitler's letter ran around her brain until she almost felt dizzy. *Test subjects will be provided?* Was he working on some new form of sterilization? What did it mean? Her hands were shaking and sweaty and she had to swallow the lump in her throat.

Perhaps her new friends in Herman's apartment on Sprengelstrasse would be able to make more sense of it.

She ran the water for her shower and stepped in. It felt wonderful, like an escape. She endeavored to think of something else, and Thomas's face was on her mind as she got out. The question one of the Subversives asked her remerged in her thoughts. Could she leave him? Thankfully, it wasn't something she had to decide upon. Their immediate future was here, in Germany.

The few moments she had alone in the bathroom ended with Fiona hammering on the door, demanding she let her in to shower before dinner. Maureen wrapped a towel around herself and, letting her wet hair fall to her shoulders, opened the door and walked past her sister without a word.

Dinner was ready thirty minutes later. The family sat at a table beside glass doors overlooking the lake. Maureen was first in her seat and stared out at the darkening expanse of the Wannsee as her family filled the chairs around her. The letter was on her mind. It was impossible to think of anything else

Dr. Walz sat down opposite her, a glass of red wine in his hand. Michael was being silly, and Karen, who had the giggles, almost fell off her seat. She excused herself as Conor covered his mouth to hide his sniggering.

Lisa and Seamus brought the food in and forked generous chicken breasts onto each of their plates, along with the salad they prepared. Everyone over the age of sixteen drank wine or beer, and despite Fiona's protestations, she was consigned to drinking cola.

The conversation was dominated by their various days at the lake.

They finished the main course as Dr. Walz poured himself another glass of wine. He tried to do the same for Karen, but she put her hand over the top of her glass, protesting that she'd had far too much already.

Dr. Walz toasted Lisa. "Who's proud of my little girl, the movie star! Can you believe what she's achieved?"

"Congratulations, Frau Ritter. It's so exciting," Karen said.

"It's nothing to be excited about," Lisa responded. "It's a low-budget movie of questionable content."

The atmosphere around the table soured like milk left in the sun.

"Is this something to do with your visit to the Führer's office yesterday?" Michael asked. "I deal with Nazi Party members all the time at the track. I just tell them what they want to hear and get back to running. You should do the same."

"I wish it were as simple as that," Lisa said.

"I can't believe you met the Führer," Fiona said. "He's the savior of Germany. I would die for him."

Her father threw his napkin down on the table and cursed under his breath before regaining his self-control.

"Children, how would you feel about moving back to America?" he asked.

Maureen's fork slipped from her hand and made a loud crack against her plate.

"What?" Michael asked. "Why?"

"No one's made any decisions yet," Seamus said, "but would you be open to it? What about you, Fiona? Don't you miss America?"

"What are you talking about, Father?" Maureen asked. "Are you thinking about selling the factory and moving back to the States?"

"It's a possibility—nothing more than that. We have certain decisions to make. One choice could mean we end up moving back to America."

Maureen looked across the table at Michael. He threw down his napkin and was staring at his plate.

"I miss my cousins and Aunt Maeve, and I still think about my friends," said Fiona. "But I love Germany."

"What about my training?" Michael burst out. "And the

Olympics here in Berlin next year? I'd never have time to set up and get on the US team if we moved back."

"I'm well aware of that, son," Seamus said. "We haven't forgotten about all the hard work you've put in over the two years. It's in my mind all the time."

"And what about my university? Am I meant to just drop out? What about Thomas?" Maureen asked. She felt her voice rising with each word, and the ire inside with them. "You can't just spring this on us like this. What about Lisa's career? You're being so selfish."

"I won't make any decisions without you, I promise. Whatever we do has to be as a family."

"If everyone's finished…" Lisa got up to start clearing the plates. "Lay off your father, please. It is only an idea."

"Lisa, sit down," Maureen said. "We'll take care of the dishes. Come on, Michael—Fiona, Conor."

In the kitchen, Michael was furious. "He wants us to leave? He said we were a family."

"I think I know why," Maureen said. "He's worried about the politics in Germany and how it's changing us."

"You're sticking up for Father now?" Michael asked.

"Just explaining where he's coming from."

"I don't miss America as much as I thought I would. I'm not focused on going back," Michael said.

"We know what you're focused on," Maureen said.

"What do you think, Conor?" asked Fiona.

"I don't know," the boy replied. "I remember the house in Newark, and sharing a room. It's much better here."

"I don't want to go," said Fiona. "I don't think Germany is changing me at all."

"You and I are going to have a discussion about your *beloved Führer* soon," Maureen said.

Now wasn't the time. Perhaps the Subversives could help Fiona see the light. Maureen shook her head and turned away.

The four of them began the task of washing the dishes.

The family reconvened around the dining room table once more after dinner to play cards. All talk of moving back to America was banished, but it simmered under the surface the entire time. Dr. Walz took his leave around ten o'clock, and Maureen's father and Lisa went out for a walk. Michael went to bed soon after, as he had to get up early to run around the lake. Maureen stayed with Conor and Fiona before they all retired to bed around eleven.

Three hours later, Maureen was in bed in the room she shared with Fiona. The house was silent. The only sound was the gentle wind and the lake lapping up against the shore like a thirsty dog.

July 26 in Babelsberg. The words of the letter reappeared in her mind. She'd only had seconds to read it. What if she missed something? Maybe it was something innocent? The doctor was a kind, upright man. It must have been something innocuous. But then, why the secrecy? Why would Hitler himself write to him about a minor experiment? Questions bobbed up in her mind like corks in a pond—no matter how hard she attempted to push them down, they just popped back up again.

Maureen waited a few seconds before swinging her feet over and getting out of bed. She pulled back the curtain and peeked outside. The moon was high in a cloudless sky and shone down ghostly light over the lake and everything else below. The study was only a few steps away at the end of the hallway. She took a deep breath and tiptoed toward the door, making sure to keep off the most trodden routes—with the loudest squeaks. It was just like being in Maeve's house again, sneaking out to meet Leo.

The door opened without a sound. She waited for any noise —anything to deter her from going on. Nothing came. The doors were all closed, and no one was moving. Her bare feet were silent on the hardwood floor, and once more, she kept to the walls to prevent creaking. The sound of snoring from the doctor's room reassured her, and she entered the study with renewed confidence, wishing she'd originally waited until now. The window was still open, and a warm summer breeze drifted in.

Even with her increased comfort levels, she didn't want to waste time and went straight to the bookshelf to where *Racial Theory as a Guide to a Better Future* was and pulled it back. The key was in the same place, and she picked it up and plunged it into the lock on the desk drawer. She took a breath and another moment to listen before opening it. The stack of letters was in the same place.

She picked it up and flicked through, but didn't find anything from the Reich Chancellery. Thinking she'd missed it, she went through the letters again; the same ones she saw earlier were still there, but the letter from Hitler was gone. Her hands were shaking so much that as she locked the drawer, she dropped the key. It clattered on the floor, like it weighed fifty pounds, and she froze. She stood still for thirty seconds and retrieved the key when she was sure no one was coming. Only when she was sure the coast was clear did she sneak back to her bed, where sleep did not come easily.

Maureen was last at the breakfast table the following day and took her place as her siblings were finishing the sliced meat and bread laid out for them. Her father was in the kitchen, and Lisa and Hannah were at the table. Dr. Walz was at the end of the table, reading the newspaper.

The doctor lowered it and asked, "Did you sleep well?"

"Yes," she replied, trying to hide the nervousness in her voice.

"That's strange. I thought I heard you up during the night," Dr. Walz said. "Was I wrong?"

"I went to the bathroom, but apart from that, I slept like a baby."

"Perhaps I heard something else," he said and raised the newspaper again.

It was a warm morning, and the sun was streaming in through the windows, but Maureen felt cold. She left her food and made her way out to the yard, where Michael was doing pushups while Fiona and Conor sat reading.

A voice behind her interrupted her thoughts.

"Is everything ok?" Lisa asked. Hannah let go of her mother's hand and ran to the water's edge.

"I'm fine," Maureen replied.

"Is it the talk about the move back to America? That's just conjecture. We only heard about it yesterday afternoon. My head's spinning about it too. I've never even imagined living anywhere other than Germany."

"No, it's not that. I understand."

The thought to tell Lisa flared up and burned out in her mind within a fraction of a second. What if she was wrong? She couldn't do that to her.

Maureen, Michael, Fiona, and Karen spent the day at the beach, just the four of them. Thankfully, the two lovebirds scaled back their flirting, and everyone had a good time.

The sun was setting red, orange, and gold over the lake as they returned, in time to get changed for the ride home to the city. Their father was packing the car.

"Hurry and get dressed," he said, looking at his watch. "I want to try to get back to the city in the next hour or so."

They quickly obeyed, and Maureen was last to the car. Her father was already behind the wheel with the engine running. Michael, Fiona, and Conor were in the back seat. Dr. Walz was saying goodbye to Lisa and Hannah when Maureen arrived. Lisa got into the passenger seat, with the little girl in her lap. The doctor turned around, and Maureen found herself face to face with him.

"Thank you for having us this weekend."

"Of course. You know you're always welcome here," he said.

She smiled as best she could before starting to walk past him. He spoke again. "Just one thing, Maureen. I don't think we'll be needing you at the clinic anymore." Her heart dropped. "It's just that we have plenty of nurses, and you're so experienced now that I don't feel you can learn much from them anymore."

"I understand."

"I don't want you to think I don't want you there. It's just—"

"It's fine, Dr. Walz. Really, it is. I've enjoyed my time with you, but to be honest, I was thinking of moving on too."

"I must have read your mind," he said with a smile. "I don't want this to come between us."

"It won't—you have my word. I'm so grateful for everything you've done for me."

"It was my pleasure."

Without thinking, she hugged him. His return embrace was mechanical, cold. She let go and shuffled to the car, squeezing in the back with her siblings.

Dr. Walz stood to wave goodbye, the sun setting behind him. Maureen looked back as they turned the corner onto the road, but he was gone.

13

Monday, June 17

The traffic thickened as Seamus and Gert made their way into the center of town. It took them more than half an hour to get to Gerichstrasse in the working-class neighborhood of Wedding.

"This man of yours had better be worth it," Seamus said as they got out of the car.

"I know he's expensive and we had to wait a while to see him, but he'll find this Gosens, or no one can."

Bernheim led him up to a red door with a small gold-plated sign with *Alfred Leder, Private Detective,* embossed into it. A large man with a curling red mustache answered the door and invited them in. He led them down a dark hallway and along a threadbare carpet before they came to another door. He held it open for them before shaking both men's hands.

Leder was muscular and fit. His skin was reddened by the sun, and his large mustache mostly covered the pockmarks underneath. Seamus imagined he looked like a strong man from a circus, except in street clothes. His fine gray suit looked tailored.

"So, what brings you here today? You're looking for an arsonist? Herr Bernheim filled me in on a few of the details."

"We have no proof of that, but Gosens is a strong lead," Seamus said.

"That's a strange accent—where are you from? America?"

"Yes, New Jersey."

The private detective nodded and reached for a pack of cigarettes on the desk. He lit one with a match he shook out in the air. "You see any action in the war?"

Seamus was taken aback. His role in fighting against the Germans in the Great War wasn't something he spoke of often. He wasn't sure Bernheim knew. He stared into Leder's eyes as he answered. Why should he hide?

"Yes. I was in Marne in '18. Saw some things there I could never forget."

"We came up against the Yanks a few times all right. Tough—tougher than I thought." He offered the men a cigarette. Seamus accepted.

Bernheim went through the details of the case again. Leder cut him off halfway through.

"I know all this already—it was in the brief. I'll go and talk to this Kurtz first off. Someone knows where Gosens is, that's for sure. And if he did set that fire, it wasn't for fun. Someone paid him. Who might that have been? Any enemies? Anyone who'd want to see you ruined?"

"My cousin and my father-in-law have since tried to buy me out and send me back to America."

"Is that so?" Leder said and jotted down some notes.

"And you've heard of Otto Milch?"

"The fat cat? I've seen him in the newspapers."

"He's been trying to force me out of business for years."

"Anything else I should know?"

Seamus thought of Ernst Milch. Knowing that Lisa killed him before Seamus helped her dispose of the body seemed pertinent, but he kept it to himself and shook his head.

"Ok, I think that's enough for now," Leder said. "I'll get working on it, but I must warn you, if Gosens doesn't want to be found, this could take a while."

"How long?" Bernheim asked.

"Ask me next year and I'll tell you how long."

Leder sat back and put his feet up on the table.

14

Saturday, June 29

Michael was already at the stadium as they arrived. Seamus parked the car, and the Ritter family got out. Lisa took Hannah's hand as Fiona, Conor, and Maureen walked with them. The Olympiastadion, the purpose-built arena for the 1936 Berlin Olympics, was still under construction, and idle diggers sat alongside piles of bricks, waiting for workers to arrive the following day. The skeleton of what would be the main arena for the games next year was finished. The massive, oval-shaped structure was already draped in Nazi flags—as if anyone had any doubt who had ordered it made. The park around the stadium was deserted, but for a few random workers working overtime, and it wasn't difficult to pick out where Michael and his trainer, Herr Voss, were standing.

Conor ran ahead and Michael hugged him. The rest of the family followed. Seamus had met Voss before, but today was different. The trainer contacted him to meet after Michael told him his father was thinking about taking the family back to

America. Propaganda was a part of life in Germany now, and Seamus suspected this visit was no different.

Herr Voss shook his hand. He was in a blue tracksuit. The swastika armband he usually wore was conspicuous by its absence. Voss represented Germany in the 1912 games—the last event before the war. He brought home a silver in the 200 meters and was tipped to go one better next time, but that was the last Olympics that Germany participated in until 1928. By that time, Voss's best days were long behind him.

"Thank you for coming along today, Herr Ritter."

"Delighted to be here."

"This must be your lovely wife, Lisa." He shook her hand. "And Maureen, I've heard all about you and your college experiences." She smiled and looked at Michael as Voss greeted her. "Fiona, Conor, and Hannah, are you looking forward to seeing your brother running in that stadium next year?"

"Do you think he'll make it?" Fiona asked.

They all laughed. "If Michael keeps training like he is, he can achieve anything. Take it from someone who knows. I was at Stockholm in 1912 when I was just a couple of years older than your brother is now. It was an experience I'll never forget."

Michael was dressed for a race, in shorts and a singlet. Seamus knew what would happen next, but was happy to give his son this moment.

"We're very proud of Michael," Lisa said.

Voss put his hand on the back of the young man's neck. "So am I. Talent without hard work is useless. I've seen the quickest young men and women waste what the Lord bestowed on them because of laziness or alcohol or other distractions. That's not the case with your son. He's steadfast in what he believes he can achieve, and is one of the hardest workers I train."

A swell of pride filled Seamus as he beheld his son. "Well done, young man."

"We have plenty of time before the race," Voss said. "I

thought you'd like to look around before we leave for the track."

Michael was due to run that afternoon in a local race against a quality field. It was a qualifying event for the Olympics—if he ran the requisite time.

"Let's take a look inside the stadium, shall we?" Herr Voss asked. The trainer led them across a lawn area toward the hulk of the stadium.

"Construction began last year and is well on schedule to be finished in advance of the games next year," he said. "The Olympic complex will be 132 hectares in all, with the crowning achievement being the Olympiastadion itself. The capacity will be 120,000 people. Can you imagine running in front of all those people?"

"Yes!" Conor said. "Michael talks to me about it all the time."

Voss ruffled the young boy's hair and laughed. "He's excited. So am I. I've dreamed about the Olympics coming to my home city my whole life, and next year it'll be a reality."

Voss led them through an opening at the front, and the interior of the stadium came into view. Conor and Fiona gasped in wonder at the sight of the enormous arena. Seamus had never seen anything like it, even in America.

"It's going to be one of the greatest arenas in the world—a monument to German greatness."

Seamus noticed how Voss was holding back on the National Socialist rhetoric, but the implication was there even without him saying it. The Nazi flags already blowing in the summer breeze left little doubt about who this stadium was being built to honor.

"What do you think, Michael?" Seamus asked.

"It's incredible," he replied. "I've been here a few times now, and it gets more impressive each time."

"Won't you be nervous running in front of all those people?" Conor asked. "What if you trip?"

"That would be so embarrassing!" Fiona said.

"I'll take my chances," Michael replied.

"My team and I are here to help your brother prepare so things like that don't happen," Voss said. "But thank you for your concern, children."

The trainer motioned for them to follow him. Seamus and his family walked around the edge of the stadium before ascending some steps to a finished seating area that overlooked the track below. Seamus saw the enthusiasm in the young man's eyes. How could he deny him this? It was his dream. America could wait, or he could follow them home later. Either way, this was a priority.

They sat for a few minutes before they all got up together and returned to the car. They drove back into the city to the less impressive track at the university, where the race was taking place. Michael rode with his trainer.

Seamus parked the car, and he and the rest of the family sat in their usual spot in the stands, along with about 300 other spectators. The 200-meter race was first. The athletes were already limbering up on the track as the Ritters sat down.

Michael appeared at the bottom of the stand with his trainer. Seamus got up and descended the steps and hugged him. "Good luck, young man."

"Thanks, Father."

"We have to go," Voss said.

Michael was beaming as he followed his trainer toward the changing rooms. Seamus jogged back to the rest of the family.

Lisa put her hand on his and smiled at him. Not all of Voss's athletes received this kind of access to the Olympiastadion, or this treatment at all.

"He must really want to keep Michael," Seamus said.

"Apparently," Lisa replied.

Michael emerged from the dressing room after the 200-meters concluded. Voss clapped him on the back as they walked to the start of the 100-meter section of the track.

"I can't take him away from this," Seamus said.

"You were never going to, were you?" Lisa answered. Hannah, on her knees, pointed down at Michael and shouted as he jogged up and down the track.

"What about you?" he asked Maureen. "Have you thought about what I said about going back to America?"

"I can't leave Thomas," she said. "My future is with him. I don't know if I'll be in Berlin long term, but at least until I finish college."

"What about the political situation?" Seamus asked.

"If everyone gave up on a country because of the politicians running it, what kind of a place would be left?"

"You feel that much of an attachment to Germany, even though you've only been here less than three years?" Lisa asked.

"This place is in my blood. I don't feel like a foreigner here. We have so much more here than we did in America."

Michael was finishing his warm-ups, almost ready to begin.

⁓

The pursuit of speed had become his obsession. Everything he did, thought of, ate, and drank was focused on the one goal of going faster, getting to the finish line in the two-tenths of a second less that would guarantee his path to the Olympics next year. School was little more than a distraction. With extra attention from his teachers and pressure from his father, Michael kept his grades up, but his studies didn't interest him. Everything else paled to his time on the track. He knew the trip to the Olympiastadion with his family was a tactic to convince them to let him stay, but Coach Voss had little reason to motivate him. The truth was, he barely thought past next year's Olympics. Perhaps August 17, 1936—the day after the Olympic Games would end—did exist, but he never thought about it. His father was sincere in his intentions, and he stayed in school to honor him, but he resented those wasted hours sitting at a desk. The older athletes trained all day. How was he expected to keep up with them when he had to divide his time between his studies and the pursuit of speed?

Coach Voss was at the finish line, stopwatch in hand. Michael looked at the athletes he was facing. His trainer had arranged some of the other preeminent sprinters in the city to race. With no trials, the members of the German national team would be chosen from those who met certain times. Anything below 11 seconds would see him through, but his personal best was 11.1 so far. Michael knew several of the other sprinters he'd been racing against on and off for two years. Time was when he would have lost to any of them. Today, he knew he was the favorite. Three were his age or a little older, but the other four were college age or beyond. None of the runners spoke as they completed their warm-ups.

It was time. The starter called out and each man squatted to the starting position. Michael was in the middle. He regulated his breath, feeling the power in his thighs and arms. The track was empty in front of them, Herr Voss a dot at the end of it. The starter called out again, and Michael heard a voice in his ear.

"You shouldn't be here, Yank."

Erich Breitner, a twenty-two-year-old from Wedding, grimaced at him before focusing down the track once more.

Michael smiled to himself. He'd never beaten Breitner before. Today he would show him who belonged.

The starter's gun sounded, and Michael sprang forward like a hare out of a trap, launching himself down the dirt track. His legs and arms started pumping. The sound of his breath whooshing in and out of his nose and mouth was all he could hear. No one was in front of him, but as he glanced to the side, he saw Breitner even with him on the left. Every muscle in his body was in perfect synchronicity. He kept the words Breitner said to him in his mind, using them as fuel to drive himself forward.

He could see the look of studied concentration on Herr Voss's face now, and the silver stopwatch in his hand. Michael looked around at Breitner, now two strides behind him, and felt a smile come to his face as he reached the finish line. He heard the clicking of the stopwatch. Air rushed in and out of his lungs as his legs stopped pumping and slowed down. He bent over as the screams of his muscles subsided.

"Michael!" came Voss's voice.

He jogged over to his trainer. Breitner had already walked off the track. The excitement in his coach's voice was mirrored on his face.

"Look at this," Voss said, holding up the stopwatch. He put it in the young man's hand. "Ten point nine," the coach said. "You did it! This is going to be good enough to qualify for the games next year."

Michael took the watch in his hand, incredulous at first. He looked at his trainer's smiling face and felt him clap him on the shoulder.

"I did it!" Michael said.

"Yes."

Some of the other athletes came over to congratulate him. Breitner did not. Michael felt a swell of pride in his chest and wished both his parents were here to see this. His mother was with him at that moment, and all he wanted was to tell her what he'd done.

He looked up at the stands. His family was jumping up and down, screaming with delight.

"I need to go to them," he said. "I have to tell my father."

"Go ahead," Voss said. "Take some time to celebrate, but the work is only beginning."

"I know."

Voss shook his hand and patted him on the shoulder. The coach reminded him that only complacency could stop him now, and Michael ran to see his family.

"I did it! I ran 10.9. I qualified for the Olympics!"

His father exploded in joy that he'd never seen in him and ran over, throwing his arms around him. Lisa was screaming and his siblings ran to him. Soon they were all hugging him.

"I'm so proud of you!" his father said.

"We knew you'd do it!" Maureen said.

Fiona and Conor were dancing in the evening sun. It was the most perfect moment of his life.

Maureen took him aside to where the crowd around them couldn't hear their conversation. "Congratulations, little brother. You don't have any qualms about running against the Americans next year?"

"We live here, and we've always been as German as American," he answered. "I don't love the Nazis either, but it was my Hitler Youth leaders who introduced me to sprinting. Who knows if I ever would have even taken it up without their guidance?"

"So you'll stand there next year and give the Hitler salute in front of all those people?"

"I'm not thinking about that. I just want to be the best I can be."

"Karen will be proud as well."

He laughed. "I don't know about that. We'll see."

15

Sunday, June 30

Lisa spent an hour in front of the mirror—longer than she had on her wedding day. It seemed like looking her best might offer some protection against what she was about to face.

She thought back to her meeting with the Führer. It was brief, but the impressions she garnered of him were strong, and stayed with her. It was as if an awkward twelve-year-old boy had taken over the body of the most powerful man in Europe. He had seemed ill at ease in their company and made eye contact only two or three times in the entire time. The women around Germany who screamed at him at his rallies, or offered coquettish smiles as he walked by, were as wrong about him as they could be. But then, millions of people were. Lisa wondered what they'd really think of him if they met the insecure man-child she had tea with in the Reich Chancellery.

Once finished with her makeup, Lisa stared at herself for a few seconds in the mirror. Perhaps she could keep her secret from the public forever and learn to live with herself. Wouldn't becoming the biggest movie star in Germany offer some comfort? A tear rolled down her face and she cursed out loud. She'd been considering quitting the movie more and more these last few days, but would doing so put Hannah in more or less danger? What would post-Nazi Germany think of such a film in years to come? But who knew if she'd ever even see such a time?

"What if the Nazis are here for the next thousand years, as they always say?" she said out loud to the woman staring back at her in the mirror. "What if this doesn't end, and you've just wasted the chance you've been waiting for your whole life?"

She wiped the tear from her face and set about reapplying the eyeliner that had left a black streak along her cheek.

"What difference does it make if it's me or Petra or someone else? They're still going to make the movie. The funding's in place now. Nothing's going to stop it."

She reached down and picked up a framed photograph of Hannah and felt warmth fill her heart.

It took three more minutes to refinish her makeup, and she turned off the lights around the mirror and left the bathroom. She locked up the house and went to the car.

Thoughts of who she was, and her Jewish roots, entered her mind as she started the car. Would the Nazis even consider her a Jew? It didn't make any sense. But then she remembered her father's work—eradicating certain traits from the population. It dawned on her that the Nazis would view her as an aberration to be eliminated from the gene pool. It didn't make any difference to them if she knew she was a Jew or not, the same as it didn't make a difference to a shopkeeper if the rats in their basements knew they were vermin or not. Whatever Hitler and his Nazis abhorred so very much was in her. It was in her blood, and Hannah's too. Whatever they were afraid of, or repulsed by, was a part of who she was as a person. *For what are we, if not the sum of those who came before us?*

A smile flickered across her face as she imagined her Jewish ancestors struggling against pogroms and prejudice, but remaining steadfast and, despite it all, staying alive. Was there some way of making a sanitized version of the movie, and getting out of this situation with her and Hannah's secret intact?

Hagen lived alone in a mansion even larger than the one she shared with her family. He was a trust-fund child—the only son of a wealthy industrialist—and had inherited a fortune upon his father's death.

The stones under the wheels hissed as she halted on the gravel driveway outside the house. Hagen was expecting her, but not what she had to say to him. Her hands were shaking as she shut the car door behind her.

Hagen answered the door in a colorful silk dressing gown that flowed in the breeze as he led her inside. She took a seat at a table on his enclosed back porch. The garden beyond was a pristine lawn surrounded by manicured hedges. Hagen sat opposite her as the servant he called brought them tea.

"Did you get a chance to look at the script?" he asked.

"I read it."

"I take it you don't approve of the changes?"

"The Jewish moneylender who rapes Ursula's sister and then joins with the Soviets? It's as ridiculous as it is offensive."

Hagen sat back in his seat and stared out at the garden for a few seconds. The explosion she expected didn't come.

"What did you expect? The Nazis are running the show now. We have to jump through their hoops for the funding."

The thought to reveal herself to him came like a flaming arrow across the bow of her consciousness. She wanted to confide in this man.

"I can't portray the role as they want me to."

"It's acting, Lisa—that's all. You're playing a part."

"My daughter and stepchildren will see me cursing Jews

and leading the villagers in a violent pogrom against them. I can't let the Nazis use me like that."

Hagen was more measured and calmer than she expected. "You know that if you leave this picture, you'll be thrown out of the guild and you'll never work in Germany again."

"Surely we have some recourse to change the script back to what it was?"

"The National Socialists *are* Germany now. We all have to accept that. You think this is the movie I wanted to make? The original script was bad enough, but this?" He reached down and picked a copy of the screenplay off the coffee table and shook it in the air. "But I can't do anything else. If I want to pursue my passion—the one thing I care about in this world—I have to play by their rules."

"Can we change some of the dialogue, perhaps make the Jewish character more real?" she asked. "I don't think I can make the movie as it is."

"We have no choice. All our creative power over the project died when Goebbels walked on set. Don't fight this, Lisa. The Nazis are powerful enemies. You met with Hitler himself about this production. If he hears that you refused to make it—"

"You think he cares about me?"

"I know his lapdog has taken on this film as a pet project."

Hagen threw the script onto the table. It knocked over his tea, and the cup broke on the tiled floor. He didn't move to pick it up.

"I don't want to make this anti-Jewish trash any more than you do, but if you leave, you'll draw the wrong kind of attention to yourself. That can be fatal these days."

"This isn't why I became an actress."

"What do you think you'll change by pulling out of the picture? The only person you'll be hurting is yourself."

"I need to be able to look at myself in the mirror. I'll be able to raise my daughter without fear of her seeing me as a Nazi puppet."

"Make the picture. Bite your lip before every scene, but don't pull out," he said. "As much for your own sake as the movie's. I can't promise we'll be able to make the script any better, but we can make different choices next time. Goebbels doesn't oversee every picture. Far from it. The chance to make something great still exists. This could be a gateway to that."

Lisa got out of her seat. She stared out the window as she spoke, her voice dull and low.

"If *The Dark Moon* is successful, the Reich Minister for Propaganda said that Petra and I could make more movies for the government. They're contemplating a star system like the Hollywood studios use. We could be the new faces of National Socialist propaganda."

Hagen threw up his hands. "You won't have to do that if you don't want to. There'll be 100 excuses you can make—scheduling, family. Other projects." Hagen got up and stood behind her. "You're not the only one who's trapped. The Nazis have us all in the grip of their vise. We need to finish this project the best that we can and move on."

Lisa never knew the director could be so considerate. It was rare that she'd seen him treat anyone with even the most basic modicum of respect before. Perhaps that was his way of asserting his authority on set. He seemed a different man today. She longed for the release that revealing her secret to him would afford her, but wasn't going to repeat the mistake she made with Petra.

"I'll make the movie," she said. "What other choice do I have?"

16

Monday, July 1

Maureen finished her day at university and walked to the corner where she and Thomas met every week before traveling north together to meet with the other members of the Subversives. The weekend she'd just spent at Dr. Walz's house weighed on her mind to the point where she could think of little else. The day's lectures had passed her by as the words of that letter from the Führer ran around in circles inside her mind.

Thomas came with his usual smile, which melted when he saw her.

"Can we talk for a few minutes before we go to the meeting?" she asked.

"Something on your mind? Of course." He took her hand. "Let's go to the café around the corner."

Neither spoke as they walked. Maureen was still deciding what to tell him, and then the group. Was this their business? Should she just trust Lisa's father? He was a decent man and had been so kind to the family. This

Babelsberg Experiment was about procuring a cure for insanity, or alcoholism, for all she knew. She felt ill, and despite the warmth of the early summer evening, a cold chill ran through her.

They took a seat at a table outside. Most of the patrons were students enjoying a drink in the sun after a day of lectures. Loud laughter filled the air around them as a waiter arrived to take their orders. They both asked for beer.

Thomas waited until they were alone to begin. He leaned forward, keeping his voice down so only she could hear. "What's the matter? Is it something I did?"

"No." She almost laughed. "It's nothing to do with you."

He looked relieved but leaned forward and asked again.

"I found something in Dr. Walz's desk at the weekend."

She told the story of how she snuck into his office and recounted the wording of the letter. It took him a few seconds to digest what she said before he spoke.

"July 26?"

"Yes."

"That's all the letter said?"

"I went back to check the wording again, but it was gone. Then he fired me."

"He fired you? What?"

The beers arrived, and both were silent until the waiter left again.

"Wait a minute, now. Did he see you with the letter?"

"No. I put it away just before he came in, but it seems like a bit of a coincidence that he let me go the day after."

"Did he say anything in the past about winding up your position?"

"In passing. He said I'd need more time going forward for my studies."

"I think it's safe to assume he wants a little space from you, but you said he wasn't angry?"

"No. It was a little awkward, but he said he didn't want it to come between us."

Thomas rubbed a bead of condensation off the glass. She knew that sparkle forming in his eyes. "I don't think he knows. He was just playing it safe."

"Ok, but what does that mean?" she answered.

"He doesn't know what you know."

She put her hand on her beer and forced herself to take a gulp in the hope that it'd make her feel better—it did. It doused the fire inside her, if only for a few seconds.

"You heard him talking to Hitler about it on the telephone, and then saw a letter confirming the experiment would take place in Babelsberg in July?" Thomas asked. "I think that's enough to go to Clayton."

"I don't know." The thought of spying on Dr. Walz didn't sit well with her. She already felt like a traitor.

"Let's put it to the others tonight, shall we?"

"They're going to tell me to double down and go back to his office…"

"No, they're not. Who do you think they are? No one wants to put you in any danger. They're a valuable resource is all—people we know we can trust. They'll steer us right."

"Us?"

"Of course," he said with a smile. "You didn't think you were going to have to do this alone, did you?"

"Come here," she said with a wave of her hand. "I want to tell you something." He leaned across the table, and she took his face with her hand and kissed him. The worries consuming her melted away for a few seconds. "I'm so glad to have you," she said and sat back down. This wasn't like when she left Leo. That was youthful infatuation. This was real—the man she would one day marry.

"I have something else I wanted to talk to you about before we go to the meeting." He took a sip of beer and sat back, listening. "My father is thinking about taking the family back to America."

His face went white at her words, and he put the beer down. Suddenly his eyes were on the floor. She reached across the table and took his hand.

"If he did, would you go too?" he asked. The tone of his voice was unlike anything she'd heard from him before. He sounded like a little boy lost.

"No one's made any decisions yet, but I'm an adult now. I'll make my own decisions about my life."

She didn't know what she wanted until that moment, but she could see now. The haze cleared. Her future was sitting across the table.

"I'm not leaving you, no matter what."

Thomas's massive smile was contagious, and they reached across the table to kiss again. A wild thought that he might propose there and then came into her mind as they sat back down, but she let it go.

"You'll stay by yourself?"

"I don't see Michael leaving either. He's far too involved with his training. A move back to New Jersey would scupper everything he's been working toward for the last two years. I'd have him if I stayed."

"And me too."

"I don't know what's going to happen. I don't think Lisa wants to go. She has her career, but my father is worried about the way things are going here, with the Jews, among other things." Her voice was so low he had to lean forward again to hear her.

"I wouldn't blame him for that. It seems to get worse for them month by month. I sometimes wonder where it's all going to end."

She wanted to talk about a future where they were together. The vision of a house and children of their own appeared in her mind. The scourge of Hitler and the Nazis would pass and this country would be free again. But she couldn't say that out loud, even under her breath.

They finished their beers. Renewed, she took his hand and led him toward the U-Bahn and the meeting on Sprengelstrasse.

Herman answered the door and hugged them both. The other members of their select club arrived one by one, and half an hour later, they were all sitting at the table. Maureen took her place in between Thomas and his father, waiting to speak as thoughts that could change the direction of her life swirled around inside her head.

This was the time to bring up what she found out, but she couldn't find the words. Thomas put his hand on hers.

"I found something else out. I saw a letter referring to the conversation I overheard in the doctor's office, signed by Hitler himself." The mere mention of that name changed the atmosphere in the room. A couple of silent seconds passed before Herr Schultz spoke.

"What did it say?"

It didn't take long to detail the exact wording of the letter. They asked the same questions Thomas did in the café, but she couldn't answer most of them.

"I wonder what this experiment could be?" Herman asked. "But this seems like the solid evidence we were speaking about last week. This could be the key to getting your American journalist friend involved, and breaking the story."

"What are you suggesting?" Herr Reus asked. "If this doctor is working for the government, he has the protection of the SS and the Gestapo. I don't think we should advise Maureen to do anything to put herself in danger."

"Of course not," Leon said. "Who knows what security they might have..."

"I know Babelsberg," Gilda said. "My cousin is in the

hospital there. As far as I know, they have some research facilities there, and a lot of mental patients, of course."

"They must mean to sterilize them en masse, perhaps with some new technique," Herr Schultz said.

"Who knows what they're doing? What were you planning on doing with this information, Maureen?"

"I don't know yet, Herman. It's unlikely I'll find anything more from here, though. The doctor had removed the letter when I tried to check it again. And now that I won't be working at the clinic..."

"He's wise to your curiosity, but nothing more," Thomas said. "If he thought you'd discovered a government secret, the Gestapo would have already come knocking."

Just hearing those words sent an icicle of fear sliding down Maureen's spine.

"Tread carefully," Herr Reus said. "You're young, and I know you want to solve the world's problems, but we learned how ruthless the Nazis are last summer on the Night of the Long Knives."

"As if we didn't know already," Herr Schultz said. "If you do want to find out what's going on, we're here to help." The other people around the table nodded in agreement. "Just don't do anything rash. Whatever you do, run it past us first."

"Go and see your journalist friend. See what he needs—it'll be a lot more than the mere sight of a letter signed by Hitler. If you want to break the story, you might need to take a trip to Babelsberg in July, but we can help you with that," Herman said.

"No, it's too dangerous," Herr Schultz said.

"I'm not suggesting she does anything remotely unsafe, but perhaps Gilda could visit her cousin and Maureen could stay out of sight and monitor the doctor's movements from afar," Herman answered. "This could be important. International pressure is key to bringing the Nazis down. What if this were the first domino to fall?"

Maureen knew she should have been afraid, but that wasn't what she felt at all. "I'll talk to my father's friend," she said. "But I do think we should see what it is about. Too many people have suffered already. Perhaps this is an opportunity to stop this insanity before it goes too far."

The Subversives applauded her. "You're right," Gilda said. "It's about time we did something. This is our chance to make a difference instead of just talking about it."

~

Thursday, July 4

Thomas was waiting with Gilda Stein as Maureen arrived. Gilda was wearing a blue sundress that matched her eyes, and her blond hair was tied up. Thomas had on khaki summer pants and a white polo shirt Maureen had picked out for him. It was a hot, humid day, and both were standing in the shade the trees afforded. They greeted her with embraces and kisses on the cheek. The Tiergarten was busy, but the sheer size of the place assured Maureen that they'd find the solitude they required.

Clayton arrived a few minutes later. Maureen kissed him on the cheek and introduced him to the others.

"Thomas," he said as he shook Maureen's boyfriend's hand. "Have I ever heard a lot about you!"

"I hope I don't disappoint you," he said as he shook the American journalist's hand.

"This is Gilda," Maureen said. "She's a friend—someone we can trust."

"It's a pleasure," Clayton said, hat in hand.

"Thank you for coming to see us today," Gilda said.

"Anything for Maureen."

"Shall we?" Thomas asked and gestured toward the path in front of them. The four strolled together, making small talk about the park and how long Clayton had been in the city. It took a few minutes to get away from the crowds of people eating lunch or trying to escape the summer heat. They found a bench where no one else was around. Maureen and Gilda took a seat while the men stayed standing.

"So, why did you really ask me here?" Clayton asked. His words were hushed. "Don't get me wrong, I enjoy a little jaunt in the park, but I'm sure you have another reason in mind for meeting today."

"Perceptive, as always," Maureen said.

"That's why I earn the big Reichsmarks."

"We might have a story for you," Gilda said.

Clayton reached into his pocket for a notebook and pencil.

"Off the record for now," Thomas said.

The journalist put them back. "You have my attention."

"I overheard Lisa's father on the phone with the Führer."

"As in the overlord of the Reich?" Clayton asked. Maureen nodded. "What did you hear? What did Hitler say to him?"

"I could only hear Dr. Walz, but he said something about an experiment down in Babelsberg—something top secret."

"Isn't Lisa working down in the studios there? Is it something to do with that?"

"We think it's more likely connected to the mental institution there," Gilda responded. "My cousin is a patient. I know the place well."

"Did he mention what the experiment was about?"

"No, but he did say that any waste would be disposed of onsite," Maureen responded.

"That could mean anything," the journalist said. "Do you have anything else? This isn't going to be enough. Not nearly."

"I also found a letter signed by Hitler in his study."

"You've been snooping around? Oh, Maureen, I hope you were careful. What did it say?"

"It was only a few lines, but that the experiment would be in Babelsberg on July 26."

"In three weeks," Clayton said. "Do you have this letter?"

"No. I put it back, but when I returned to look at it again it was gone."

"So he caught you?"

"No," she responded. "He didn't mention anything about it."

"What exactly are you trying to expose here? The sterilization program? That's old news, I'm afraid. I'm sorry to be the one to burst your bubble."

"We think the doctor's experiment might be taking his eugenics research in a new direction," Thomas said.

Clayton pushed out a breath. "Enderis would eat this up and spit it back in my face."

"Who?" Thomas asked.

"My boss. Let's just say he's eager not to insult our gracious Nazi hosts. If I'm going to have any chance of printing this, the evidence has got to be ironclad. We're going to need documents, witness statements, photographs. And even then, Enderis will probably sit on it."

They quieted down for a few seconds as a young couple ambled past. Clayton waited until they were long gone to begin again.

"I can't believe you were snooping around. Your father will flay me alive if anything happens to you. The Nazis don't mess around either. People they view as a threat go missing every day."

"If your boss won't print this, is there anyone else you could send us to?" Gilda asked.

"Let's just worry about getting the story first. At the moment, all we have is a letter that disappeared and an overheard phone call, albeit to the Führer himself. It's a start, but we'll need a lot more."

"You think we might be on to something?" Thomas asked.

"If there's something here—and I sense there is—we could be in business."

"I was hoping you'd say that," Maureen said. "If we're to go to Babelsberg, we're going to need your help."

"You're planning on going down there?"

"What other way do you suggest?" Gilda asked.

"I'm guessing—and hoping—that you have a plan in place already."

"I go down to visit my cousin at least every month or two. I'll arrange a trip down there and hang around."

"Maureen and I are going to accompany her down to the hospital, but stay back. We won't be able to get too close. We'll watch from the woods behind."

"Seems smart not to take too many chances, but what are you going to see from there? He'll be inside, in the laboratory."

"We'll take note of everyone coming in and out of the building, and perhaps even snap some photographs. You could accompany Gilda and see what you can find out from the staff, or even the patients. The letter said 'test subjects will be provided on-site.' That can only mean the patients themselves," Maureen said.

"They're going to sterilize them all at once," Clayton said. "But how?"

"That's what we mean to find out," Maureen said.

"Are you sure you want to do this? He's your step-grandfather."

"I know who he is, and what I have to do."

"Does your father know anything about this?" Clayton asked.

"No."

"Good. Keep it that way." Clayton took off his hat and

rubbed the sweat from his brow with his forearm. "So, it looks like we'll be taking a little day trip to Babelsberg."

"I know what you're going to say," Maureen said.

"What's that?"

"Don't tell anyone, and be careful."

"I must be getting predictable in my old age."

The trees above them rustled in the summer breeze. Clayton took off his hat and used it to fan himself. "You're not going to do anything dangerous, are you?" he said to Maureen.

"Would I?"

"I was afraid you'd say that."

17

Thursday, July 11

Lisa wasn't sleeping much, and showed up to the studios every day with black bags under her eyes. Afraid of what Hagen might say, she took to avoiding him in the mornings before the people in makeup worked their magic on her tired face. The joy she once derived from making movies had all but drained away—it was more like working on a chain gang than creating the art her soul craved. What was artistic or beautiful about a picture that ended in a pogrom?

Lisa dreaded shooting the upcoming scenes where she rallied the villagers to their final destiny—rising up to defeat the evil forces of the Bolshevist-Jewish conspiracy. Sometimes she wondered if the script was so outlandish that no one could take it seriously. She tried to comfort herself with that thought in her dark moments—of which there were many.

Seamus had noticed her frame of mind when she was at home in the few hours away from the studio. Who wouldn't? Misery had become her default mood. Even the company of her family offered scant comfort. Her husband had marked the scheduled last day of shooting on the kitchen calendar and was marking off each day as it passed. August second couldn't come quickly enough.

Lisa sat in her changing room in the studio, waiting for the call. They were shooting the scene where Petra's character told her she had been raped by the Jewish moneylender today. It was one of the many scenes she had dreaded since she first read the script.

A tap on the door roused her from her thoughts. Lang pushed the door open.

"Do you have time for a word?" he asked.

"Yes. Come in."

"Are you ready for the scene today?"

"Of course."

"We've noticed your enthusiasm for the role waning these last few days. Your attitude hasn't shown in your work yet, but I'm worried. If you don't want to be here—"

"I'm fine," she said. Lisa wanted to grab him by the lapels and tell him that this was the last place on earth she wanted to be right now, but she looked down at a framed photo of Hannah on her dresser. She picked it up and put it back down.

"I'm here to do the job, and I'll finish it."

Lang looked unconvinced, but nodded his head. "They're ready for you now."

Petra was already on the set, pacing up and down, going over her lines. She was dressed in torn rags, but her beauty still shone through. Lisa hadn't seen or talked to her in days. Clayton hadn't heard from her in longer.

Everyone got into position. The visit to Hagen's house must have had some effect, as he'd been a gentler version of himself ever since...at least to her.

"Ok," he said. "Petra's coming in after Ezekiel raped her. Lisa, you're the only person in the world she can speak to, the only one who understands the agony she's going through."

Lisa didn't have to dig deep to channel the misery required to act out the scene.

Petra didn't greet her as she walked onto the set, but she took that as the young actress getting into character. Lisa sat in the wooden chair and waited for the knock on the door that would signify the beginning of the scene.

Hagen called action and Lisa became Ursula, soon-to-be leader of the local resistance. Lisa cast aside all thoughts apart from those Ursula would have in that moment. Petra opened the door and stumbled into the room, tears running down her face. Lisa took her in her arms.

The studio door opened and Hagen exploded. "Who is coming onto my set in the middle of shooting?" he roared. He quieted down as he saw two men in suits holding up badges. Both gave the Hitler salute, which the director and most of the crew reciprocated.

"What's this about?" demanded Hagen.

"I'm Kriminalinspektor Diels of the Gestapo. This is my colleague, Kriminalinspektor Jodl. We'd like Frau Ritter to come along with us for questioning."

Lisa's heart exploded. She couldn't move.

"On what charge?" Hagen asked.

"A complaint has been made against your leading actress. We're here to take her in for questioning."

"Someone denounced her?" Hagen asked. "What was the accusation?"

"We're not going to talk about that here," Jodl said. He was in his midforties, with a brown beard. His colleague was much younger and six inches taller than he was. Diels was blond with a chiseled chin and dark blue eyes. In another light, he might have even been considered handsome.

"Frau Ritter can come with us of her own accord, or we can arrest her. The choice is hers," Diels said.

"What are you going to do with her?" Hagen asked. "I need her here, on set!"

"It's just routine questioning," Jodl said. "Nothing to be concerned about."

"Where is she?" Diels asked.

One of the cameramen held up a shaking finger and pointed at her.

Terror gripped Lisa to the point where speaking was difficult, but she knew she had no choice. She had to go with these men.

Jodl approached her. "Come with us, Frau Ritter."

She shook her head. "There must be some mistake. I haven't done anything."

"There's no mistake," the man answered. "Come with us."

Lisa's legs seemed like they were made of lead. She looked over at Petra. She seemed as shocked as everyone else, but didn't speak.

"Did you—?" Lisa asked as Diels hauled her to her feet.

Petra shook her head and backed away.

Lisa held the tears back. She didn't want Petra to see her cry.

"Where are you taking her?" Hagen asked.

The two Gestapo men were calm, almost bored. "It's just routine. We'll have her back home later tonight."

"I'll call your husband, Lisa," Hagen said.

Lang was standing in the background, shaking his head, powerless. The Gestapo answered to no one.

"Thank you," Lisa said and shrugged off the Gestapo man's grip. Petra was nowhere to be seen.

Lisa walked out to the parking lot with the two men. Evening was falling, but the air was still sticky and warm.

What will this mean for Hannah? Lisa thought as Diels sat her in the back seat of the car.

The two men made small talk as they drove into the city. Lisa sat terrified and alone on the back seat.

They parked outside Gestapo headquarters on Prinz-Albrecht-Strasse—an address known to all Berliners now.

"Let's go," Jodl said in an unruffled voice.

The two men led her inside and sat her on a bench beside a man in his fifties. Neither dared say a word as the Gestapo men processed them. The clock on the wall said it was just after five. Finally, at almost seven o'clock, Jodl came back, took her by the arm, and led her through a door and down a long hallway to an interrogation room. He offered her a seat in front of a desk in the otherwise bare room. Diels joined them a few seconds later with some papers in his hand.

"Do you know why you're here?" Jodl asked. Both sat down opposite her. The other man was still shuffling through the papers in his hand.

"I have no idea."

The pressure inside her was building to breaking point already.

"We received notice that you are attempting to conceal the fact that you were born a Jew."

Lisa stared on, unable to speak.

"Do you deny this?" Jodl asked.

She knew she had only seconds to answer, but what was the point in lying now? They would find out the same way her father did. They probably knew already.

"I was born and raised Lutheran."

"Do you deny that your mother was a Jew?" Diels asked and put the papers down.

Lisa decided it was best not to lie to people who saw through lies for a living. "No, I don't. She hid my ancestry from me my entire life. I only found out when she died in '33."

"So, you admit you're a Jew?" Diels asked and leaned forward.

"In the strictest definition of the word, yes."

"Why didn't you register as such when you found out?"

"I didn't know I had to do such a thing, or that it mattered at all."

Diels shook his head. "We're seeing this more and more as we investigate people's backgrounds, but you should have told us, and not tried to hide it. According to our records, you met with the Führer himself to discuss the film you were working on."

"That's true."

"How would the Führer react to knowing he was in the presence of a Jew?" Jodl roared and thumped the table with his fist. The Gestapo man's anger flared up like a kick from a horse's hind leg.

Lisa jumped, and an errant tear ran down her cheek. She wiped it away as quickly as it came.

"It wasn't my intention to insult the Führer. I was fulfilling his wish to see me and another actress. Herr Goebbels invited us. I couldn't say no."

Jodl laughed. "She couldn't say no! Do you know what an honor it is to meet the Führer?"

"I realize how fortunate I am to have met him. It was the greatest privilege of my life."

"You have a daughter," Diels said. "But on her birth certificate, no father is listed. Was he a Jew?"

An image of Ernst Milch appeared in her mind. "No. I was a dancer in a nightclub. The father was a charlatan who ran as soon as I told him I was pregnant. I didn't want my daughter to even know who he was."

"How convenient," Jodl said. "She will be placed on the register as a Jew, just as you will be."

"But her father was a German—a military man. My own father was the same. She's only part Jewish."

"Your birth certificate is missing. Who was your father?" Diels asked.

She remembered what her father told her about not revealing him, but what if the Gestapo caught her lying?

"My mother never told me. She tried to hide our heritage after she converted. She was a loyal German, as I am."

"You have no idea who your father was?" Diels asked.

"I'm still trying to figure that out myself."

"We'll follow that up to see if what you say is true," Jodl said, jotting down something on a pad.

"My daughter isn't a Jew. She's only one quarter Jewish. I'm only half."

"Those matters are up to the government to decide. Guidance on such is coming soon, I believe," Jodl said.

The two men got up and left without another word.

Ten minutes later, Diels appeared once more. "You're free to leave, Frau Ritter. I'll escort you out."

The words came like icy water on a raging fire. Her legs were weak as she stood up, and she stumbled a little on the way to the door. Diels brought her out to the street.

"Realize, Frau Ritter, that the government considers you a Jew now, and you will be subject to any regulations that affect them."

Lisa nodded, and he went back inside. A sudden urge to get as far away from this place as possible caused her to start running. A great mourning settled over her consciousness like a fog. She went several blocks before breaking down in tears, her head in her hands as she collapsed to her knees on the side of the street.

18

Wednesday, July 17

Seamus went upstairs to his wife, who was lying on the bed in her dressing gown, staring at the ceiling. He sat beside her and took her hand.

"How are you?"

"About as well as someone whose dreams have been flushed down the toilet could be, I suppose. Filming for *The Dark Moon* begins again today, with new starlet, Petra Wagner, in the leading role. At least we know who denounced me."

"I can't believe she'd do that."

"The Nazis know the secret my mother tried to hide all those years, and Hannah is registered as a Jew."

Seamus searched for the words that could offer her some semblance of comfort.

"We'll look after Hannah, and I'd rather be with you than Petra. Your integrity is still intact. I couldn't be prouder of you."

She didn't turn her head to face him. He took both her hands in his, but it didn't seem to make any difference.

"Being me doesn't feel great."

"You must be glad not to have to play that role. Imagine what people will think once the Nazis are gone?" He was floundering.

"You think the Nazis are going to vacate their position of ultimate power anytime soon?"

"Perhaps if the French and the British apply the right pressure," he said, not really believing his own words. "The Americans could oust them."

"The British and the French are terrified of another war, like the last one, and the Americans? Are you serious? They want nothing to do with the situation here. Hitler has his own fan club there—at least according to the German newspapers that fawn over him."

"Whether or not it's the Nazis in power, could you have lived with yourself if you played that role?"

"No." She shook her head. The word came as a whisper.

He gulped back his feelings about his own guilt and continued.

"I know you, my darling. You're too good to play that trash. Let Petra sell her soul if she values it that little."

"My dreams are dead."

"Better now than later. Imagine if Goebbels and his cronies found out after the movie came out."

Tears welled in her eyes. Seamus embraced her, but she seemed numb.

"I thought this was it," she said. "After all these years of struggling, this was my break. But it's not. It's the end."

"I'm so sorry. I'm proud of what you achieved."

"What? Nothing? I'm a nobody. I've exposed my daughter's background to those wolves."

She stood up and Seamus followed her. She went to the mirror in the bathroom, staring into her own eyes.

"You haven't done *nothing*, and you're not a nobody. You're the most important person in the world to me and your daughter and the other kids, and you're the best example they could ever have."

"So, you agree with them?"

He leaned against the doorway. "Who?"

"The Nazis. They've achieved their goal again—another woman forced to abandon her career: *kinder, küche, kirche*."

"Children, kitchen, church," murmured her husband.

"That's all we're good for, after all—churning out babies to feed their war machine."

"Maybe you can start over if we move to America. You could try the stage in New York, or even Hollywood."

"And who would I play? The German housemaid? I don't speak the language."

"Marlene Dietrich made the move—why couldn't you?"

"She was the biggest star in Germany before she got a contract with Paramount. I'm a nobody who just passed up the biggest break of my career."

"I believe in you."

"I'm thirty-two, Seamus. I'm past it in this game. It's too late to start over anywhere."

"Not for someone with your talent and drive. That anti-Semitic nonsense would have tainted your soul forever. This society isn't set up for women to succeed—you and Maureen say it all the time. You've done more than most women can in a lifetime of toil."

Lisa seemed to ponder what he said for a few seconds before asking a question herself.

"Have you decided? Are you going to supply the army with bullets?" She washed her hands and soaped up her face.

"Do I have a choice?"

The lather on her face was thick as she looked at him in the mirror. "People are still going to need knives and forks."

"Yes, but we've lost a lot of contracts. With the fire, this is the only way I can see for the factory to survive."

Lisa washed the soap off her face and went to him. She put her arms around his neck. "Do what you think is right."

She kissed him and went back to the sink.

"History won't judge those who pandered to the Nazis kindly," he said.

"What use is history to us? We're just trying to survive."

He was downstairs ten minutes later when the sound of the phone ringing cut through the silence of the house. Seamus picked up the receiver and held it to his ear.

"Herr Ritter," came the familiar voice down the line. Seamus cringed. "Otto Milch here. I hear you have some decisions to make about the future of your business."

A flash of Milch's son's bloodied face appeared in Seamus's mind before he answered.

"Who told you?"

"People talk. Everyone likes to gossip. What does that matter, anyway?"

It matters a great deal, Seamus thought. He knew there was little point in pushing the old man as to whether he was working with Helga or someone else on the inside. He'd never tell.

"What does matter is what I can offer you," Milch continued. "I know your business has taken a hit after the unfortunate fire at your premises."

"You wouldn't happen to know anything about how that started, would you?"

"What are you implying, Herr Ritter?"

Seamus knew he'd said too much already and held his tongue. "What's your offer?"

"I'll buy the business—at a discount, of course. Ritter Industries isn't the attractive proposition it once was. I offered you 400,000 back in '33. I'll give you 350,000 now."

It all fit too well. Leder, the private detective, was still looking for Sebastian Gosens, but when he found him, would

Otto Milch's name be on the fugitive's lips? Perhaps Milch had silenced him already.

"Thank you for the generous offer, Herr Milch, but I'm afraid I must decline. I've explained before that in the event of a sale, all proceeds go to my cousin."

"She'll give you half. You know that."

Lisa appeared behind him and gestured to ask if it was ok to stand and listen. He replied it was as Milch began to speak again.

"Don't be too hasty," the older man said. "You could put this nasty episode in Germany behind you. It's common knowledge you're no fan of the National Socialists. Imagine never having to deal with them again."

"Thank you for the call. I must go. I'll speak with my business partner in due course, if you haven't already."

"No. I came to you first," he said. "I wouldn't deal with a woman in business matters."

Seamus hung up the phone and explained to Lisa what had happened.

"You think he set the fire?" she asked.

"I wouldn't put it past him." He put his arms around his wife. "You want a drink?"

"I could use one."

He went to the cabinet and poured two tumblers of whiskey. They went to the patio behind the house together, sat down, and let the liquor do its work.

19

Friday, July 26

The day came. Clayton picked them up in town, cautious to the end, and they drove to Babelsberg—and whatever waited there—together. Insects collided with the windshield, sticking to the glass. Gilda was in the front seat, and despite the relative coolness of the weather, had her window cracked open. Maureen sat in the back seat with Thomas. They hadn't seen much of Lisa's father these past few weeks. He was too busy to join them in his house at Wannsee, and they'd spent the last two weekends there alone. It wasn't easy to hear Lisa mention him in casual conversation when Maureen knew this day was coming.

Twenty-five minutes later, Gilda directed Clayton off the highway toward the hospital. When she told him they were a minute away, the journalist pulled off to the side of the road and stopped to go over the plan. He turned around to face Maureen and her boyfriend.

"You know what you need to do? Is the camera working?"

"Yes," Thomas said. He held it up.

"Remember: if we have to hightail it out of there, or get separated, we'll meet you in Café Bolero on Steinstrasse. It's only a few minutes away, in town."

"Got it," Maureen said. "And don't try and do anything stupid."

"You're saying that to me?" Clayton asked. "I know better than to mess with the Nazis. You should too. If there's the slightest sign of trouble, you run for the hills, got it?"

"Of course," Maureen said.

"Thomas, tell me you're not going to take any chances," Clayton said.

"You have my word."

Gilda looked at her watch. "It's nine thirty now. How long do we stay around if we don't see anything?"

"We'll give it until three o'clock at least," Maureen said.

"That's going to be a long wait on the perimeter for us," Thomas said.

"You'll be with me," Maureen said. "Every moment will be one to cherish."

"Just keep your heads down." Clayton started the engine. The concrete walls that marked the institution's perimeter came into view a few seconds later. Clayton stopped just outside the grounds and the two college students jumped out. The car sped down the road and slowed to pass through the gates of the institution. The hospital was set in an idyllic vale, with a rich green lawn, with forest and hills in the background. It was like a painting above a fireplace in a stately home.

"Uh-oh," Thomas said as they walked past the entrance on the other side of the road.

Clayton's car was stopped, and an SS man was leaning in the open window.

"Looks like they have some security in place already," Maureen said.

"Are you sure we should do this?"

"I didn't come all this way to turn around at the first sign of trouble."

Maureen took her boyfriend's hand and led him along the outside wall of the hospital grounds, which was about eight feet tall.

"Built to keep the inmates caged in," Thomas said.

They kept on until the wall ended, cut off by a hill covered in trees.

"I hope you have good climbing shoes on," she said and grabbed a small tree for balance.

Thomas followed her through the undergrowth. Neither grumbled as sharp branches scraped at their exposed skin like tiny daggers. Maureen had several scratches as they crested the hill, which looked down on the hospital. The trees descended toward the grounds, and they followed them until a razor-wire fence ended their progress.

They were about a hundred yards back from the hospital, looking down from a height of about twenty yards. They fell first to their haunches, and then crawled along the dry ground to the fence.

"A good view from here," she whispered.

"Of the back of the hospital."

She reached into her bag. "That's why I brought these." Maureen brandished a pair of binoculars.

"This can't be your first time doing this."

Maureen smiled and brought the binoculars to her eyes. "I can see Clayton's car parked in the lot. They must be inside. Get the camera ready."

Maureen felt cold, and her hands were shaking as she held the binoculars now. The SS man who'd stopped them was standing with one of his colleagues. They seemed to be chatting. Two other SS men were in the empty lot below them. All were armed with rifles. She remembered what Clayton said about leaving at the first sign of danger, but she repressed the fear inside her—tried to control it.

"More security," she said.

"Can I see?"

She handed Thomas the binoculars. Why would a simple experiment require SS men prowling the exterior of the building? She shifted her body to peer around at the parking lot where Clayton's Ford sat.

"You think they can see us up here?" he asked.

"Not if we stay low down to the ground. Why are they stopping cars driving up to the hospital?"

"I don't know, and we might not find out up here," Thomas said. "But by my count, twelve SS men are patrolling the perimeter of the building. I'm starting to think this is too risky. What do we say if they catch us up here? Those fanatics don't mess around."

He handed her back the binoculars. "You might be right," she said.

Was this worth it when all they were going to see was the outside of the building? Maureen was just about to ask Thomas if he wanted to leave when she noticed something at the front door and brought the binoculars up to her eyes once more.

Two SS men were escorting their friends out the door.

"They're kicking Gilda and Clayton out of the hospital."

She saw Clayton turn around and try talking to them, but one took his rifle off his shoulder and used the flat end to force the American down the steps. He stumbled a little, dusted himself off, and returned to the car with Gilda. More people emerged from the hospital dressed in civilian clothes, but then doctors and nurses too.

"They're evacuating the staff." Maureen handed the binoculars to her boyfriend.

"You think Gilda and Clayton gave the game away somehow?" Thomas asked. "I'm getting nervous."

Their companions got into Clayton's car and drove up the driveway toward the road into town.

"They couldn't have been in there more than twenty minutes," Maureen said. "Why are they clearing the entire facility?"

Several more visitors were herded into their cars to leave, while a small group of doctors and nurses were still on the steps, arguing. An SS officer emerged through the doors and said something that sent them to a waiting truck. A soldier herded them in and then got in the cabin and started the engine. A minute later, they were all gone. The only people visible outside the hospital were those in SS uniforms.

Maureen took the binoculars back and peered down, trying to make out anything through the barred windows of the hospital. It was impossible. She shifted to the soldiers themselves. They looked like they were on holiday, laughing and joking with each other, smoking cigarettes. It was quiet enough that she could hear what the men were saying to each other.

"I don't like this," Thomas whispered. "We should go."

Maureen was just about to respond when an ambulance drove down the driveway, followed by two unmarked white vans. The ambulance drove around the hospital to the now-empty parking lot to its rear. The white vans followed and parked beside each other, a few steps behind the other vehicle. The doors opened, and Maureen's blood ran cold as Dr. Walz stepped out of the ambulance. An SS man in uniform got out with him, and two other SS from the vans. The officer who'd thrown out the staff came around to shake their hands.

"It's him—the doctor." Maureen swept a fly from her face and handed the binoculars back to her boyfriend.

The main gate was closed now, guarded by another SS soldier with his rifle drawn. Walz and the soldiers were obviously determined that what they were about to do remained secret.

"We should get to the café in town," Thomas murmured. "The others will be wondering what happened to us."

"You go."

Dr. Walz walked around to the back of the ambulance and opened the doors. It was hard to see from their vantage point, but it seemed the vehicle was empty and dark inside.

"Get the camera out," she whispered.

"It's all ready," the doctor said in the quiet.

"But will it work?" the SS officer asked.

"It'll work," Dr. Walz replied.

"What's going on?" Thomas's voice was so low that she had to strain to hear. "Is it some kind of mobile sterilization unit?"

"I don't know. Maybe."

Thomas snapped a couple of photographs.

Neither dared move. They waited in breathless silence for two minutes until the back door opened. Two SS men emerged and set up a bench at the wall of the hospital. A few seconds later, more SS came out, but this time, bringing patients with them. The twelve of them, ranging in age from about fifteen to well over sixty, were dressed in white pajamas. The older ones were hunched over. The SS men helped them along. One young man wandered off, and Dr. Walz jogged after him to shepherd him back to the bench with a kind touch.

"Some of those men look too old to have children." Thomas took several photos of them.

All thoughts of leaving before the sick ballet being played out in front of them ended were dispelled. It was hard to believe that the man who bought a house at the lake just to share it with her family was below them, herding mental patients onto benches in a parking lot.

Once the patients were all sitting down, Dr. Walz stood back and began to speak.

"This is going to be a day to remember. We're taking a trip together. Does anyone want to do that?"

Several of the patients nodded and smiled. One stood up to cheer. An SS man sat him down with a smile.

"You're excited," Dr. Walz continued. "How wonderful! Let's get into the ambulance and off we go. We're going to travel in it to make sure no one gets sick."

He motioned to the SS men, who helped, herded, or carried the twelve back to the doors of the ambulance. One by one, the patients got inside and sat on the benches on either side of the interior. Once the last man was in, an SS soldier closed the doors and bolted them over.

"What are they going to..." Thomas's words trailed off.

Two SS men got into the other vans. A few of the others opened up the back and took out long hosepipes. They fit them to the exhaust pipes of each truck and carried them over to the ambulance.

"No," Maureen hissed. "They can't mean to do this."

Her whole body constricted, and she felt the air being compressed out of her lungs as if she was being squeezed by some coiled, muscular serpent.

"Take more photos."

The SS fit the hosepipes to what looked like specially made vents in the back door, and then the other men started the vans' engines. Banging on the inside of the ambulance began a few seconds later. Dr. Walz stood with a stopwatch in his hand, like Michael's trainer at the beginning of a race. The other SS stood around. One of them lit up a cigarette.

"How long is this going to take?" the SS officer asked.

"That's what we're here to measure," the doctor replied.

Maureen wept in silence. Thomas's skin was cold, and gray as the clouds above their heads. The SS men in the vans revved the engines again, drowning out the conversation between Dr. Walz and the SS officer. All they could hear now was the banging coming from inside the vans. This wasn't about sterilization.

It took fifteen minutes or so for the thumping and screaming from inside the trucks to fade out.

Maureen wept as Dr. Walz walked up to the doors of the ambulance. Thomas had the camera ready and she heard the shutter snapping as he took more photographs.

Walz hesitated a few seconds to say something, and then opened the ambulance. Several corpses tumbled out like rag dolls and he had to skip back to save them falling on his feet. The bodies were heaped on top of one another at the door, their limbs intertwined as if they were engaged in some ghastly wrestling match.

"Take a photograph," Maureen whispered.

Thomas was white, his body frozen. She repeated the order and heard the shutter snapping inside the camera.

Walz stood back as the SS picked up the bodies and loaded them back into the ambulance. Certain things could never be unseen. Maureen knew she was changed now, but also knew if the SS caught them, they'd be the next to die.

"We've got to get out of here," she whispered.

"Ok. If they catch us with this camera—"

"You don't think I know that?" she snapped.

Maureen replaced the binoculars in the case with ice-cold, shaking hands. Thomas slipped the camera in after. They rose to their haunches and inched back through the trees. The ghosts of the people Walz and his SS cohorts murdered seemed to swirl around her as they went. They moved in careful silence. It took almost twenty minutes to get back to the road. Earlier it had taken them less than five.

Maureen had a horrible feeling that the SS had posted a guard at the end of the wall where they entered, but no one was there when they came down through the trees.

Neither of them spoke as they reached the road. It was only a few minutes' walk into the city of Potsdam, through the affluent neighborhood of Babelsberg, home of the German film industry. Maureen bent over on the road to vomit. Thomas held her hair, rubbing her back.

Cars passed them as the country subsided to suburban Potsdam. It was only when she felt the safety of houses, shops, and other people that Maureen dared speak.

"I can't believe what we just saw."

They walked on another block in silence until they saw the sign for Steinstrasse, and then Café Bolero.

Clayton and Gilda were at a table together, drinking coffee. They both stood up as Maureen and Thomas came in.

"Are you all right?" Clayton asked under his breath. "You're bleeding."

She looked at her arm, which was streaked with a line of crimson. Gilda took a handkerchief from the table and wiped it off before holding it on the site of the wound.

"What happened to you? We were only in there a few minutes before the SS threw us out. We saw nothing," the journalist said.

"Not even my cousin," Gilda added.

Clayton started to sit back down, but Maureen shook her head.

"Not here. We can't talk here. Let's go to the car."

Clayton threw a few coins down on the table and all four left. The sun was glinting gold from behind the clouds. It seemed inappropriate in every way. The car was just down the street, and Thomas opened the door for Maureen as Gilda and Clayton got in the front.

She waited until the doors were all closed. "They killed twelve patients."

"Who did?"

"Dr. Walz and the SS men. They drove in a specially constructed vehicle disguised as an ambulance, hooked up some pipes to two vans they brought, and pumped gas in."

No one in the car spoke for a few seconds. Gilda looked like she couldn't breathe.

"Did you see the bodies?" Clayton asked.

"I have photographs," Thomas answered.

"And Dr. Walz directed it all?"

"He was holding a stopwatch to see how long it took for the carbon monoxide to work," Maureen said. A tear slid down her cheek. "He's a monster, and this is only the beginning."

"I knew it," Gilda said. "The Nazis will stop at nothing to achieve their twisted ends."

"We can't let that fiend get away with this," Maureen hissed. "They murdered a dozen men in front of our eyes, and their only concern was how long it took."

"I believe you," Clayton said. "I believe every word you say. We'll get the photos developed in my lab, and I'll speak to my editor. This is a big story. This is State-sanctioned murder of defenseless people."

"What about my cousin?" Gilda asked. "Was one of the men in his thirties, with thinning brown hair and a limp? He usually walks with a cane."

"I don't know," Thomas said. "It was hard to make each of them out. They were in the ambulance so quickly."

"I'm sure your cousin's fine," Clayton said.

"How do you know that?"

He had no way to answer. "Let's get back to the city," he said. "Not a word about this to anyone until we figure out what we're going to do."

They all agreed. Maureen settled back in her seat as the car started. What was she going to tell Lisa? How would she ever look Walz in the eyes again?

20

Monday, July 29

None were immune to the giddy thrill of meeting the Führer in person. It still affected Dr. Walz every time. It was difficult to explain, but most who met him experienced the same emotions. Hitler wasn't perfect, by any means. Some of his policies put the doctor in an awkward spot, but who else could have turned the country around so quickly? He was just the man the Reich needed.

Their meetings were professional and brief—heaven knows how busy the man must have been—but they still excited him. It was testament to the man and his vision that he met with a doctor endeavoring to improve humankind. Hitler believed in learning from the past, but always with a view to moving forward. His vision was inspiring, and Walz felt a deep desire not to disappoint him.

A warm sense of accomplishment filled him as he approached the gate of the Reich Chancellery. How many thousands more mental patients languished in various institutions around the country? So much work to be done. As for the patients themselves? He didn't give them a second thought.

Hitler referred to them as "useless eaters" and "unworthy of life." Who was he to argue with such a man? Those people had no business passing on their defective genes to the next generation, and if liquidating them was the way to make sure of that, then so be it. He was proud to be a part of an exciting movement to secure the safety and prosperity of the German people for generations to come.

The guard at the front gate recognized Walz and nodded to him before asking for his papers. Nothing was left to chance here. And why should it be? Enemies of the State were everywhere—the Führer warned against them every day. The SS guard handed the papers back to Walz, and he proceeded through the gate to the now-familiar second security check, and then to the third. A new man met him and led him through the hallways.

"Where is Schengen?" Dr. Walz asked the new adjutant.

"Family emergency. His wife is having a baby."

The aide brought him to Hitler's office, where his secretary greeted him by name. Walz refused the offer of coffee and took a seat. Five minutes later, the door opened, and the Führer invited him inside.

"Good to see you again, Dr. Walz."

"And you, my Führer. It's an honor, as always."

"I don't believe you've met Reichsführer Himmler."

"I've not yet had the pleasure."

Himmler rose out of an armchair and shook Walz's hand. The head of the SS was in full uniform, his pasty skin slick. The man had an unhealthy glow about him. His hair was cut short, and struggled to cover his scalp. His head reminded the doctor of a potato.

"It's a pleasure to meet you," Himmler said.

"The pleasure is mine, Herr Reichsführer. It's such a privilege to be here with you both today."

"I believe some of my men helped you with the experiment you carried out at Babelsberg," Himmler said.

"They were exemplary in their actions. I couldn't have asked for better."

Hitler gestured at the two men to take seats in front of his desk. He sat behind it and asked if either man wanted tea or coffee. They both declined.

"I'm eager to get the full report on your experiment," the Führer said. "I didn't want to wait until the written document came through; hence, I called you here to see me."

"It's always the ultimate honor to be called to the Reich Chancellery. We carried out the experiment on Friday morning, on the grounds of the mental institution in Babelsberg. The SS men cleared the hospital of potential witnesses before we proceeded."

"What about the other patients?" Himmler asked.

"A bunch of babbling fools—no one would believe them. Their word against the SS, or a respected doctor? I don't think so."

The doctor paused to gauge the men's reactions. Once satisfied, he continued. "The specially prepared ambulance was brought onto the hospital grounds, along with two unmarked vans to provide the carbon monoxide required to liquidate the subjects." He chose the word *liquidate* with great care. No use humanizing the patients, particularly in front of these men.

"The ambulance was designed to trap air inside, giving the subjects no other option but to breathe in the gas pumped in from the vans."

"How difficult was the process?" Hitler asked.

"Not problematic at all. It was a simple case of connecting the hosepipes from the exhausts of the vans to the vents set up on the ambulance. Once connected, all we had to do was wait."

"How long did it take to liquidate the subjects, and how many were there?" Himmler asked.

"A dozen. It was a tight squeeze in the ambulance, but that was deliberate. Our intention was to have them use up all the oxygen in there as quickly as possible."

"To quicken the process?"

"Precisely, my Führer."

"What were the successes of the project and, in your opinion, were there any failures, or even shortcomings?" Hitler asked. He picked up a pen and played with it as he sat back to listen.

"The success of the experiment was that it worked. The subjects were indeed liquidated, with relative ease. The ambulance was most useful insofar as it was easy to bring it in, and once we had the subjects in it, we could transport the waste to wherever they were to be disposed of."

"And the failures?" Himmler asked.

Both men stared at him. Walz took a breath before answering. "The main issue was the amount of time it took to eliminate the subjects. It didn't work as quickly as I hoped. It took fifteen minutes, and that led to the other problem: the noise. The SS men were steely in their determination and professional to the core, but not all men are that way. The noise from inside the ambulance—banging and wailing and the like—could prove disturbing to those with less stringent training."

"Did you find it disturbing, Dr. Walz?" Himmler asked.

The doctor knew what the Reichsführer was trying to do... Anything to undermine someone else in front of the Führer.

"Not at all," he replied. "It was a scientific experiment and I treated it as such. I gave the subjects no more thought than I would a mouse or some other animal. It's the end product that's important—the advancement of knowledge."

"All right," Hitler said. "Enough of that. What would be

your overall impression of the process, Dr. Walz? Would you recommend it?"

"For now, I think it's a viable option with enough benefit, until something better comes along. It depends on how you want to use it, and who'll be operating the vans and pipes. Steely SS soldiers aren't everywhere."

"I'm sure I could spare enough men to accommodate whatever plans the Führer comes up with," Himmler said.

"Thank you for your work, Dr. Walz," Hitler said. He put the pen down and reached out to shake his hand again. "I'll be in touch in the coming weeks. In the meantime, please continue the excellent research you're doing. It's vital to the future of the Reich that we remove all contaminants from the gene pool. It's imperative that we become the strongest we've ever been to prepare for the expansions ahead."

"The German people are secure in your hands, my Führer," Walz said.

Himmler looked jealous that he hadn't thought of that line and stood up to offer a limp handshake.

"I'll submit my full report this week," the doctor said as he walked to the door.

"I look forward to receiving it," Hitler said. "And Dr. Walz?"

He had his hand on the doorknob and turned to face the Führer once more.

"This is only the beginning. I'm going to need great men like you by my side to secure the future of the Reich."

"Thank you, my Führer," he replied and shut the door behind him.

The adjutant approached, but the door to Hitler's office opened behind them and Reichsführer Himmler emerged. The aide scuttled away.

"A word, Herr Doktor," Himmler said. "It's come to the attention of the Gestapo that your illegitimate daughter, Lisa

Ritter, hid her Jewish roots in order to gain fame and ingratiate herself with the Führer."

Walz was taken aback. "I had no idea—"

"I'm not here to argue, just to tell you to make good of the situation. The Führer is pleased with your work, but doesn't look kindly on such matters. Deal with your past mistakes as you see fit, but make sure you act with due haste. The Führer's patience will only last so long."

Himmler went back inside without another word.

Walz felt sick. Was this the end of his research? Something had to be done, and quickly. Sacrifices were necessary for great work to prosper, and this would be his. The Führer was a wise man and valued his work above the mistakes of the past.

The doctor was shaking as the adjutant showed him onto the street.

21

Thursday, August 1

Lisa kissed him again. "I trust you," she said. "Do what's right—not just for us, but for the workers too."

He stood holding her for a few seconds before he said goodbye and made his way to the door.

He rubbed the tiredness from his eyes as he traipsed to his car. The sun was hidden behind clumps of gray clouds, and the morning breeze provided a level of comfort absent these past few weeks.

The car started, and he pulled out onto the road outside the house his uncle left him. His promise to Uncle Helmut to keep the factory together and take care of the workers, no matter their religion or nationality, returned to him. Milch wouldn't hesitate to fire the Jews and Eastern Europeans if he took over.

The stark fact was that the business his uncle had left him in charge of was ailing. Unfulfilled orders were driving their most loyal customers to their competitors. Milch, like any shark, smelled the blood in the water and had rushed in to feed.

He drove for a few minutes. Helga had chosen the Kaiserhof Hotel for their meeting, perhaps because of the proximity to the chancellery and Hitler himself. It didn't matter why or where the meeting was. The pressure of what he was about to decide was like a stone slab on top of him. The time had come to decide.

Seamus drove out of his way, knowing that he'd be late for his meeting with Helga not deterring him. Five minutes later, he was at Gert Bernheim's front door.

"I wanted to see you before I met Helga."

"You've decided what kind of a factory we're going to be? Or are you going to sell to Milch?"

"What do you think? How would rearming the German Army sit with you?"

"What's the point in delaying the inevitable? If you sell, they'll be making bombs and bullets before the ink's dry on the contract. If you don't, and we continue on as before, we might not survive," Gert said.

"The fire crippled us," Seamus said.

"Who's to say that the people who set it won't come again? Maybe the Nazis will lay off if we're supplying the Wehrmacht. Securing the future of the firm has to come first. Have we even retained enough business to go on as before?"

"Maybe. But at half of what we were. We'd have to lay off 150 workers. Maybe more."

"People are relying on you for their livelihoods. I don't think you have much of a choice," Gert said with no joy.

Seamus thanked his friend and got into his car and drove into the city.

Helga was sitting alone in the lobby of the Kaiserhof, dressed in her familiar black dress with a Nazi Party pin on her breast. She greeted him with a hug.

"How is Lisa?"

"Devastated, but taking it day by day."

The story he told Helga, and everyone else, was that Lisa and Hagen had a falling out, and she left the movie because of it.

Seamus took a seat opposite his cousin, who was drinking red wine. He needed something stronger and ordered a whiskey.

"Have you come to a decision about the direction of the company? Or the other matter?"

Seamus sat back in his chair. He could see the rest of his life unfolding in front of his eyes one way or another.

"Have you been in contact with the members of the Trustee Council?"

"Yes. They're eager for you to make a decision one way or another. They're hurting, Seamus, like all the workers. They need security."

"I had a call from our old friend, Otto Milch. He offered to buy the factory. Did you speak to him?"

"No, of course not," Helga spluttered. "Who do you think I am? I don't want him getting hold of my father's factory and breaking it up."

"He mentioned the fire."

"Are you still trying to find whoever set it?"

"I have someone looking into it."

The waiter returned with his whiskey. Seamus accepted it with thanks.

"You want to know what I think?" she asked.

"About the fire?"

"Yes. It was arson, but what does it matter?"

Seamus almost stood up but controlled himself. "You don't care who sprinkled the strychnine in our soup? You don't care?"

"What's the point? The fact is, we're in trouble either way, and whoever set—or ordered—the factory ablaze is most likely powerful enough to kill the investigation. The best revenge is to take this government contract and become so huge that no one can ever do this to us again."

"And there's only one way to get that big that quickly," he said.

"You agree to take the government contracts?"

Seamus took a gulp of whiskey and nodded. "I wish there was some other way."

"There might be."

Helga raised her arm in the air and Lisa's father stood up from a seat at the bar.

"What's going on?" Seamus asked.

Dr. Walz was dressed in a blue pinstriped suit and approached them with a smile.

Seamus wondered if the doctor had heard from the Gestapo yet. He hadn't returned his daughter's calls since she'd been taken in for questioning.

"We haven't seen you in a while, Josef," Seamus said.

"I've been so busy. This new project with the government is the most time-consuming thing I've ever done. Every time I issue a report, they want another. I'm sorry I haven't been around, or even able to return Lisa's calls. She must think I'm a monster."

"Not at all. We appreciate that you've been snowed under."

Helga greeted him with a kiss on the cheek, and the trio sat down.

"Why are you here, Josef?" Seamus asked. "Is there a problem?"

The doctor sat down. "I wanted to talk to you about the factory. I believe you and Helga were about to relaunch the business to supply arms to the military. What if there was another way?"

"What's the other way?" Seamus asked.

"Let Helga buy you out. Take the family back to America

with enough money to buy yourselves a house in New York, or California, or wherever you'd care to go."

Seamus put his glass down. "Are you considering this?" he asked his cousin. "Do you even have that kind of money?"

"No. I'd need an investor."

"Who would you..."

He turned to Lisa's father. The doctor crossed his arms as a smile spread across his lips.

"I have enough. A lifetime of earning money with no children to spend it on has been good for my bank balance."

"What do you know about running a factory?" Seamus asked.

"About the same as you did when you arrived in the city back in '32, but running the place wouldn't be for me. I'd be a silent partner. We'd work out the details."

Helga nodded.

"How long have you been talking about this?" Seamus asked.

"Only a few days," Helga said. "But it makes sense."

"What about the children?" he asked the doctor. "You'd be happy to see them leave?"

"Of course not, but I'm not thinking about myself." Dr. Walz turned to Seamus. "I know how concerned you are about the direction this country's moving in. This could be your chance to get away, to leave the National Socialists and their policies behind."

"What about the workers?" Seamus asked.

"What about them?" Helga replied.

"I'm sure Benz and the other members of the Trustee Council would approve of getting rid of me," Seamus said. "They could have the Jews and the foreigners removed."

"I won't let that happen," Helga said.

"Imagine returning home with all the money you'd ever need to start again," Walz said.

This was everything he'd dreamed when he was riding the rails looking for work for two years. This was the dream that kept him away from his children so long—and he'd returned penniless. But things were changing. Seamus never thought the prospect of returning to America as a wealthy man would have caused him so much consternation. Yet… He knew Helga would bow to the pressure of the Trustee Council, and the Jewish and Eastern European workers would be on the street as soon as his ship left harbor. His promise to Uncle Helmut to watch over them would be betrayed.

"I can't do that," Seamus said. "Thank you for your generous offer, but I must decline."

"What are you talking about?" The doctor was astonished. "You can't turn this down."

Helga shifted in her seat, looking uncomfortable.

"This is the offer of a lifetime," Walz said.

"I can't leave Germany. I won't abandon my workers. And besides, Michael and Maureen won't come. I'd rather sell out and make armaments—for a while, at least."

"Your children are falling prey to the National Socialist propaganda," he hissed under his breath. "Fiona loves Hitler more than you."

His words were like daggers, and Seamus had to take a moment to absorb the pain.

"I will talk to her. She's as easily influenced as any thirteen-year-old."

"You have no concern for your children," Dr. Walz said.

The instinct to respond to his insult was difficult to resist.

"Leaving Michael here just isn't an option, and we can't bring him back to America for another year at least."

"Then you are a bad husband and father," Walz said.

Seamus could see the doctor was struggling to control himself in the public setting. He'd never seen him lose his temper before.

"If you care about your children's welfare, you will get my daughter and granddaughter out of this country now!"

"I don't think you need to be quite so hasty, Dr. Walz—" Helga said.

Once again, he cut her off. "You are a woman. You have no idea what I need to do or not do."

"You have no call to speak to her like that, sir," Seamus said.

Why was he so desperate to see them leave? Did he know something they didn't? Was it really to do with the children's well-being, or was it something else?

"Helga, do you mind if I take the doctor for a walk? We need to talk. I'm sure you understand."

"I do. Please, work out whatever you need to."

"Are you willing to talk, Josef?"

The doctor stood up. "If you'll listen to reason."

The two men stepped out into the bright sunlight. Kurfürstendamm was busy as always, and they remained silent as they moved toward the haven that the zoological gardens offered. No way was Seamus talking on the street. Both forewent the formality of small talk. Seamus couldn't put his finger on it, but somehow the doctor was emitting disturbing energy. It was as if something wasn't quite right.

Ten minutes later, they entered the relative safety of the zoological gardens and found a bench in a deserted corner. Seamus lit up a cigarette.

"Why do you want us to leave so much? If you hate what Hitler is doing, why did you join with him?"

"That's nothing more than a marriage of convenience, you know that."

Do I? Seamus thought but didn't say out loud.

"Things are going to change here, in ways that liberal-minded people like you and Lisa won't appreciate," Walz said.

"You're going to have to be more specific if you want me to break up my family because of that. In a year's time—"

"Fiona and your children will be card-carrying Nazis by then, and God knows what Hitler intends to do with the Jews."

Seamus recoiled at the venom in the doctor's voice and the mania in his eyes. It was frightening. The impression that Walz was lying to him was difficult to shake also. The man who bought the lake house to be closer to them seemed far away at that moment. It was like this was a different person.

"Where are you getting this from? Did Hitler tell you something in one of your meetings?"

"I hear things...from the Führer, and other people. They have plans in store for people like you."

Walz was sweating profusely, his eyes wild.

"You haven't given me any specifics yet."

Serious worries about the doctor's mental health formed in Seamus's mind. Did he really want Helga to partner with this man? And what about the workers? Was he to leave them in this man's hands?

"Get them out of the country now, while you still can." He grabbed Seamus by the shoulders. "Take my money and get out of the country, or you'll regret it."

"I appreciate that we're going to have to be careful. If anything bad happens, we'll leave, but I can't break up my family because of your words. I won't make that mistake again. Who knows? Things might improve. Maybe the reasons to leave won't exist this time next year. We love living in the city. Maureen might stay forever."

"What if the Gestapo come back and beat Lisa and her daughter to death in front of your eyes? Will you believe me then?"

"Wait a minute." Seamus was flustered and searched for words that didn't seem to want to form in his throat. Fear gripped him as the image of the Gestapo returning to do what Walz suggested polluted his mind. He'd read about pogroms and spoken to Lil Bernheim about what happened to her family on the streets of Kishinev back in '03, but nothing like that had happened here. If it did, or if he had any credible evidence that it might, he'd up and leave. But all he had to go on was the word of a man who seemed increasingly less in charge of his own mental faculties as the conversation continued.

Then he realized what was going on, and why the doctor was so desperate for them to leave.

"None of this is about Lisa or Hannah at all, is it?"

"What are you talking about?"

"This is all about you and your work, and the fear that if Hitler finds out your little secret, then he'll cut off your funding."

"I have no idea where you're getting that theory from, Seamus, but believe me, Lisa and Hannah are in grave danger. I'm offering you a fortune to leave. I won't be so generous next time."

"Say what you mean, Doctor."

"You don't want me as an enemy."

Seamus rose to his feet. "I'll go back to the hotel and convey to Helga what we spoke about. Please don't tell her or anyone else about Lisa and Hannah. We don't know how to handle that yet."

"Take Lisa and the children and go to America. Michael will be fine. We'll watch over him. Say you'll do it—now."

Seamus walked away. The doctor called after him, but he didn't turn his head. His mind was made up.

∼

Thursday, August 1

Maureen was in her room, poring over books at her desk. The sun was fading over the horizon, and she peered out at it. The specter of what she witnessed in Babelsberg still haunted her. Gilda's cousin wasn't one of the unlucky ones chosen to take part in Dr. Walz's hideous experiment, but she wondered what the Nazis would tell the families of those who had been. They'd never admit to what they did. The families would receive death notices stating that their loved ones died in their sleep, or slipped in the shower. The other members of the Subversives recoiled in horror when she and Thomas recounted the story to them. They all agreed that exposing Walz and his experiment was the only recourse, and the only way to extract some kind of justice for those he murdered. But Clayton was silent, and had been since Babelsberg. She could only hope his editor would see sense and agree to run the story. Frustration at her powerlessness rippled through her, and she threw the pencil on the desk.

No one had seen or heard from Lisa's father since the experiment. Did he even know Lisa had been dragged in for questioning by the Gestapo, or that she'd been outed as a Jew? How would he react to his crimes being revealed? She hoped it hurt him—that it destroyed his credibility with Hitler, and somehow brought the eugenics movement to a halt. It felt good to think he'd feel some of the pain he'd doled out to others.

Lisa was rational about the Gestapo knowing she was a Jew. As Maureen's father reasoned, she wasn't a part of the workforce and had no plans to attend university. The things Jews had been banned from didn't affect a stay-at-home mother with a rich husband, and besides, they could return to the United States if they had to, where prejudice existed, but was not an official part of government policy, at least.

Her father's voice from downstairs interrupted her thoughts. He had some business meeting with Helga earlier that afternoon, but hadn't shared any details.

"Maureen, the telephone!" he shouted.

She got up from her seat and went downstairs.

"It's Clayton," he said. "He said he wants to talk to you about some project you're working on?"

"Oh, it must be about one of my courses I was telling him about," she said. It didn't feel good to lie to her father, but he accepted what she said and gave her the handset. She made eyes at him to give her some privacy. Her father nodded his head and went into the living room with the rest of the family.

"Maureen?" Clayton asked. "Can I come and pick you up in five minutes? I need to talk to you."

"Did you get the photographs developed?"

"Yes, but let's not talk about that now."

"What will I tell my father?"

"You'll think of something."

He hung up and Maureen went into the living room. Conor was playing with toy soldiers, and her father was on the couch playing cards with Fiona. Lisa sat in an armchair, reading Hannah a book. Maureen stood against the frame of the door for a few seconds, just watching. How could she tell her stepmother about Walz? She was just getting over her ordeal with the Gestapo. Best to wait until she spoke to Clayton, or maybe even until the article came out. Perhaps she wouldn't have to tell her at all. Could she maintain her confidentiality as the source of the story even in the face of her own family? What good would telling them do?

"I'm going out for a walk," she said.

"Ok," her father said.

She made sure to be at the door when Clayton pulled up outside and ran out to the car before he stopped. She climbed in and he drove off.

"So, where are the photographs?"

He pointed to an envelope by the gear stick. Seeing the scene again, even in black and white from afar, almost brought her to tears. It was hard to make out the faces of the men in pajamas as the SS men led them to the ambulance, but anyone would have recognized Dr. Walz as he locked the doors. She stopped at the photo of the bodies at his feet, the ambulance doors gaping like some huge mouth that had devoured those men.

"Can you print these?"

"I don't know. I need you to talk to my editor. Maybe you can make him see sense."

"He doesn't want to print the photographs?"

"He doesn't want to run the story at all."

They pulled up outside Clayton's office a few minutes later. "Maybe the Nazis got to him. I don't know, but tell him exactly what you saw, and what you're hoping will happen if the story runs."

Maureen nodded, unable to fully believe what she was about to do. What kind of a newsman wouldn't want to print this story? She walked in behind the young journalist. He led her straight to his editor's office, whose name was embossed on the glass in gold lettering.

He was a small man with a dark tan and jet-black hair to match his eyes. His legs were up on the desk and he didn't move them as they walked in.

"Guido, this is Maureen Ritter, the witness I was telling you about."

Enderis looked unimpressed, but dropped his legs off the desk and stood up to shake her hand.

"It's a pleasure to meet you," she said.

"I was at your house a few weeks ago, for your stepmother's party. Shame what happened, but Hagen is known to be difficult."

"Yes."

"Maureen put her life on the line for these photographs and this story." Clayton threw the envelope full of photos on the desk. "We have to run it."

"And say if we do, what happens then?"

"We expose the Nazis for what they are," Maureen said.

"And the doctor who performed these horrific acts is your step-grandfather, is that correct?"

"That has nothing to do with it."

"Is this something personal? Are you trying to get back at him for something?"

"I am now. I'm trying to expose his work, and stop it."

"How do you expect that to happen? Do you think the Americans are going to invade because you saw twelve poor unfortunates gassed?"

"It's our job to report the news," Clayton said. His anger showed.

"We won't be able to report anything if the Nazis kick us out of the country!" Enderis said.

"You're not going to print the story because you're afraid of the Nazis?" Maureen asked.

"If I run this, we're all done. The Nazis will deport us and, Maureen, they'll find you, I promise that. You and your boyfriend will be sent to a KZ. Do you even know what they are?"

"KZs? Of course." She had heard the term in her meetings with the Subversives: der Konzentrationslagers. Her father's friend, Hans Litten, was languishing in one.

"They're prison camps for enemies of the people. The Gestapo will come in the middle of the night and take you away. Everything you know in your life will end."

"We'll keep her confidentiality," Clayton said.

"So, you're confident of standing up to torture, are you?" Enderis asked. "I admire you. I don't think I could, however."

"What are we in this city for?" Clayton asked. "To go out to fancy dinners and get drunk?"

Enderis ignored him. "Maureen, forget this story. Warn your family, and get away from that reprehensible doctor."

"You can't just ignore what he did!" Maureen said. "We

risked our lives. If no one stands up to the Nazis, they'll continue to do whatever they please."

"I can't—"

She cut him off. "You think this is the end of the experiment? They're perfecting the process. Walz has been working his whole life toward this. Who's to know where this will end?"

"I'm sorry, Maureen. You're a fine young woman, but I won't print this story. It's just too dangerous, and to be honest, I don't think anyone back home would care."

They stayed to argue for another few minutes, but she knew it was no use. Clayton drove her home, dejected. As they pulled up outside the house, he handed her a slip of paper.

"This is the article I wrote. It's short, but be careful with it. Read it and destroy it."

She took the piece of paper without looking at it and got out of the car. She was in a daze as she walked into the house. Her father and Lisa were sitting listening to the radio. It was hard to look at them, knowing what she had to do now. She would wait until morning to show Lisa the article and reveal her father's true self.

22

Friday, August 2

The house was still as Lisa awoke. Seamus took Fiona and Conor to summer camp that morning and let her rest after a night of fractured sleep. What Seamus told her about her father had unnerved her—not the fact he wanted to buy the factory as much as how he'd reacted when her husband refused. A feeling of uneasiness haunted her as she lay awake. It was as if something inside her knew bad things were going to happen. Her eyes felt like someone had poured sand in them, and her throat ached. Golden beams of sunlight shone through the chink in the curtains. It was almost eleven o'clock.

Seamus was at the dining room table with Maureen as she arrived downstairs and she knew that the feelings from the night before were correct. Seamus was red-faced, and stood up, holding a piece of paper. Maureen seemed to cringe and a tear ran down her face.

"What's going on?" Lisa asked.

"We need to talk to you," Seamus said.

"Where's Hannah?"

"She's in the playroom," Seamus answered. "She's fine. This isn't about her."

"Is it the Gestapo?"

"This isn't about you either."

Her husband took her by the arm. His hands were ice cold. Maureen seemed as if she were in mourning.

"Clayton gave me this article," she said. "He tried to publish it, but his editor wouldn't let him. He was too afraid he'd upset the Nazis. But I thought you deserved to see it."

"Is it about the movie? I'm done with—"

"It's best you read it," her husband said.

Lisa took the paper from Seamus and held it up.

NAZI EUGENICS PROGRAM TURNS DEADLY

THE NAZI GOVERNMENT UNDER HITLER HAS, SINCE 1933, UNDERTAKEN A CRUEL AND RUTHLESS POLICY OF STERILIZATION OF ITS LESS DESIRABLE CITIZENS, ALL IN THE NAME OF SCIENCE. THIS NEW FIELD IS CALLED *EUGENICS*, AND THOUGH IT ORIGINATED IN CALIFORNIA, THE NAZIS HAVE TAKEN TO IT WHOLEHEARTEDLY. IT BEGAN WITH THE LAW FOR PREVENTION OF HEREDITARILY DISEASED OFFSPRING, ENACTED IN JULY OF 1933, JUST A FEW SHORT MONTHS AFTER HITLER BECAME CHANCELLOR. NO ONE KNOWS QUITE HOW MANY PEOPLE WERE SENTENCED BY THE SPECIALLY SET UP HEREDITARY HEALTH COURTS TO BE STERILIZED BECAUSE OF SO-CALLED WEAKNESSES PERCEIVED BY THE NAZIS. BUT ESTIMATES ARE IN THE TENS OF THOUSANDS. THE PEOPLE TARGETED BY THE NAZIS INCLUDE THOSE WITH CONGENITAL COGNITIVE AND PHYSICAL DISABILITIES, AND ESPECIALLY THOSE THE GOVERNMENT LABEL "FEEBLE-MINDED." OTHERS VICTIMIZED BY THE NAZIS INCLUDE DISSIDENTS, DEGENERATES, AND HOMOSEXUALS.

Lisa felt her husband's hand on her leg but didn't stop reading.

BUT RECENTLY, IT SEEMS LIKE THINGS ARE CHANGING. THE NAZIS HAVE BEGUN KILLING OFF THOSE THEY SEE AS UNFIT TO BREATHE THE SAME AIR AS THEMSELVES. A RECENT EXPERIMENT, UNDERTAKEN BY A RENOWNED PHYSICIAN, DR. JOSEF WALZ, ENDED IN A DOZEN PATIENTS IN A MENTAL INSTITUTION BEING MURDERED. THE PATIENTS WERE TAKEN TO A VAN DISGUISED AS AN AMBULANCE. AIRTIGHT DOORS WERE CLOSED BEHIND THEM AND DEADLY CARBON MONOXIDE GAS WAS PUMPED IN. THE WITNESSES WERE IN FEAR FOR THEIR LIVES AND FLED THE HEAVILY GUARDED SCENE. IT IS THOUGHT THAT AT LEAST A DOZEN PATIENTS WERE MURDERED IN THE NAME OF SCIENCE THAT DAY AT THE BABELSBERG MENTAL HOSPITAL, NEAR BERLIN. WHO KNOWS HOW MANY MORE IT WILL BE NEXT TIME AS THIS CRUEL REGIME CONTINUES UNCHECKED?

"This is ridiculous," Lisa said. "Clayton wrote this?"

"There are photographs of the day," Maureen said. "I saw them myself. Dr. Walz was there, and just like the article says, he murdered those men."

"Photographs?" Lisa spluttered. "How do you know so much? Why would he go to you?"

Maureen hesitated and looked at her father. He nodded to her to continue.

"Because I was in Babelsberg that day. I saw it happen with my own eyes."

Lisa stood up. Everything was spinning. Seamus took her hand and sat her back down. She focused on her breath, in and out of her lungs.

"Why would you spread these lies about my father, Maureen? I've been good to you. I love you as if you were my own."

"I'm sorry, Lisa." Tears rolled down her face. "I wish this

wasn't true, but it is. You need to know what your father is doing for the Nazis."

Lisa went to the window and stared out into the garden. She couldn't control herself. Her legs seemed to fall away and she was on the floor in seconds, sobbing.

Seamus took her in his arms, holding her head tight against his chest. "I'm so sorry, my darling," he whispered.

"It can't be true. There must be some mistake."

"I'll go out for a couple of hours," Maureen said.

"I think that's best," her father answered.

Her mother and brothers, and the man who raised her, were dead. Aside from the people under this roof, Josef Walz was the only close family she had left in this world. A niggling voice in the front of her mind repeated that Maureen's story was a lie, that she had gotten it wrong somehow. How could the kind, generous man who treated the homeless for free do these horrific things? It didn't make sense. She thought back to when Andrei Salnikov's daughter was sick. The foreman in Seamus's factory went to her father as a last resort, and when tragedy struck, the doctor even paid for the funeral.

Seamus got her a drink. She knocked it back and regained some of her senses.

"I honestly don't know what to think," she said. "First he offers to buy you out, and then this? I need to talk to him."

"What if it's true?" Seamus asked.

"Then we cut him out of our lives forever. I won't have him around Hannah ever again."

They sat at the table talking in circles for an hour. Lisa's heart rate settled and rational thoughts returned.

"I'm so sorry," Seamus said.

"You think it's true, don't you?"

He nodded his head.

"Can you give Hannah lunch?"

Turning her back, Lisa went back upstairs and ran herself a bath. Time drew out like a file across the enamel of her teeth.

She wanted nothing more than to stay in the bath, and maybe to drown in there.

An hour passed before she realized she couldn't stay in the water forever, so she climbed out and got changed.

She was coming back downstairs when the sound of the phone ringing jarred her frail nerves. Seamus answered it. She could tell by the tone of his voice that it wasn't her father or anything to do with him. He replaced the handset and turned to her.

"That was Leder, the private detective. He found Gosens. He has him in his office across town."

"The arsonist? Where did he find him?"

"At his ex-girlfriend's house in Dresden."

"Did he admit to setting the fire?"

"He's not talking yet, but wants to see me. Apparently he wants to make a deal." Seamus took her hand. "Will you be ok alone?"

"Of course. I'm all right now—over the shock."

"His office is in Wedding. I'll be as quick as I can."

"I'm fine. I'll see you in an hour or two."

She kissed him on the mouth.

"I'm going to leave Leder's phone number here by the phone if you need it," Seamus said, holding up a piece of paper.

"Ok, good luck," she said.

She saw him to the door, kissed him again, and he was gone.

A half hour of trying to read more than a few lines, or even listen to the radio, ended when she heard a knock on the front door. She went to get it, ready to apologize to Maureen. But it wasn't her stepdaughter. Her father was alone, hat in hand, with a strange look on his face that was somewhere between anger and sorrow.

"Can I come in?"

She didn't move for a second or two, just stared into his eyes as if the answers might be there. They weren't, and never had been.

She turned around and walked back into the house. He followed her inside. Was this the last time he'd ever be here? The last time she'd ever see him?

She stopped and turned to him in the living room, her arms crossed.

"What are you doing here?"

"I was in the area, and wanted to see you." His face changed to pity. "Is something the matter?"

Hannah peeked out of the playroom. "Go back and play, sweetheart."

The little girl disappeared before the doctor had a chance to greet her. The time was now—his reaction would tell her everything. Maybe there was some rational explanation for this.

"Come with me," she said.

The piece of paper was still on the table. She handed it to him, watching his face turn from surprise to disgust to fear as he read it.

"I've never been so infuriated in all my life. It's liberal propaganda! That journalist friend of your husband's should be deported immediately. I can't believe his nerve, spouting lies like this."

"Lies?"

"Of course. You don't really think I'd be part of something like that, do you? I became a doctor to help the sick, not kill them!"

∽

Bernheim was waiting as Seamus pulled up outside Leder's office. The factory manager greeted him with a handshake before motioning to go inside. Seamus was happy to cut out the idle chat. The curiosity coursing through him almost had him running in. Bernheim knocked, and a few seconds later, the burly private detective answered.

"Wait until you get a load of this guy," he said and led them down the hallway to his office.

"How did you get him?" Gert asked.

"This came in handy," Leder said and showed them the gun in a leather holster under his armpit.

Sebastian Gosens was sitting on a wooden chair in the corner. He was reading a newspaper, which he folded up and put down as the other men came in. In his late thirties, his handsome, clean-shaven face was tanned by the sun. He was thin and wiry, but looked tough. His brown eyes danced as he spoke.

"So, these are the guys? The Yankee and the Jew. Quite the pair," Gosens said.

"What do you know about us?" Bernheim asked.

"Just what Leder told me."

"I'd take a more respectful tone if I were you," Leder said. He sat behind his desk and directed the two men to use the chairs in front. "Took me a while to find him. Slippery as a wet fish, this one. He was all over the place, but I caught up with him eventually."

Gosens shook his head. "You've got nothing on me."

"Maybe not," Leder responded. "But it seems your old friend from the bakery, Olaf Kurtz, isn't a man to be trifled with, and he wants to speak to you. He's not the type of man it's wise to steal from, is he, Sebastian?"

"He's a gutter rat."

"He's not quite the respectable business owner he comes across as, and he means to deal with you with extreme prejudice."

Seamus felt like he was at the pictures, or watching a show. It didn't seem right to interrupt them, but Bernheim did.

"So, are you going to tell us who set the fire at the factory?"

"Not for nothing," Gosens replied. "You let me go and I'll tell you everything you want to know. If Kurtz gets a hold of me, I'm dead."

"It's up to you," Leder said. "We can turn him in to the police, but they won't have a lot to charge him with. The only solid thing they have him for is stealing the truck, and if Kurtz gets his way, our friend here will never make it to court."

"Tell us," Seamus said.

"And you'll let me go? You give me your word?"

"If you convince us," Seamus said. "If you're lying—"

"Ok. You swear to let me go?"

"Start talking," Bernheim said.

"All right," Gosens said. "You got a cigarette?"

Seamus reached into his pocket and threw the pack to him. Leder handed over a lighter, and a few seconds later, a cloud of gray smoke hung in the air between them.

"I did the fire, ok?"

"You admit it?" Leder asked.

"Off the record."

"Who paid you?"

"A guy came into the bakery. I'd never heard of your factory before, but I needed the money, and I wanted out of there."

"Who came into the bakery?" Seamus asked.

Gosens took a deep drag on the cigarette, seemingly realizing there was no way back from the precipice he found himself on. "It was a doctor, with a clinic down on Hobrechtstrasse. I'd seen him a few—"

"On Hobrechtstrasse?" Seamus asked in disbelief.

"Yeah. He wouldn't tell me his name, but I followed him down there one night after he came in, saw him go inside with his patients. Dr. Josef Walz is his name."

Gosens took another drag on the cigarette.

～

Lisa wanted to believe him. He was the only direct family she had in this world, and she'd only just found him. This wasn't fair.

She searched his cold eyes for the good she'd seen in them once, but none remained. It was as if it had all been drained away.

He had his leather case in his hand. "I know the Gestapo came for you. It's only a matter of time before they come back. The treatment of Jews is going to get worse—more than you can imagine. You have to get out of this country now," he said. "You can't hide from them. The only way is to get out of the Reich."

Lisa put her hands on her head and walked to the kitchen for a glass of water. Her throat was dry, her hands shaking.

"Why are you saying this? They registered me as a Jew, but I'm not a civil servant or a university professor. If things get worse—"

"You have no idea!" he roared.

"Seamus won't break up his family again. We can live with the Nazis."

"Please, Lisa. Get out while you still can."

"You don't care about us. It's your career, isn't it? You're terrified Hitler is going to discover your dirty little secret—that you have a Jewish daughter—and he'll kick you off the project. That's why you want us to move home so much."

"Nonsense," her father said. "You're hysterical. I'll get you a sedative, my darling. You need to calm down."

He reached into his bag, turning his back to her.

"I don't need a sedative. Just for you to leave."

"Please, don't do this." He turned to face her again.

"You don't care about me—only the sick pseudoscience you follow. I know the report is true, just admit it!"

"Then you give me no choice."

His hand came up faster than she could react. She tried to deflect it, but he grabbed her arm and held it behind her back, pinning her against the sideboard as he brought a handkerchief up to her face. She tried to grab it away with her other hand, but his grip was too strong. He pressed it over her nose and mouth.

"Just breathe," he said. "That's better. It'll all be over soon."

The strength leaked from her body like water from a broken pipe, and her vision dimmed and faded to black.

~

Michael sprinted a few seconds along the sidewalk, then relented, then ran at full speed once more. His muscles worked in perfect unison. The mansions on either side of the streets of Charlottenburg were little more than a blur as his father's house came into view around the corner. The afternoon sun was warm, but he ignored the sweat pouring down his brow. *The Olympics are in August—it's going to be hot then too. This time next year, I'll be in the stadium, in front of all those people, and the Nazi flags fluttering in the breeze.*

He was the only one of Coach Voss's athletes he never mentioned politics in front of. All of the others seemed to be running to impress Hitler. He only wanted to impress himself. And then, maybe he could leave and set to work on becoming a great American athlete.

He sprinted the last few steps and turned into his father's driveway, already thinking about the shower he was going to have, when the front door opened. Dr. Walz emerged from the house, carrying Lisa in his arms.

"What's going on?" Michael asked. "Is something wrong with Lisa?"

"She took some pills," the doctor replied. "I think it was stress over the movie—perhaps the shame." The doctor carried her limp body down to his car. "Help me get the door open, I have to get her to my clinic."

Michael obeyed and spotted Hannah lying on the seat. Walz laid Lisa out beside her daughter. Both were unconscious.

"What's wrong with Hannah?"

"Her mother gave her something—tried to hurt her too. She's gone mad. I have to get them to my office."

"All the way across town? There's a hospital—"

"I have the drugs they need. I can save them. They could die, waiting somewhere else."

"Ok. I'm coming."

"No. You stay here and wait for your father. I'll look after them. You'd only get in the way."

"But—"

"Let me do my job, boy! My daughter's going to die if I can't help her."

The doctor got into the front seat and reversed out. The car was gone before Michael had the chance to say another word.

The house was deserted, but something caught his eye in the kitchen. Five or six little white pills littered the floor, and an empty bottle of morphine sat on its side on the kitchen table.

He took a few deep breaths and ran to the phone. A note in his father's handwriting sat beside it. He picked up the handset and asked the operator to put him through to the number on the piece of paper. Just as the voice came on the line, his sister walked back through the door.

"What's going on?"

∼

"Dr. Josef Walz?" Gert asked. "Why on earth would he want to burn down the factory?"

"I don't ask why—just when I'm getting paid," Gosens said. "The doctor approached me. Paid me good money too. He said he knew the cop in charge and paid him off. It seemed he had it all figured out. I have no idea why he did it, and I don't care. Can I go now?"

The phone on Leder's desk rang. The private detective picked it up and put it down again.

"Can I leave? If you turn me over to Kurtz, I'll be floating face down in the Spree tomorrow."

"Is that it?" Seamus asked.

"That's all I know."

"How do we know you're telling the truth?" Bernheim asked.

"I believe him," Seamus said.

"It's his word against a respected doctor, a hero to the working classes and a confidant of the Führer himself," Bernheim said.

"So, do we have a deal?" Gosens asked.

"Go back to your girlfriend in Dresden," Seamus said.

"Ex-girlfriend."

The phone rang again. "Can I get that?" Leder asked. Both Seamus and Bernheim motioned for him to go ahead. "Yes, he's here," the investigator said. "It's for you." He handed the handset to Seamus.

"Father?"

"Michael? Why are you—"

"It's Lisa. I came home from a run and Dr. Walz was here. He took her and Hannah to the clinic. He said she took some pills and gave some to Hannah. He carried her out to the car. They were both unconscious and I didn't know who to call. I just found this number."

A creeping black dread filled Seamus's insides. "He took her to the clinic? When?"

"About ten minutes ago, maybe. I tried to call a minute ago, but the person hung up on me. I'm so sorry. Maureen's here with me now. She told me about Walz. We're going to the clinic."

"I'll be there as soon as I can." Seamus hung up. He jumped out of his seat. "Walz has Lisa and Hannah. They're both unconscious. He took them to the clinic."

"Just like with Bruno Kurth back in '33," Gert said.

"He's got a head start on us—it's twenty minutes from here. Let's go."

"I'm coming too," Leder said.

The three men ran out to the street. Seamus got in the driver's seat and was speeding down Gerichstrasse before Leder closed the door.

Seamus detailed Clayton's story as they went.

"You think Lisa took pills?" Bernheim asked when he finished.

"It's a setup. Lisa is a Jew. Her mother converted, but never told her. Walz wanted us gone—his dirty little secret erased before his Nazi overlords found out and cut off his funding. I guess he figured I'd cut and run back to the States as soon as the insurance check came through. He even tried to buy me out on the proviso that I leave immediately with Lisa and the family. The fact that taking over the factory will make him a rich man was just a bonus."

"That's why he wanted you to return to America so badly?" Bernheim asked. "That's insane."

"So is killing a dozen mental patients in a disguised ambulance with carbon monoxide. Lisa always said she wanted to know who her father truly is. I guess we know now."

∽

Maureen found Lisa's keys and ran to the car with Michael. She never thought she'd be in the clinic again. Not like this, anyway. Neither of them spoke as she raced through the city. Walz's car was outside the clinic. They jumped out and ran across the pavement, but the door was locked. Maureen reached into her pocket—the doctor never asked for her key back when he fired her. They burst through the door toward the sounds in Walz's surgery at the back.

~

Seamus's hands were wet on the wheel as he pulled up outside the clinic. He thought he saw Lisa's car, but didn't stop to check.

"Take this." Leder handed him his revolver. Seamus didn't wait for the others. The door to the clinic was ajar, so he took the pistol and ran in.

The light was on in the surgery. He heard Maureen and Michael's voices, and stopped dead as he reached the door. Lisa was lying on the table, with her eyes closed. Hannah was on the floor.

"What are you doing?" he roared.

A transparent tube was feeding something into a needle in his wife's arm. Michael lunged for it.

"Don't touch that!" Walz shouted. He drew a scalpel from his pocket and slashed at the young man's arm. A line of blood streamed out. Walz's hand shot to Lisa's throat.

"Take another step, and I'll cut her throat."

"Put it down," Seamus said, levelling the pistol.

"Drop the gun or she dies," Walz shouted.

Seamus didn't move.

"Have it your way, then." He pressed the blade into the soft flesh of Lisa's neck. Seamus pulled the trigger, and a loud *bang* erupted in the confined space. Dr. Walz dropped the scalpel. Only a tiny drop of blood dribbled down Lisa's neck.

Walz stumbled backward as crimson stained his shirt. He brought his hands to the bullet hole in his chest.

"My work," he said. "My research." He stumbled back against the closet and fell to the floor.

Seamus dropped the gun and went to his wife. He yanked the needle out of her arm and pressed a cloth to her neck. The wound didn't seem deep.

"Check Hannah!" he roared.

Maureen was already with her. "She's alive."

Michael was on the floor, clutching his arm. Bernheim came around the table and lightly slapped Lisa on the face. "Lisa? Wake up!" he said.

Seamus could hardly see through his tears.

Maureen examined the bag that was feeding down into Lisa's arm. "It's potassium chloride," she said. "I've heard of it. It'll stop her heart."

"Lisa, please," Seamus said. "Come back to us!"

"This is a doctor's office," Maureen said. She wiped the tears away from her face. "Keep talking to her." She rifled through the cabinets for a few seconds before she found a small bottle. She plunged a needle in and drew out the liquid.

"What is that?" Seamus asked.

"Epinephrine. For her heart."

Maureen took the needle, stabbed it into her chest, and Lisa's eyes shot open. Seamus roared with joy and held his wife's face against his. Bernheim was holding Hannah, who was awake. Lisa's eyes were clouded over and her complexion milky, but she was alive.

"You came for me," she said.

Seamus could only nod as he held her against him. The tears prevented anything else.

They stayed in that position for a minute before Leder pulled Seamus aside, out of the office and into the empty reception area.

"How are we going to explain this? You just killed a high-ranking Nazi doctor."

"Who was about to kill my wife."

"I was a detective in Berlin for twelve years. The police will be here in a few minutes, but I can make this go away. Give me the gun."

Seamus picked it out of his pocket and handed it to the private investigator. He took a handkerchief and wiped it down, barrel to grip.

"I'll say I shot him, but I'll need a bonus on top of my fee."

"Ok, how much?"

"Five thousand."

Seamus nodded and shook the man's hand before returning to his family.

23

Monday, September, 16

Walking through the new factory was a strange mix of joy and melancholy. The modern hardware was calibrated and ready to pump out ammunition for the Wehrmacht. The government contracts were in place, and soon, money would start rolling in. The furor over Walz's death faded in days. Leder took Seamus's cash along with full responsibility for the doctor's death and was a free man. It seemed the Nazis were eager to forget about him and his Jewish scandal. The newspapers embraced the story the private detective told them and declared Walz was driven mad by guilt over his lies to the Führer.

Seamus ran his finger along a machine designed to make high-caliber rounds for aircraft. Helga was happy, and the workers had jobs. Why did he feel like Faust, the man who sold his soul to the Devil? He'd been here since dawn, getting ready for the first day. Helga was in her new office, just down from his. The sound of her speaking on the telephone reverberated around the empty factory. A friendly voice behind him interrupted his thoughts.

"Big day," Gert said.

"Yes. Today is the day I become a war profiteer."

"The workers have jobs. The foreigners and Jews owe their livelihoods to you. You read the letter they sent you in thanks."

"It's framed, behind my desk," he said. "Just in case Uncle Helmut ever comes back and decides to visit. I want him to see it."

"You did the right thing, Seamus. After what happened with Walz, what other choice did you have? To sell to Milch?"

"'The right thing.' That's an interesting concept. Sometimes it seems there is no right thing—just a choice between bad and worse."

"I want to thank you myself," Bernheim said and took his hand.

"You're welcome, my friend." The two men embraced.

"It's almost time to open the doors," the factory manager said, looking at his watch. "How is Lisa, and Hannah? I know she had a tough time after what happened."

"She's doing a lot better now. It all hit her hard...everything that happened. But she's strong as an ox again, and the smile's back on her face. Sometimes, at least. And Hannah's the same as she ever was.

"Gert, do you remember what I told you the doctor said about Hitler and the Jews, how there was a storm coming?"

"That's not the type of thing you forget easily when you're a man in my position."

"What do you think? I mean, we all dismissed it at the time. Do you think he really did know something?"

"I think the same as you do—that he made it up to fit his narrative. He wanted to get Lisa out of the country at any price, for his own sake. Hannah too. But as for the Nazis? Who knows? Hitler has never wavered in his obsession with us. I wonder what we ever did to cause this level of hatred in him, or anyone else, for that matter. We'll see what tomorrow brings."

"It's easy to blame the things we see in ourselves on someone else, especially a minority group like the Jews. Doing that means not accepting responsibility for anything, and that nothing that ever goes wrong is your fault."

"Yes, people have been blaming us for their ills since Christ was nailed to the cross. I don't suppose they'll ever stop."

"These four walls will be a safe haven," Seamus said. "If Benz and the other members of the Trustee Council start their bullyboy tactics in here, I'll toss them out."

"I appreciate the sentiment, but that's not going to be easy when the government gives them carte blanche. Best just to stick to the plan of separating them from us."

Helga emerged from her office and descended the staircase to the factory floor. The two men stopped talking to wait for her.

"You ready for this?" she asked.

"As ready as I'll ever be. Do the honors, partner," Seamus said to her.

The bolt on the door came back with an audible *clack* and the morning sunshine streamed in through the open doors. Andrei Salnikov stood at the door with Leonard Greenberg and Judith Starobin, two Jewish workers. They were first in.

Helga greeted them with a handshake. They wished her good morning before approaching Seamus.

"We just wanted to thank you again," Judith said.

"For making you produce bullets for the Wehrmacht?"

"For securing our jobs and giving us somewhere safe to make a living," she responded.

"You've done so much for us," Salnikov said.

The sadness at knowing Walz killed Salnikov's daughter with one of his failed experiments was still there to see in the man's eyes. Seamus supposed it always would be.

"You have a home here."

The Russian thanked him before walking over to his new workstation. He would supervise the smelting of steel helmets with the other foreigners and Jews working under him. The Trustee Council would oversee the bullets and bombs.

The first morning, and then lunchtime, passed without incident. It was just after three o'clock and Seamus was at his desk when Bernheim came in with a newspaper.

"Remember that conversation we had earlier?" He threw the paper on the desk. All the news media was controlled by the government now. Seamus seldom listened to anything other than foreign broadcasts, but only from the safety of his own home. He picked up the newspaper. The headline read: JUSTICE FROM NUREMBERG.

Seamus read through the article as Bernheim stood in front of him.

"This can't be," he said when he finished.

"The Nazis convened a special meeting of the Reichstag at the annual rally to their own greatness."

Seamus had seen the pictures from their rallies, and Nuremberg was the biggest of them all—an orgy of Nazi flags, SS, Brownshirts, Hitler Youth, and grandiose Aryan imagery. A cast of thousands proclaimed undying, unquestioning loyalty to their demigod on earth, Adolf Hitler.

"They've rescinded German citizenship for all Jews!" Seamus said.

"We're now to be classed as State subjects without any citizenship rights. But did you see this part?" Bernheim pointed at the end of the middle of the article.

THE LAW FOR THE PROTECTION OF GERMAN BLOOD AND GERMAN HONOR FORBIDS MARRIAGE AND ANY SEXUAL RELATIONS BETWEEN GERMANS AND JEWS.

Seamus dropped the newspaper in disgust.

"My son was to be married next year."

A sudden desire to be with Lisa overwhelmed him. He was shocked she hadn't called yet.

"Gert, I have to go home. Have you spoken to Lil and the boys?"

"She was the one who told me to read the newspaper. I never usually do."

"How is she?"

"How do you think?"

"I'm sorry, my friend," Seamus said as he got out of his seat. "Go home if you need to."

"Ok," Bernheim said. "I'll just tidy up first."

Seamus rushed to Helga's office and told her he had to leave early. She nodded and said goodbye. Several workers asked him what the matter was as he ran through the factory.

"Everything's fine," he answered, wishing his words were true. He kept on until he reached his car.

Lisa was in the backyard with Hannah as Seamus came home. The other children were still at school, but would be back within minutes. His wife tried to smile as she saw him, but it came as a grimace instead. Hannah hugged him and then saw something in the bush more interesting and ran off.

"Did you see the newspapers today?"

"I heard the radio," she said. "The Nazis were kind enough to disenfranchise the entire Jewish population of Germany on a Sunday so we could get this news on a Monday morning."

"Does this mean that our marriage...?"

"No," she said. "It doesn't apply to those already married to Jews."

"But Hannah?" he asked. "Growing up without a citizenship?"

The little girl was in the corner of the garden chasing a butterfly. She turned to smile at them.

"I called Clayton when I heard," Lisa said.

"Not me?"

"I didn't want to disturb you on your first day back..." Seamus let the sentiment slide as she continued. "...and I knew you'd come home as soon as you found out. You've been very attentive since what happened with Walz."

Lisa always referred to her father as "Walz" now.

"What did Clayton say?"

"That the Nazis were going to play nice until the Olympics. The prosecutions won't begin until all the foreign press go home."

The front door slammed shut, and Seamus knew the other children had come home.

"What do we tell them?"

"That the National Socialists are securing the future of the Aryan race by excluding Jews from the gene pool. It's just what Dr. Walz would have wanted. We'll also tell them that Hannah and I are Jews."

"Ok," Seamus replied. "After the Olympics, we'll rethink our plans." Seamus took her in his arms and she kissed him on the lips. "We'll talk to the children later, when Maureen and Michael get home. We'll explain about you and Hannah, and why we never told them before."

"What about Fiona?"

"We'll steer her in the right direction. She's a child still. I mean, how seriously do you take what a thirteen-year-old thinks? I'll take the appropriate action—whatever that might be."

"It's so strange," she said. "I never knew, but it's only now, with the Nazis bearing down on us, that I feel connected to my heritage. My mother's parents were Jews."

"That's the side that makes you Jewish."

"And their parents were before them," she continued. "It's taken the horrific threat the Nazis pose to make me realize who I am, and I'm proud of that. The lies they spread every day, the propaganda in the newspapers, don't take away from who my ancestors were, and who she is."

Lisa pointed at her daughter.

"I couldn't be prouder of the person you are."

Seamus went into the house. Fiona and Conor were taking the bookbags off their backs. He went to them and asked how school was. Their replies were the usual mix of boredom and lack of detail. Maureen wouldn't be home until later that evening, and Michael was at training until just before dinnertime. The two children followed him out into the garden. Lisa was sitting in the afternoon sun, watching her daughter play.

Conor ran to the shed and got a soccer ball. Seamus set up goalposts with two flowerpots and threw the old leather ball to Fiona, who smashed it back at him with all the intensity only a thirteen-year-old can muster. It flew past him and she cheered. Lisa called out too, and Seamus ran to get the ball.

Still together, he thought, and picked the ball out of the hedge. He punted it high into the air. Conor took it on his chest and brought it under control before passing it to his sister. She belted it past Seamus in goal, taking even more pleasure in beating him this time. He traipsed back to get the ball once more, unable to keep the smile from his face.

The End

The next installment in the Lion's Den Series— THE GRAND ILLUSION—is coming in July 2022.

I hope you enjoyed my book. Head over to www.eoindempseybooks.com to sign up for my readers' club. It's free and always will be. If you want to get in touch with me send an email to eoin@eoindempseybooks.com. I love hearing from readers so don't be a stranger!

Reviews are life-blood to authors these days. If you enjoyed the book and can spare a minute please leave a review on Amazon. My loyal and committed readers have put me where I am today. Their honest reviews have brought my books to the attention of other readers. I'd be eternally grateful if you could leave a review. It can be short as you like.

ACKNOWLEDGMENTS

I'm incredibly grateful to my regular crew, my sister, Orla, my brother Brian, my mother, and my brother Conor. Thanks to my fantastic editors. Massive thanks to my beta readers, especially Carol McDuell, Kevin Hall, Frank Callahan, Ave Jeanne Ventresca, Vickie Martin and Michelle Schulten. And as always, thanks to my beautiful wife, Jill and our three crazy little boys, Robbie, Sam and Jack.

ALSO BY EOIN DEMPSEY

Finding Rebecca

The Bogside Boys

White Rose, Black Forest

Toward the Midnight Sun

The Longest Echo

The Hidden Soldier

The Lion's Den

A New Dawn

Made in the USA
Coppell, TX
08 August 2022